'You know what people are saying about you and Mortimer?'

She recoiled a little.

'I neither know nor care,' she retorted.

'I would not have you dishonour your husband's name, madam.'

Her eyes darkened angrily.

'How dare you suggest I would do that?'

Her eyes darted fire, and she moved forward as if to engage with him. Jack could not look away: his gaze was locked with hers and he felt as if he was drowning in the blue depths of her eyes. She was so close that her perfume filled his head, suspending reason. A sudden, fierce desire coursed through him. He reached out and grabbed her, pulling her close, and as her lips parted to object he captured them with his own. He felt her tremble in his arms, then she was still, her mouth yielding and compliant beneath the onslaught of his kiss.

AUTHOR NOTE

Every book is special to its author, and DISGRACE AND DESIRE is no exception. It is the story of exceptional friendship and loyalty as well as love.

Eloise's childhood friend Alex sums her up perfectly when he says of her, 'She was loyal to a fault, and often took the blame for our pranks… She spent most of her time rescuing us from our more outlandish scrapes.'

This was the premise for my story of a widow who is so fiercely loyal to the memory of her husband that she will go to almost any lengths to protect his good name, even risking her own reputation. She is aptly named, too, after Heloise, the lover of Peter Abelard and a woman revered for her fidelity and piety.

I wanted a very special hero to complement my heroine, and Major Jack Clifton came striding onto the scene. Darkly handsome, an honourable soldier and intensely chivalrous, Jack comes from the bloody battlefield of Waterloo to the glittering ballrooms of London to fulfil a promise made to a dying colleague, and he finds Lady Allyngham is not the shy, retiring widow he was expecting! He is captivated by her beauty but increasingly intrigued by her behaviour: is her reputation as a wicked flirt merely a façade?

Eloise discovers that she is attracted to the dashing Major in a way she has never experienced before, and she is torn between her new love and old loyalties. She doesn't want Jack to think badly of her, and she needs his help, yet she is not prepared to confess to him her secrets—secrets that she says are not hers to share.

Eloise needs to protect the reputation of her friend and the good name of Allyngham, and also defeat the villain who threatens to expose her before she can even consider winning Jack's love. It's a tall order, but this is, after all, a romance, so there must be a way. I hope you enjoy her story.

DISGRACE AND DESIRE

Sarah Mallory

First published in Great Britain 2010
by Mills & Boon, an imprint of Harlequin (UK) Limited,
Large Print edition 2011
Eton House, 18-24 Paradise Road, Richmond, Surrey TW9 1SR

© Sarah Mallory 2010

ISBN: 978 0 263 21855 8

Harlequin (UK) policy is to use papers that are natural, renewable and recyclable products and made from wood grown in sustainable forests. The logging and manufacturing process conform to the legal environmental regulations of the country of origin.

Printed and bound in Great Britain
by CPI Antony Rowe, Chippenham, Wiltshire

Sarah Mallory was born in Bristol, and now lives in an old farmhouse on the edge of the Pennines with her husband and family. She left grammar school at sixteen, to work in companies as varied as stockbrokers, marine engineers, insurance brokers, biscuit manufacturers and even a quarrying company. Her first book was published shortly after the birth of her daughter. She has published more than a dozen books under the pen-name of Melinda Hammond, winning the Reviewers' Choice Award in 2005 from Singletitles.com for *Dance for a Diamond* and the Historical Novel Society's Editors' Choice in November 2006 for *Gentlemen in Question*.

Previous novels by the same author:

THE WICKED BARON
MORE THAN A GOVERNESS
  (part of *On Mothering Sunday*)
WICKED CAPTAIN, WAYWARD WIFE
THE EARL'S RUNAWAY BRIDE

For Dave, Roger and Norman,
my very first heroes!

Praise for
Sarah Mallory

'Sarah Mallory's name
is set to become a favourite with readers of
historical romantic fiction the world over!'
—*Cataromance*

'MORE THAN A GOVERNESS is a richly
woven tale of passion, intrigue and suspense
that deserves a place on your keeper shelf!'
—*Cataromance*

Prologue

Major Jack Clifton dragged one grimy sleeve across his brow. The battle had been raging all day near the little village of Waterloo. The tall fields of rye grass had been trampled into the ground as wave after wave of cavalry charged the British squares between bouts of deadly artillery fire. A smoky grey cloud hung over the battlefield and the bright colours of the uniforms were muted by a thick film of dust and mud.

'Look,' said his sergeant, pointing to the far ridge. 'That's Bonaparte up there!'

A nervous murmur ran through the square.

'Aye,' Jack countered cheerfully. 'And Wellington's behind us, watching our every move.'

'So 'e is,' grinned the sergeant. 'Well, then, let's show the Duke we ain't afraid of those Frenchies.'

Another cavalry charge came thundering towards them, only to fall back in a welter of mud, blood and confusion. Jack rallied his men, knowing that as long as he stayed calm the square would hold. A sudden flurry of activity caught his attention and a party of soldiers approached him, carrying someone in a blanket.

'Lord Allyngham, Major,' called one of the men as they laid their burden on the ground. 'Took a cannonball in his shoulder. He was asking for you.'

The bloodied figure on the blanket raised his hand.

'Clifton. Is he here?'

Jack dropped on one knee beside him. He averted his eyes from the shattered shoulder.

'I'm here, my lord.'

'Can't—see—you.'

Jack took the raised hand.

'I'm here, Tony.'

His calm words seemed to reassure Lord Allyngham.

'Letters,' he muttered. 'In my jacket. Will you see they are sent back to England, Jack? One for my wife, one for Mortimer, my…neighbour. Important…that they get them.'

'Of course. I'll make sure they are sent tonight with the despatches.'

'Thank you.'

Jack glanced up at the sergeant.

'Take him back, Robert, and get a surgeon—'

'No.' The grip on his hand suddenly tightened. 'No point: I know I'm done for.'

'Nonsense,' growled Jack. 'We'll have the saw-bones patch you up—'

The glazed eyes seemed to clear and gain focus as he looked at Jack.

'Not enough left to patch,' he gasped. 'No, Jack, listen to me! One more thing—do I still have my hand?'

Jack glanced at the mangled mess of blood and bone that was his left side.

'Aye, you do.'

'Good. Can you take my ring? And the locket—on a ribbon about my neck. Take 'em back to my wife, will you? In person, Jack. I'll not trust these damned carriers with anything so dear. Take 'em now, my friend.' He gritted his teeth against the pain as he struggled to pull a silk ribbon from beneath his jacket.

'Be assured, Tony, I'll deliver them in person,' said Jack quietly, easing the ring from the bloodied little finger.

Allyngham nodded.

'I'm obliged to you.' He closed his eyes. 'Good woman, Eloise. Very loyal. Deserved better. Tell her—' He broke off, wincing. He clutched at Jack's hand again. 'Tell her to be happy.'

Jack dropped the locket and the ring into his pocket and carefully buttoned the flap.

'I will, you have my word. And if there is anything

I can do to help Lady Allyngham, be sure I shall do it.'

'Thank you. Mortimer will look after her while she is in mourning but after that, keep an eye on her for me, Jack. She's such an innocent little thing.'

A sudden shout went up. Jack looked up. For the past few moments he had been oblivious of the noise of the battle raging around him. Allyngham opened his eyes.

'What is it, why are they shouting?'

All around them the men were beginning to cheer.

'The French are in retreat,' said Jack, his voice not quite steady.

Allyngham nodded, his cracked lips stretching into a smile.

'Damnation, I knew the Duke would do it.' He waved his hand. 'Go now, Major. Go and do your duty. My men will look after me here.'

An ensign at his side nodded.

'Aye, we'll take care of him, sir,' he said, tears in his eyes. 'You may be sure we won't leave him.'

Jack looked down at the pain-racked face. Lord Allyngham gave a strained smile and said, 'Off you go, my friend.'

Jack rose and followed his men down the hill in pursuit of the French, who were now in full flight.

'Steady, lads,' he called, drawing his sword. 'We'll chase 'em all the way to Paris!'

* * *

In the drawing room of Allyngham Park, Eloise stood by one of the long windows, gazing out across the park, but the fine view swam before her eyes. There were two sheets of paper clutched in her hand and she glanced down at them before placing them upon the console table beside her. It would be useless to try to read while her eyes were so full of tears. She took out her handkerchief. It was already damp and of little use in drying her cheeks.

'Mr Mortimer, my lady.'

At the butler's solemn pronouncement she turned to see Alex Mortimer standing in the doorway. His naturally fair countenance was paler than ever and there was a stricken look in his eyes.

'You have heard?' She forced the words out.

'Yes.' He pulled a letter from his pocket. 'I came over as soon as this arrived. I am so very sorry.'

With a cry she flew across the room and threw herself upon his chest.

'Oh Alex, he is d-dead,' she sobbed. 'What are we going to do?'

She felt a shudder run through him. For a long while they sat on the sofa with their arms around each other. The shadows lengthened in the room and at last Eloise gently released herself.

'It says he d-died at the end of the day, and…and he knew that the battle was won.' She dabbed at her eyes with the edge of the fine linen fichu that covered her shoulders.

'Then at least he knew he had not died in vain.' Alex had turned away but she knew he, too, was wiping away the tears. 'I had the news from a Major Clifton. He enclosed Tony's last message to me.'

Eloise rose and took a deep breath, striving for some semblance of normality. She walked over to pick up the papers.

'Yes, that is the name here, too. He says Tony gave him our letters to send on.' She swallowed painfully. 'Tony knew what danger he was facing. He… he wrote to say goodbye to us.'

Alex nodded. 'He bids me look after you, until you marry again.'

'Oh.' Eloise put her hands over her face. 'I shall never marry again,' she said at last.

Alex put his hands on her shoulders.

'Elle, you do not know that.'

'Oh, I do,' she sobbed, 'I doubt there is another man in the world as good, and kind, and generous as Tony Allyngham.'

'How can I disagree with that?' He gave her a sad little smile. 'And yet you are young, too young to bury yourself away here at Allyngham.'

She held up Tony's last letter.

'He has asked me to ensure that our plans for the foundling hospital go ahead. You will remember we discussed it just before he left for Brussels.' She sighed. 'How typical that when he was facing such danger Tony should think of others.'

He took her hand, saying gently, 'My dear, you will be able to do nothing until the formalities are complete. You will need to summon your man of business, and notify everyone.'

'Yes, yes.' She clutched his fingers. 'You will help me, will you not, Alex? You won't leave me?'

He patted her hand.

'No, I won't leave. How could I, when my heart is here?'

Chapter One

It was more than a year after the decisive battle at Waterloo that Jack Clifton returned to England. As he rode away from his comrades and the army, which had been his life for more than a decade, there were two commissions that he had assigned himself before he could attend to his own affairs. One was to return Allyngham's ring and locket to his widow, but first he would make a trip to a small country churchyard in Berkshire.

The little village outside Thatcham was deserted and there was no one to see the dusty traveller tie his horse to the gatepost of the churchyard. Jack shrugged off his greatcoat and threw it over the saddle. The rain that had accompanied him all the way from the coast had eased and now a hot September sun blazed overhead. He strode purposefully between the graves until he came to a small plot in one corner, shaded by the overhanging beech trees. The grave was marked only by a headstone. There were no flowers on the grassy mound and he was momentarily surprised, then his lip curled.

'Who is there but me to mourn your passing?' he muttered.

He knelt beside the grave, gently placing a bunch of white roses against the headstone.

'For you, Clara. I pray you are at peace now.'

He rose, removed his hat and stood, bareheaded in the sun for a few moments then, squaring his shoulders, he turned away from the grave and set his mind towards London.

Eloise clutched at her escort's arm as they entered Lady Parham's crowded reception rooms.

'I am glad you are with me, Alex, to give me courage.'

'You have never wanted courage, Elle.'

She managed one speaking look at him before she turned to greet her hostess, who was sweeping towards her, beaming.

'My dear Lady Allyngham! I am delighted to see you here. And honoured, too, that you should attend my little ball when everyone is quite *desperate* for your company! Some expected to see you in the summer, but depend upon it, I said, we will not see Lady Allyngham until the Little Season. She will not come to town until the full twelve months' mourning is done. As the widow of a hero of Waterloo we should not expect anything less. And Mr Mortimer, too. Welcome, sir.'

Lady Parham's sharp little eyes flickered over Alex. Eloise knew exactly the thoughts running through her hostess's mind and felt a little kick of anger. Everyone in town thought Alex was her lover. Nothing she could say would convince them otherwise, so she did not make the attempt. Besides, it suited her purposes to have the world think she was Alex's mistress. She had seen too many virtuous women hounded by rakes and roués until their resolve crumbled away. At least while the gentlemen thought she was living under Alex's protection they might flirt with her but they would not encroach upon another man's territory. Yet occasionally it galled her, when she saw that knowing look in the eyes of hostesses such as Lady Parham.

Twelve months of mourning had done much to assuage the feelings of grief and loss that had overwhelmed Eloise when she had learned of Tony's death. Through those lonely early weeks Alex had always been there to support her and to share her suffering. He was a true friend: they had grown up together and she loved him as a brother. She did not want the world to think him a deceitful womaniser who would steal his best friend's husband, but Alex assured her he was happy to be thought of as her *cicisbeo*.

'If it satisfies their curiosity then we should let it

be,' he told her, adding with a rueful smile, 'Much less dangerous than the truth, Elle.'

And Eloise was forced to admit it kept the wolves at bay. Now she fixed her smile as she regarded her hostess, determined no one should think her anything less than happy.

'Mr Mortimer was kind enough to escort me this evening.'

'La, but you need no escort to my parties, dear ma'am. I am sure you will find only friends here.'

'Yes, the sort of friends who smile and simper and cannot wait to tear my character to shreds behind my back,' muttered Eloise, when her hostess had turned her attention to another arrival. Angrily she shook out the apricot skirts of her high-waisted gown.

'They are jealous because you cast them all into the shade,' remarked Alex.

'I did not think it would be so difficult,' sighed Eloise, 'coming back into society again.'

'We could always go back to Allyngham.'

'If I were not so determined to get on with fulfilling Tony's last wish to build a foundling hospital I would leave now!' muttered Eloise angrily. After a moment she squeezed Alex's arm and gave a rueful little smile. 'No, in truth, I would not. I have no wish to be an outcast and live all my life in the country. I am no recluse, Alex. I want to be able to come to London and—and *dance*, or visit the theatre, or join a debating society. But I could do none of these things if you were not with me, my friend.'

'You could, if you would only hire yourself a respectable companion.'

She pulled a face.

'That might give me respectability, but I would still be vulnerable. Even worse, it might make people think I was on the catch for another husband.'

'And is there anything wrong with that?'

'Everything,' she retorted. 'I have been my own mistress for far too long to want to change my situation.'

'But you might fall in love, you know.'

She glanced up at him and found herself responding to his smile.

'I might, of course, but it is unlikely.' She squeezed his arm. 'I have some experience of a sincere, deep devotion, Alex. Only a true meeting of minds could persuade me to contemplate another marriage. But such a partnership is very rare, I think.'

'It is,' said Alex solemnly. 'To love someone in that way, and to know that you are loved in return, it is the greatest blessing imaginable.'

Eloise was silent for a moment, considering his words.

'And I could settle for nothing less,' she said softly. She looked up and smiled. 'But these are grave thoughts, and unsuitable for a party! Suffice it to say, my friend, that I am very happy to have you as my protector.'

'Then you must also accept the gossip,' he told her. 'It is no different from when Tony was in the Peninsula and I escorted you to town.'

'But it *is*, Alex. Somehow, the talk seems so much more salacious when one is a widow.'

He patted her arm.

'You will grow accustomed, I am sure. But never mind that now.' He looked around the room. 'I cannot see Berrow here.'

'No, I thought if he was going to be anywhere this evening it would be here, for Lord Parham is an old friend. Oh, devil take the man, why is he so elusive?'

'You could write to him.'

'My lawyer has been writing to him for these past six months to no avail,' she replied bitterly. 'That is why I want to see him for myself.'

'To charm him into giving you what you want?' asked Alex, smiling.

'Well, yes. But to do that I need to find him. Still, the night is young; he may yet arrive.'

'And until then you are free to enjoy yourself,' said Alex. 'Do you intend to dance this evening, my lady?'

'You know I do, Alex. I have been longing to dance again for the past several months.'

He made her a flourishing bow.

'Then will my lady honour me with the next two dances?'

Alex Mortimer was an excellent dancer and Eloise enjoyed standing up with him. She would not waltz, of course: that would invite censure. She wondered bitterly why she worried so about it. Waltzing was a small misdemeanour compared to the gossip that was spreading about her after only a few weeks in London—already she was being called the Wanton Widow, a title she hated but would endure, if it protected those she loved. Eight years ago, when Lord Anthony Allyngham had first introduced his beautiful wife to society everyone agreed he was a very lucky man: his lady was a treasure and he guarded her well. During his years fighting in the Peninsula he had asked Alex to accompany Eloise to town, but it was only now that she realised the full meaning of the knowing looks they had received and the sly comments. It angered her that anyone should think her capable of betraying her marriage vows, even more that they should think ill of Alex, but since the truth was even more shocking, she and Alex had agreed to keep up the pretence.

The arrival of the beautiful Lady Allyngham at Parham House had been eagerly awaited and Eloise soon had a group of gentlemen around her. She spread her favours evenly amongst them, giving one gentleman a roguish look over the top of her fan while a second whispered fulsome compliments in her ear and a third hovered very close, quizzing glass raised, with the avowed intention of studying the flowers of her corsage.

She smiled at them all, using her elegant wit to prevent any man from becoming too familiar, all the time comfortable in the knowledge that Alex was in the background, watching out for her. She was surprised to find, at five-and-twenty, that the gentlemen considered her as beautiful and alluring as ever and they were falling over themselves to win a friendly glance from the widow's entrancing blue eyes. The ladies might look askance at her behaviour but the gentlemen adored her. And even while they were shaking their heads and commiserating with her over the loss of her husband, each one secretly hoped to be the lucky recipient of her favours. Eloise did her best to discourage any young man who might develop a serious *tendre* for her—she had no desire to marry again and wanted no broken hearts at her feet—but she was willing to indulge any gentlemen in a flirtation, secure in the knowledge that Alex would ensure it did not get out of hand.

It could not be denied that such attention was intoxicating. Eloise danced and laughed her way through the evening and when Alex suggested they should go down to supper she almost ran ahead of him out of the ballroom, fanning herself vigorously.

'Dear me, I had forgotten how much I enjoy parties, but I am quite out of practice! And perhaps I should not have had a third glass of—oh!'

She broke off as she collided with someone in the doorway.

Eloise found herself staring at a solid wall of dark blue. She blinked and realised it was the front of a gentleman's fine woollen evening coat. She thought that he must be very big, for she had always considered herself to be tall and yet her eyes were only level with the broad shoulder to which this particular coat was moulded. Her eyes travelled across to the snow-white neckcloth, tied in exquisite folds, and moved up until they reached the strong chin and mobile mouth. For a long time she felt herself unable to look beyond those finely sculpted lips with the faint laughter lines etched at each side. It was quite the most beautiful mouth she had ever seen. A feeling she had never before experienced thrummed through her. With a shock she realised what it was. Desire.

Summoning all her resources, she moved her glance upwards to meet a pair of deep brown eyes set beneath straight black brows. Almost immediately she saw a gleam of amusement creep into those dark eyes.

'I beg your pardon, madam.'

He spoke slowly but did not drawl, his voice deep

and rich and it wrapped around Eloise like a warm cloak, sending a tiny *frisson* of excitement running down her spine. Really, she must pull herself together!

'Pray think nothing of it, sir…'

'But I must, Lady Allyngham.'

She had been enjoying the sound of his voice, running over her like honey, but at the use of her name she gave a little start.

'You know who I am?'

He gave her a slow smile. Eloise wondered if she had taken too much wine, for all at once she felt a little dizzy.

'You were described to me as the most beautiful woman in the room.'

She had thought herself immune to flattery, but she was inordinately pleased by his words. She did not know whether to be glad or sorry when she felt Alex's hand under her elbow.

'Shall we get on, my lady?'

'Yes,' she said, her eyes still fixed upon the smiling stranger. 'Yes, I suppose we must.'

Really, she felt quite light-headed. Just how many glasses of wine had she taken?

The stranger was standing aside. The candlelight gleamed on his black hair and one glossy raven's lock fell forwards as he bowed to her. Eloise quelled an impulse to reach out and smooth it back from his temple.

Alex firmly propelled her through the doorway and across the hall to the supper room.

'Who is he?' she hissed, glancing back over her shoulder. The stranger was still watching her, a dark, unfathomable look in his eyes.

'I have no idea,' said Alex, guiding her to a table. 'But you should be careful, Elle. I saw the way he looked at you. It was pure, predatory lust.'

She sighed. 'That is true of so many men.'

'Which is why I am here,' replied Alex. 'To protect you.'

She reached for his hand.

'Dear Alex. Do you never tire of looking after me?'

'It is what Tony would have wished,' he said simply, adding with a rueful grin, 'besides, if you had not dragged me to London, I should be alone in Norfolk, pining away.'

'And that would never do.' She smiled and squeezed his hand. 'Thank you, my friend.'

When supper was over, Eloise sent Alex away.

'Try if you can to discover if Lord Berrow plans to attend,' she begged him. 'If he does not, then we need not stay much beyond midnight. Although I think you must do the pretty and dance with some of the other ladies in the room.'

'I must?'

His pained look drew a laugh from her.

'Yes, you must, Alex. You cannot sit in my pocket all night. Several of the young ladies are already looking daggers at me for keeping you by my side for half the evening. You need not be anxious about me; I have seen several acquaintances I wish to talk to.'

When he had gone, Eloise moved around the room, bestowing her smiles freely but never stopping, nor would she promise to dance with any of the gentlemen who begged for that honour. Her eyes constantly ranged over the room, but it was not an acquaintance she was seeking. It was a dark-haired stranger she had seen but once.

Suddenly he was beside her.

'Will you dance, my lady?'

She hesitated.

'Sir, we have not been introduced.'

'Does that matter?'

A little bubble of laughter welled up. All at once she felt quite reckless. She held out her hand.

'No, it does not matter one jot.'

He led her to join the set that was forming.

'I thought you would never escape your guard dog.'

'Mr Mortimer is my very good friend. He defends me from unwelcome attentions.'

'Oh? Am I to understand, then, that my attentions are not unwelcome?'

Eloise hesitated. This encounter was moving a little

too fast and for once she was not in control. She said cautiously, 'I think you would be presumptuous to infer so much.'

His smile grew and he leaned a little closer.

'Yet you refused to stand up with the last four gentlemen who solicited your hand.'

'Ah, but I have danced with them all before. I like the novelty of a new partner.' She smiled as the dance parted them, pleased to see the gleam of interest in his eyes.

'And does my dancing please you, my lady?' he asked as soon as they joined hands again.

'For the moment,' she responded airily.

'I agree,' he said, his eyes glinting. 'I can think of much more pleasant things to do for the remainder of the evening.'

She blushed hotly and was relieved that they parted again and she was not obliged to answer.

Eloise began to wonder if she had been wise to dance with this stranger: she was disturbed by his effect upon her. Goodness, he had only to smile and she found herself behaving like a giddy school-girl! She must end this now, before the intoxication became too great. When the music drew to a close she gave a little curtsy and stepped away. Her partner followed.

'I know I have not been in town for a while,' he said, 'but it is still customary to stand up for two dances, I believe.'

She put up her chin.

'I will not pander to your vanity, sir. One dance is sufficient for you, until we have been introduced.'

She flicked open her fan and with a little smile she walked away from him.

Alex was waiting for her.

'Our host tells me Lord Berrow has sent his apologies for tonight. He is gone out of town. However, Parham expects to see him at the Renwicks' soirée tomorrow.'

'How very tiresome,' said Eloise. 'If we had known we need not have come.' She tucked her hand in his arm. 'Let us go now.'

'Are you sure? You will disappoint any number of gentlemen if you leave now: they all hope to stand up with you at least once.'

Eloise shrugged. If she could not dance with her dark stranger she did not want to dance with anyone.

'There will be other nights.'

She concentrated on disposing her diaphanous stole across her shoulders rather than meet Alex's intent gaze.

'What has occurred, Elle? I mislike that glitter in your eyes. Did your last partner say anything to upset you?'

She dismissed his concern with a wave of one gloved hand.

'No, no, nothing like that. He was a diversion, nothing more.'

'He was very taken with you.'

'Did you think so?' she asked him, a little too eagerly.

Alex frowned.

'Does it matter to you that he should?'

Eloise looked away,

'No, of course not. But it is very flattering.' She tried for a lighter note. 'He was very amusing.'

Alex looked back across the room to where the tall stranger was standing against the wall, watching them.

'I think,' he said slowly, 'that he could be very dangerous.'

'Hell and damnation!'

Jack watched Lady Allyngham walk away on Mortimer's arm.

It would not have taken much to have Parham present him to the lady. That had been his design when he had first arrived, but the sight of Eloise Allyngham had wiped all intentions, good or bad, from his mind.

He had carried Allyngham's locket with him for the past year and was well acquainted with the tiny portrait inside, but he had been taken aback when he saw the lady herself. The painting only hinted at the glorious abundance of guinea-gold curls that framed her face. It had not prepared him for her dazzling smile, nor the look of humour and intelligence he observed in her deep blue eyes.

He had intended to find the lady, to hand over the bequests and retire gracefully, but then Lady Allyngham had collided with him and when she had turned her laughing face to his, every sensible thought had flown out of his head. He had prowled the room until she returned from the supper room and by then his host was nowhere to be seen, so Jack seized the moment and asked her to dance. He should have told her why he was there, but he could not resist the temptation to flirt with her, to bring that delicious flush to her cheeks and to see the elusive dimple peeping beside her generous mouth.

He pulled himself together. It had been a very pleasant interlude but he had a duty to perform. He sought out his hostess.

'Lady Allyngham?' She looked a little bemused when he made his request. 'My dear Major, I would happily introduce you to her, if it were in my power, but she is gone.'

'Gone!'

'Why, yes, she took her leave of me a few minutes ago. Mr Mortimer was escorting her back to Dover Street.' She gave him a knowing smile. 'He is a *very* attentive escort.'

Disappointment seared through Jack. He tried to convince himself that it was because he wanted to hand over Tony's ring and locket and get out of London, but he knew in his heart that it was because he wanted to see Eloise Allyngham again.

Jack took his leave and made his way to St James's Street, where he was admitted into an imposing white stone building by a liveried servant. White's was very busy and he paused for a while to watch a lively game of Hazard, refusing more than one invitation to join in. Later he wandered through to the card room where he soon spotted a number of familiar faces, some of whom he had seen in Lady Parham's ballroom earlier that evening. A group of gentlemen were engaged in a game of bassett. One looked up and waved to him.

'Had enough of the dancing, Clifton?'

Jack smiled. 'Something like that, Renwick.'

He looked at the little group: Charles Renwick was an old friend and he recognised another, slightly older man, Edward Graham, who had been a friend of his father, but the others were strangers to him— with one exception, the dealer, a stocky man with a heavily pock-marked face and pomaded hair. Sir Ronald Deforge. A tremor of revulsion ran through Jack. At that moment the dealer looked up at him from beneath his heavy-lidded eyes. Jack saw the recognition in his glance and observed the contemptuous curl of the man's thick lips. As he hesitated a gentleman with a florid face and bushy red side-whiskers shifted his chair to make room for him.

'Doing battle in the ballroom can be as hellish as a full-scale siege, eh, Major? Well, never mind that now. Sit you down, sir, and we'll deal you in.'

'Aye, we are here to commiserate with each other,' declared Mr Graham. 'Come along, Deforge, deal those cards!'

'Oh?' Jack signalled to the waiter to fill his glass.

'Aye. There was no point in staying at Parham House once Lady Allyngham had left.' Edward Graham paused, frowning over his cards. 'Hoped to persuade her to stand up with me later, but then found she had slipped away.'

Jack schooled his features to show no more than mild interest. Sir Ronald cast a fleeting glance at him.

'It seems Major Clifton was the only one of us to be favoured with a dance.'

The whiskery gentleman dug Jack in the ribs.

'Aye, Sir Ronald is right, Major. You lucky dog! How did you do it, man? Are you well acquainted with her?'

'Not at all,' Jack replied, picking up his cards and trying to give them his attention. 'I know very little about the lady.'

'Ah, the Glorious Allyngham.' Jack's neighbour raised his glass. 'The whole of London is at her feet. She would be a cosy armful, for the man that can catch her! We are all her slaves, but she spreads her favours equally: a dance here, a carriage ride there—keeps us all on the lightest of reins—even Sir Ronald there is enthralled, ain't that right, Deforge?'

A shadow flitted across the dealer's face but he replied indifferently, 'She is undoubtedly a diamond.'

'Rumour has it she is on the catch for a royal duke.' A gentleman in a puce waistcoat chuckled. 'Ladies don't like it, of course, to see their husbands drooling over another woman. They've christened her the Wanton Widow!'

'So they have.' Mr Graham sighed. 'But I wish she were a little more wanton, then I might stand a chance!'

Ribald laughter filled the air, replaced by good-natured oaths and curses as Sir Ronald Deforge displayed his winning cards and scooped up the little pile of rouleaux in the centre of the table. There was a pause while a fresh hand was dealt and the waiters leapt forwards to refill the glasses.

'Where did Allyngham find her?' asked Jack, intrigued in spite of himself.

'She was some sort of poor relation, I believe,' said Graham. 'Caused quite a stir when Allyngham married her—family expected him to make a brilliant match.'

'Caused quite a stir when he brought her to town, too,' remarked Renwick, pushing another pile of rouleaux into the centre of the table. 'We were all in raptures over her, but Allyngham was careful. He made sure no one became over-familiar with his new bride.'

'Except Alex Mortimer, of course,' remarked one of the players.

'Nothing surprising in that.' Edward Graham grimaced as he studied his hand. With a sigh of resignation he threw one card down. 'He is a neighbour and close friend of Allyngham. Escorted the lady to town while her husband was in the Peninsula.'

'While the cat's away,' said Sir Ronald said softly. 'And now the cat is dead do you think Mortimer plans to jump into his shoes?'

'Shouldn't be surprised if he's got his eye on the widow,' said Charles Renwick. 'Apart from the title, which died with Allyngham, his lady inherits everything, I hear.'

'In trust, I suppose?' said Deforge, dropping his own tokens on to the growing pile of rouleaux in the centre of the table.

'No,' declared Mr Graham. 'I heard she has full control of the property.'

'Making her even more desirable, eh, Deforge?' murmured Jack.

The dealer grew still.

'What the devil do you mean by that, Clifton?'

There was a tension around the table. Jack met Deforge's hard eyes with a steady gaze.

'I think you might be looking to replenish your fortune.'

Deforge shrugged.

'No sensible man takes a penniless bride.'

'Your first wife was not penniless,' remarked Jack, a hard edge to his voice. 'I hear that there is nothing left of her fortune now, save the house in Berkshire, and you would sell that if it were not mortgaged to the hilt.'

An unpleasant smile curled Sir Ronald's thick lips. He said softly, 'Your allegations have all the marks of a disappointed suitor, Clifton.'

'Gentlemen, gentlemen, this is all history,' declared the whiskery gentleman sitting beside Jack. 'If you wish to quarrel then take yourselves off somewhere and let the rest of us get on with our game!'

'Aye, let us play,' added Charles Renwick hastily. 'Deal the cards, Deforge, if you please.'

Jack spread his hands, signifying his acceptance and after a final, angry glare Deforge turned his attention back to the game. It did not last long. Luck was running with the dealer and as soon as the last card was played Sir Ronald scooped up his winnings and left.

Charles Renwick called for a fresh pack of cards.

'You caught him on the raw there,' he remarked, watching Deforge stalk out of the room. 'Damnation, Jack, why did you have to mention his dead wife?'

'Because I don't believe her death was an accident.'

Charles Renwick leaned over and placed his hand on Jack's sleeve. He said, 'Let be, my friend. It was years ago. It can do no good for you to dwell on it now.'

Jack's hands clenched into fists, the knuckles showing white against the green baize of the table. How could he be thankful that the girl he had wanted to marry, the love of his life, was dead?

They subsided into silence as the next game of bassett began. Jack played mechanically, his thoughts still on Deforge. He hated the man because he had stolen the woman he loved, but was that rational? Clara had been free to make her own choice. He had no proof that she had not been happy in her marriage, only a feeling in his gut. He gave himself a mental shake. Clara was dead. There was nothing he could do about that now. It was time to forget the past.

'I did hear Deforge is running low on funds.'

The remark by one of the players broke into Jack's thoughts.

'As long as he can pay his gambling debts, I don't care,' laughed Edward Graham.

'If he marries the Glorious Allyngham his worries will be over,' said the gentleman with the red side-whiskers.

'She won't have him,' said Jack emphatically.

'Oho, what do you know, Clifton?'

Jack shook his head. The thought of that beautiful, golden creature marrying Sir Ronald Deforge turned his stomach. He schooled his face into a look of careful indifference.

'If the lady is as rich and independent as you say she has no need to marry a man like Deforge.'

'Perhaps you think she might prefer a handsome soldier,' chuckled Graham, giving a broad wink to his companions.

Charles Renwick cocked an eyebrow.

'Fancy a touch at the widow yourself, Clifton? Well, I wish you luck.'

'I need more than that,' grinned Jack. 'We have not yet been introduced.'

The red side-whiskers shook as their owner guffawed loudly.

'What, and you stole a dance with the widow? Impudent young dog!'

'If you want an introduction, my boy, my wife is giving a little party tomorrow. A soirée, she calls it,' said Renwick. 'Come along and she'll present you to the Glorious Allyngham.'

'Thank you, I will.'

'I'll wager Mortimer won't let you breach that particular citadel,' declared Mr Graham. 'I think Renwick has the right of it and Alex Mortimer's looking to wed her himself. His principal estate marches with the Allyngham lands: I'd wager a monkey he would very much like to combine the two.'

Jack took another card and studied his hand. He did not like the conversation but knew that any remonstrance on his part would only fuel the speculation.

'That might be *his* intention, but what about the lady?' remarked Renwick, flicking a smile towards Jack. 'Our mutual acquaintances in Paris tell me the Major has gained quite a reputation over there with the fairer sex, to say nothing of the havoc he wreaked with the beauties of Spain and Portugal.'

'Ah, but the Glorious Allyngham's different: you might say Mortimer is already in residence,' chuckled Graham. 'He will protect his own interests, I'm sure.'

Jack threw down his hand.

'Deuce and a pair of fives. I am done, gentlemen.'

Mr Graham gave a snort.

'Well you know what they say, Clifton, unlucky at cards… I'll wager Lady Allyngham will be married before the year is out. Any takers, gentlemen?'

Jack smiled but made no reply to that. With a nod he took his leave of them and as he walked away he heard the man with the red side-whiskers calling for the betting book.

Jack made his way to his lodgings in King Street, where his valet was waiting up for him, dozing in a chair. He jerked awake and jumped up as Jack came in.

'You's early, Major,' he said, rubbing his eyes. 'Didn't think to see you for an hour or so yet.'

'I have an appointment with my man of business tomorrow morning.'

Jack allowed himself to be eased out of his coat and waistcoat but then waved his man away.

'Thank you, Robert. I can manage now. Wake me at eight, if you please.'

When he was alone, Jack delved into the bottom of his trunk, searching for the ring and the locket that he had carried with him since Waterloo. They were safe, tucked into a small leather pouch at one side of the trunk. On impulse he pulled out the locket and carried it to the bed, where he opened it and turned it towards the flickering light of his bedside candle. Two faces stared out at him, the colours jewel-bright. Lord Allyngham's likeness was very much as Jack remembered him, curling brown hair and a cheerfully confident smile. The other face was but a pale imitation of the original. He frowned. Tony Allyngham's image of his quiet, loyal, loving wife was sadly at odds with the glorious creature that now had all of London at her feet.

The Renwicks' narrow town house was full to overflowing by the time Eloise arrived.

'What a squeeze,' muttered Alex as he escorted

her upstairs. 'I do not know how you expect to find anyone in this crush!'

'You are too pessimistic, my friend. If Lord Berrow is here I shall find him.' She swept ahead of him to greet their hostess, and moments later they were pushing their way through the crowded rooms. There was to be no dancing, just a little music provided by those proficient at the pianoforte and the harp, and Mrs Renwick had hired an Italian singer for their entertainment.

Eloise left Alex talking to an old acquaintance and made her way to the music room in search of her quarry. A young lady was playing the harp and while it could not be said that her audience was universally enraptured, the crowd was a great deal quieter than in the other rooms. It did not take Eloise long to realise that Lord Berrow was not in the music room and she turned to make her way back to the main salon.

'Ah, Lady Allyngham!' A silk-coated gentleman approached her. His wizened, painted face looked unnaturally white in the candlelight and it made his crooked teeth look even more yellow. She forced herself to smile, not to flinch as he took her hand and bowed over it. 'My dear madam, you are looking lovelier than ever tonight.'

She inclined her head, wishing she had not dismissed Alex quite so quickly.

'And shall we hear you sing, this evening, ma'am?'

She shook her head.

'No, sir. Tonight I am a mere spectator.'

His yellow smile widened and he leaned towards her.

'You could never be a *mere* anything, my lady! Shall we find a quiet corner where we may be private?'

'Alas, sir, that will never do,' she said archly, treating him to a flutter of her dark lashes. 'I must not keep you all to myself when there are so many ladies here waiting to talk to you—I see Lady Bressington even now doing her best to attract your attention.'

The old man straightened, his narrow chest puffing out and with a murmured excuse and a flash of her lovely smile Eloise moved away, barely suppressing a shudder. How had she come to this, she wondered miserably, to have every rake and roué hounding her?

You know very well it is your own fault.

The words clattered through her head as clearly as if she had said them aloud. Her spirit sank a little lower. Yes, it *was* her own doing. When she had first come to town with her husband he had not objected to her flirting with other gentlemen. Indeed, Tony had been happy to encourage it. It had amused him to see his beautiful new bride the object of such admiration, but Tony had always been there in the background to ensure that the flirtations were not carried too far. Eloise's return to town as a beautiful young widow had aroused a great amount of interest and it had suited her plans to allow herself to be drawn once more into that heady world of flirtation, but now she wondered perhaps if she had taken the game a little too far. Respectable hostesses were beginning to look askance at her and she was for ever fending off unwanted amorous attentions. She could only be thankful that Mrs Renwick had taken her under her wing and still treated her kindly. Eloise bit back a sigh. Once she had concluded her business with Lord Berrow she would retire to Allyngham and live quietly there until the world had forgotten the Wanton Widow.

She heard her hostess calling to her.

'My dear Lady Allyngham, I have a gentleman here most eager to make your acquaintance.'

Eloise turned, schooling her face into a polite smile which changed to one of genuine pleasure when she recognised the man beside Mrs Renwick as her dancing partner of the previous evening. There was no smile on the gentleman's face, however, but a faint look of frowning disapproval. She lifted her chin. No doubt he had seen her encounter with the old roué.

'May I introduce Major Clifton, madam? He is new to town, having only recently returned to England—he was with the Army of Occupation in Paris.'

'So you are a soldier, sir?' She held out her hand.

'I was, ma'am. I have sold out.'

Major Clifton took her fingers in a firm clasp. She was not prepared for the tiny flutter of excitement she experienced at his touch. Glancing up she saw the startled look in his eyes. Was he, too, shocked by this sudden, unexpected connection? Eloise withdrew her hand and struggled to speak calmly.

'And what will you do now, sir?'

'Oh, this and that. Become a gentleman farmer, perhaps.'

His response was cool, distant. If she had not seen that look of surprise and confusion in his face she would have thought him nothing more than a polite stranger. Inconsequential thoughts chased through her head: how dark his eyes were, fringed by long black lashes. She liked the way his hair curled about his ears. She wondered how it would feel to run her fingers through those glossy black locks, to stroke his lean cheek… The major was still speaking and Eloise had to drag her mind back to concentrate on his words.

'I knew your late husband, my lady. We served together in the Peninsula and at Waterloo.'

'Ah, yes.' She gave her head a tiny shake as his words put her frivolous thoughts to flight. She must be serious now. 'Of course—you wrote to me. I am sorry; I did not recognise your name at first. You were with him when he died.' Her pleasure drained away. Instead of the laughter and chatter of a London drawing room she imagined the battlefield as Tony had described it to her, the pounding thunder of artillery, the shouts and screams of the soldiers. So much pain and violence.

'My lady? I beg your pardon, I did not mean to arouse unpleasant memories.'

'It would be unpardonable for any of us to forget, sir.' She fixed her eyes upon him. 'Why did you not tell me this last night?'

The major hesitated, then gave a rueful grin, dispelling his rather disapproving look and making him look suddenly much younger.

'Last night I was taken by surprise. Our encounter was…unusual. I did not want to ruin the moment.'

So she had not dreamed it! He had felt it, too. Eloise found herself unable to look away as she recalled her dance with a stranger. Yes, it had been special, and slightly alarming. She had never felt such an attraction before. But she must be on her guard, she could not afford to lose her head. The major was speaking again and she twisted her hands together, trying to concentrate.

'Your husband gave me a commission, to deliver to you certain items. I would like your permission to call, if I may?'

'What? Oh, yes, yes, of course, Major.'

'Thank you. Shall we say tomorrow morning, at ten, or is that too early?' She gazed up at him, fascinated by the laughter lines around his mouth, the way his eyes crinkled when he smiled. He was smiling at her now and she thought how wonderful it would be to stand with him thus all evening, letting his voice drift over her like a soft summer breeze…

'So, madam, shall we say ten?'

She blinked. 'Um…yes. I mean, ten o'clock tomorrow morning. You have my direction—Dover Street.' She swallowed. What was happening to her? She was not at all sure that she liked being so out of control. He was very striking, to be sure, but she had met many gentlemen equally good looking, so she did not think it could be his lean, handsome face that caused her emotions to riot. She needed to put a little distance between them so that she could consider these new and alarming sensations dispassionately.

Eloise dragged her mind back to what she had been doing before Mrs Renwick had brought the major to meet her. Oh, yes. She had come in search of Lord Berrow. It was important; she must put duty before pleasure.

'Now the formalities are over,' Major Clifton was saying, 'may I—?'

She interrupted him as she spotted her quarry.

'I beg your pardon, but I cannot talk now.'

'Of course.' He stood back. 'Perhaps later…?'

'Yes, perhaps.' She summoned up her dazzling society smile but directed it at his neckcloth, afraid that if she met his eyes again her resolve would weaken. 'Excuse me.'

She forced herself to walk away from him, hoping that his magnetism would fade if she put some space between them. Resolutely she fixed her eyes on the jovial-looking gentleman in a grey wig making his way towards the music room.

'Good evening, Lord Berrow.'

The Earl turned his pale, slightly protuberant eyes towards her.

'Lady Allyngham!' he smiled and took her hand. 'My dear, you are looking positively radiant!' He hesitated. 'But you have been in mourning. My lady wife sent you our condolences, did she not?'

She thought of the neat little letter she had received after Tony's death, so obviously composed and written by a clerk.

'You did, my lord, thank you. I was touched by your concern.'

He harrumphed and nodded.

'Yes, well, least we could do, m'dear! Sad business. We lost so many fine men at Waterloo, did we not? But that's all in the past now, and here you are, looking more beautiful than ever!'

'I have been hoping to meet up with you, my lord.'

'Have you now?' He beamed at her. 'Been very busy—government business.' He puffed out his chest, swelling with self-importance. 'Member of the Cabinet, you know.'

'Yes, of course,' said Eloise. 'I wanted to talk to

you—that is, my lawyer has written several times now, about the land at Ainsley Wood.'

'Has he? Well, no need to worry ourselves about that, m'dear. My steward is an excellent man. He will deal with everything.'

'Actually, he will not,' she replied, determined not to be put off. 'He writes that he has no authority to sell…'

Lord Berrow waved his hand.

'Yes, yes, we can discuss that later.' He took her arm. 'Come and sit with me, my dear, and we can listen to the soprano our hostess has brought in. She's not quite Catalini, but I understand she is very good.'

Eloise realised it would be useless to press her case further at that moment. With a smile she allowed the Earl to guide her to the gilded chairs set out for the guests. Having found Lord Berrow, she was determined she would not leave him now until she had explained to him why she needed to purchase Ainsley Wood.

Jack leaned against the wall and watched Lady Allyngham. The tug of attraction was just as strong as it had been the night before. She felt it too, he was sure, but she had not tried to flirt with him. Quite the contrary, she had seemed eager to get away. He observed her now as she took Lord Berrow's arm, smiling, turning her head to listen to the man as if he were the most interesting person she had ever met. No wonder all the gentlemen were enraptured. Alex Mortimer was on the far side of the room. He, too, was watching Lady Allyngham as she walked off with the Earl and did not seem the least perturbed. If he really was her lover then he must feel very sure of himself to allow her such freedom. Jack frowned. It demeaned Allyngham's memory to have his widow flaunting herself in town in this way. But she had been discomposed when Jack had mentioned her husband, so perhaps she did have a conscience after all. He gave himself a mental shake. Enough of this: it was no business of his how Tony's widow behaved.

Suddenly the noise and the chatter was grating on his nerves and he decided to leave. Once he had called at Dover Street tomorrow morning his mission would be complete and he need not see Eloise Allyngham again.

Chapter Two

Eloise sipped at her morning chocolate. Last night had not gone quite as planned. Lord Berrow had resolutely refused to discuss selling the land at Ainsley Wood. Despite all her efforts to charm the Earl the best she had achieved was his promise that he would talk to her when he was not quite so busy. She had had to be content with that, and when she left the Earl she had fallen into the clutches of Sir Ronald Deforge. She felt a certain sympathy for Sir Ronald. She knew him to be a widower and she thought perhaps he was lonely, but Sir Ronald with his pomaded hair and oily manner was all smug complacency, and less than twenty minutes in his company had her yawning behind her fan. Thankfully Alex rescued her and carried her off to supper before she had grown too desperate. And she had suffered another disappointment: Major Clifton had left early. Not that that mattered, she told herself, for he was calling upon her at ten o'clock.

It was her habit to breakfast early, no matter how late she had been out. While she nibbled at her freshly baked bread she looked through the morning's post, putting aside the numerous invitations and letters to be answered and reading carefully the daily report from her steward at Allyngham. This morning there was one note at the bottom of the pile that caught her attention. She did not recognise the writing, and there was no hint of the sender. She put down her coffee cup and broke the seal.

The single sheet crackled as it unfolded, and as her eyes scanned the untidy black writing her cheeks grew pale. She summoned her butler.

'Noyes, send a runner to Mr Mortimer. Ask him to join me, immediately, if you please!'

Alone again, she pushed her plate away, her appetite gone.

She hoped Alex would appear soon. He had taken a house only a few doors away but for all she knew he might still be sleeping. Thankfully it was only a matter of minutes before she heard the bell jangling in the hall. Carefully folding the letter and putting it in her pocket, she made her way to the morning room.

Alex was waiting for her. His brows snapped together when she entered.

'What is it, Elle? You are very pale—what has happened?'

Silently she pulled the letter from her pocket

and held it out to him. He scanned it quickly and looked up.

'Is this all there is?'

She nodded. He looked again at the letter.

'I know your secret,' he read. 'Very cryptic.'

'What should I do?'

'Nothing.'

'Do you...do you think someone knows, about us?'

Alex smiled.

'No names, no clues—someone is trying to frighten you, Elle. Some jealous wife or mistress, perhaps. Your return to town has put many noses out of joint.'

She spread her hands.

'Why should anyone be jealous of me? I have not stolen any of their lovers.'

'Not intentionally, but the gentlemen are singing your praises and laying their hearts at your feet.'

Her lip curled.

'I do not give the snap of my fingers for any of them. Idle coxcombs!'

Alex laughed.

'That is part of your attraction.'

She indicated the letter.

'So what do you think it means?'

'I have no idea.' He turned the letter over. 'There was nothing to say who sent it?'

'No. Noyes told me one of the footmen found it

on the floor of the hall this morning and put it with the post. Who would do this?'

'Some idle prankster.' Alex screwed the letter into a ball and threw it into the fire. 'You should forget about it. I am sure it is nothing to worry about.'

She eyed him doubtfully and he took her hands, smiling down at her.

'Truly, it is nothing.'

'Major Clifton, my lady.'

Jack followed the footman into the morning room. Lady Allyngham turned to greet him, but not before he had seen Mortimer holding her hands. Damnation, what was the fellow doing here so early in the morning, did he live here?'

Setting his jaw, Jack made a stiff bow. Unperturbed, Alex Mortimer nodded to him before addressing Lady Allyngham.

'I must go. I am going out of town this afternoon: I have business with my land agent in Hertfordshire which will take me a few days, I think.' He lifted her hand to his lips. 'Send a note if you need me, Elle. I can be here in a few hours.'

Jack watched the little scene, his countenance, he hoped, impassive, and waited silently until Alex Mortimer had left the room. There was no doubt that Mortimer and the lady were on the very best of terms. He had to remind himself it was none of his business.

'What is it you wished to say to me, Major Clifton?'

Lady Allyngham's softly musical voice recalled his wandering attention. She disposed herself gracefully into a chair and invited him to sit down.

'Thank you, no,' he said curtly. 'This will only take a moment.'

'Oh. I had hoped you might be able to tell me something of my husband.'

She sounded genuinely disappointed. He reached into his pocket.

'Before he died, Lord Allyngham gave me these, and asked me to see that they were returned to you.' He dropped the ring and locket into her hands. 'I apologise that it has taken so long but I was in Paris until the summer, with the Army of Occupation, and I had given Lord Allyngham my word that I would bring them in person.'

She looked down at them silently.

Jack cleared his throat.

'He asked me to tell you…to be happy.'

'Thank you,' she whispered.

She placed the ring on her right hand. Jack remembered it had been a tight fit for Lord Allyngham: it had been a struggle to remove it, but now the signet ring looked big and cumbersome on the lady's dainty finger. He watched her open the locket and stare for a long time at the tiny portraits. At last she said, 'I had this painted for Tony when we first married. He would not let me accompany him when he went off to war, so I thought he might like it…' Her voice tailed off and she hunted for her handkerchief.

Jack sat down.

'He was a very courageous soldier,' he said quietly. 'We fought together in the Peninsula: he saved my life at Talavera.'

She looked up and he saw that her eyes were shining with unshed tears.

'You knew him well, Major Clifton?'

He shrugged.

'As well as anyone, I think. We drank together, fought together—he spoke very fondly of you, madam, and of Allyngham. I think he missed his home.'

'His letters to me were very brief; he mentioned few of his fellow officers by name.'

'He kept very much to himself,' replied Jack.

She nodded, twisting her hands together in her lap.

'He was a very private man.' She blinked rapidly. 'Forgive me, Major Clifton. I know it is more than a year since Waterloo, but still…' She drew a steadying breath. 'How…how did he die?'

Jack hesitated. There was no easy way to explain.

'Artillery fire,' he said shortly. 'A cannon ball hit him in the chest. It was very quick.'

Her blue eyes rebuked him.

'How could that be? You said he had time to ask you to bring these things to me.'

He held her gaze steadily.

'He was past any pain by then.' He saw her eyes widen. The colour fled from her cheeks and she swayed slightly in her chair. He said quickly, 'I beg your pardon, madam, I should not have told you—'

She put up her hand.

'No, I wanted to know the truth.' She closed the locket and placed it on the table beside her, then rose and held out her hand, dismissing him. 'Thank you, Major. I am very grateful to you.'

Jack bowed over her fingers. He hesitated and found she was watching him, a question in her eyes.

'Forgive me, ma'am, but…' How the devil was he to phrase this?

'What is it you wish to say to me, Major Clifton?'

'I beg your pardon, my lady. Lord Allyngham having given me this commission, I feel an obligation to him. To his memory.'

'What sort of obligation, Major?'

He shot a look at her from under his brows.

'You know what people are saying, about you and Mortimer?'

She recoiled a little.

'I neither know nor care,' she retorted.

'I would not have you dishonour your husband's name, madam.'

Her eyes darkened angrily.

'How dare you suggest I would do that!'

He frowned, annoyed by her disingenuous answer. Did she think him a fool?

'But you will not deny that Mortimer is your lover—it is the talk of London!'

She glared at him, angry colour flooding her cheeks.

'Oh, and gossip must always be true, I suppose!'

Her eyes darted fire and she moved forwards as if to engage with him. Jack could not look away: his gaze was locked with hers and he felt as if he was drowning in the blue depths of her eyes. She was so close that her perfume filled his head, suspending reason. A sudden, fierce desire coursed through him. He reached out and grabbed her, pulling her close and as her lips parted to object he captured them with his own. He felt her tremble in his arms, then she was still, her mouth yielding and compliant beneath the onslaught of his kiss. For a heady, dizzying instant he felt the connection. The shock of it sent him reeling with much the same effect as being too close to the big guns on the battlefield, but it lasted only for a moment. The next she was fighting against him and as sanity returned he let her go. She pushed away from him and brought her hand up to deal him a ringing slap across his cheek.

He flinched.

'Madam, I beg your pardon.'

She stepped aside, clinging to the back of a chair as she stared at him, outraged.

'Get out,' she ordered him, her voice shaking with fury. 'Get out now before I have you thrown out!'

'Let me explain—' Jack had an insane desire to laugh as he uttered the words. How could he explain the madness that had come over him, the all-encompassing, uncontrollable desire. Dear heaven, how could he have been so crass?

Eloise was frantically tugging at the bell-pull, her face as white as the lace around her shoulders.

'Have no fear, my lady, I am leaving.' With a stiff little bow he turned on his heel and walked out of the room, but as he closed the door behind him he had the impression of the lady collapsing on to the sofa and heard her first anguished sob.

Eloise cried unrestrainedly for several minutes, but such violence could not be sustained. Yet even when her tears had abated the feeling of outrage remained. She left the sofa and began to stride to and fro about the room.

How dare he abuse her in such a way! He had insinuated himself into her house and she had treated him with courtesy. How had he repaid her? First he had accused her of having a lover, then he had molested her as if she had been a common strumpet! She stopped her pacing and clenched her fists, giving a little scream of anger and frustration.

'Such behaviour may be acceptable in Paris, Major Clifton, but it is *not* how a gentleman behaves in London!'

She resumed her pacing, jerking her handkerchief between her fingers. Rage welled up again, like steam in a pot, and with an unladylike oath she scooped up a little Sèvres dish from the table and hurled it into the fireplace, where it shattered with a most satisfying smash. The noise brought her butler hurrying into the room.

'Madam, I beg your pardon, but I heard...'

The anxiety in his usually calm voice brought Eloise to her senses. She turned away and drew a deep breath before replying.

'Yes, Noyes, I have broken a dish. You had best send the maid to clear it up: but tell her to be careful, the edges are sharp, and I would not like anyone to cut themselves because of my carelessness.'

When the butler had withdrawn Eloise returned to her chair. Her rage had subsided, but the outpouring of emotion had left her feeling drained and depressed. She could not deny that Major Clifton had some excuse for thinking that Alex was her lover. They had never made any attempt to deny the rumours and Eloise had been content with the situation. Until now.

She was shocked to realise how much Major Clifton's disapproval had wounded her, and he had had the audacity to compound her distress by attacking her in that disgusting way. She bit her lip. No, she had to be honest: it was not his actions that had distressed her, but the shocking realisation that she had *wanted* him to kiss her. Even when her anger was at its height, some barely acknowledged instinct had made her move closer and for one brief, giddy moment when he had pulled her into his arms, she had blazed with a desire so strong that all other thoughts had been banished from her mind. Only the knowledge of her own inadequacy made her push him away.

She hung her head, wondering if Jack Clifton could tell from that one, brief contact that the Wanton Widow had never before been kissed?

Jack strode quickly out of Dover Street and back to his own lodgings, his mind in turmoil. Whatever had possessed him to behave in that way towards Eloise Allyngham? He might disapprove of her liaison with Mortimer but he had hardly acted as a gentleman himself. Scowling, Jack ran up the stairs and into his sitting room, throwing his cane and his hat down on to a chair.

'Oho, who's ruffled your feathers?' demanded his valet, coming in.

Jack bit back a sharp retort. Bob had served with him as his sergeant throughout the war and was more than capable of giving him his own again. He contented himself by being icily civil.

'Fetch me pen and ink, if you please, Robert, and some paper. And be quick about it!'

'We are in a bad skin,' grinned Bob. 'Was the widow disagreeable?'

'Damn your eyes, don't be so impertinent!' He rubbed his chin, scowling. 'If you must know I forgot myself. I need to write an apology to the lady, and quickly.'

Jack rapidly penned his missive, sealed it and despatched Robert to deliver it to Dover Street.

The valet returned some twenty minutes later and handed him back his letter, neatly torn in two.

'She wouldn't accept it, Major.'

'Damnation, I didn't ask you to wait for a reply!'

'No, sir, but I arrived at the house just as my lady was coming out, so she heard me tell that sour-faced butler of hers who the letter was from. She didn't even bother to open it. Just took it from me and ripped it in half. Said if you thought she was the sort to accept a *carte blanche* you was very much mistaken.' He grinned. 'Seems you upset her right and proper.'

With an oath Jack crumpled the torn paper and hurled it into the fireplace. He would have to talk to her. Whatever her own morals—or lack of them—he was damned if he would have her think him anything less than a gentleman.

* * *

A few hours attending to her correspondence and a brisk walk did much to restore Eloise's composure. She had derived no small satisfaction from being able to tear up Major Clifton's letter and send it back to him. She thought it might be an apology, but she was determined not to accept it. The man would have to grovel before she would deign to notice him again! However, she could not quite forget his words and when she prepared to attend a party at Clevedon House that evening she decided upon a robe of dark blue satin worn over a gold slip and wore a tiny cap of fluted blue satin that nestled amongst her curls. She added a collar of sapphires and matching ear-drops to lend a little lustre to the rather severe lines of the gown, but even so, she considered her appearance very suitable for a widow, and once she had fastened a gold lace fichu over her shoulders no one—not even a certain disagreeable major whom she was determined never to think about—could mistake her for anything other than a respectable widow.

She was a little nervous walking into Clevedon House without Alex by her side, but she hid her anxiety behind a smile as she sought out Lord Berrow. He gave her a quizzical look as she approached.

'If you are come to talk to me about selling my land again, my dear, then you are wasting your time.'

Eloise laughed and tucked her hand in his arm.

'Allow me at least to tell you why I want the land, sir.'

'Very well.' He gave her an avuncular smile. 'No harm in my being seen with a pretty woman, eh? Come along, then. We will sit in this little alcove over here, out of the way. Now, what is it you want to say to me, ma'am?'

She conjured up her most winning smile.

'I want to found a charitable institution as a memorial to my husband. You knew Anthony, Lord Berrow; you will remember how kind-hearted he was.'

'Aye, a very generous man, and a good neighbour, too,' nodded the Earl. 'And he left no children.' He shook his head. 'Pity the Allyngham name will die out now.'

'Yes, and the title, too, is lost.'

'But everything else comes to you?'

'Yes.' Eloise sighed and gazed down at her lap. She put her left hand over the right, feeling the hard outline of her Tony's ring upon her finger beneath the satin glove. 'Being a soldier, my husband knew there was a strong possibility that he might die before me, and he saw to it that there would be no difficulties there. And we discussed doing something to help those less fortunate. It has given me something to think about during the past twelve months. I have spoken to the mayor of Allyngham and he has agreed my plans. We have set up a trust and I am giving a parcel of land for the building itself. However, when we came to look at the map there is a narrow stretch of your own land, sir, at Ainsley Wood, that cuts between the town and the proposed site. It is less than half a mile wide but without a road through it we will need to make a journey of several miles around the boundary.'

'But the woodland is very profitable for me.'

Lord Berrow's response convinced her that he had at least been giving her proposal some thought.

'Of course it is, sir, and we would give you a fair price. The wood could provide timber for the building and of course firewood. However, if the trust cannot buy it then perhaps you would allow us to put in a road, my lord. The project is not viable unless we have access to the town.'

'Well, we shall see, we shall see.' He smiled down at her. 'And just what is this project you are planning?'

Eloise clasped her hands.

'A foundling hospital, my lord. As you know, the plight of the poor is so much worse since the war ended—'

'A foundling hospital?' he exclaimed, horrified. 'No, no, no, that will never do.'

'My lord, I assure you—'

'No, no, madam. Out of the question.' He shifted away from her, shaking his head. 'I cannot support such a scheme.'

Eloise was shocked.

'But my lord, I thought you would be in favour of it! After all, you are a great friend of Wilberforce and his Evangelical set, and I read your speeches to the House, in favour of reform...'

'Yes, yes, but that is different. A foundling hospital would bring the very worst sort of women to Allyngham, and I spend a great deal of time in Norfolk. I could not countenance having such an institution in the area.' Lord Berrow stood up. 'I am sorry, my dear, but I think you should consider some other plan to honour your husband.'

With a little bow he walked off, leaving Eloise wondering what to do next. She had not expected such strong opposition from the Earl. She wondered if he would perhaps be more amenable once he had had time to think about the idea. She hoped so, and decided to renew her argument again in a few days.

Eloise noticed that several of the gentlemen were looking in her direction and she realised that to be sitting alone in the alcove might be construed as an invitation. Even as the thought occurred to her she saw one fashionably dressed gentleman excusing himself from a little group and making his way towards her. Recognising Sir Ronald Deforge, she quickly slipped out of the alcove and lost herself in the crowd.

* * *

'Lady Allyngham.'

Eloise whipped round to find Jack Clifton behind her.

'What are you doing here?'

'I came to find you.'

She hunched one shoulder at him.

'Then you have wasted your time, Major Clifton,' she said coldly. 'I will not talk to you.'

He grabbed her wrist as she turned away, saying urgently, 'I want to apologise.'

'I do not care what you want!' she hissed at him, wrenching her hand free.

Quickly she pushed her way through the crowds, never pausing until she reached the ante-room. There she glanced around and was obliged to stifle a tiny pang of disappointment when she discovered the major had not followed her. She saw Mrs Renwick coming out of the card-room and went to join her, hoping to avoid any further unwelcome attentions by staying close to the lady and her friends. The ploy worked very well, and she was just beginning to think that she might soon be able to make her excuses and leave without arousing too much speculation when a footman approached and held out a silver tray.

Eloise looked doubtfully at the folded note resting on the tray.

'What is this?' she asked, suspicion making her voice sharp.

A flicker of surprise disturbed the servant's wooden features.

'I do not know, my lady. The under-footman brought it into the ballroom and requested that I deliver it to you.'

One of Mrs Renwick's companions leaned closer.

'Ah, an admirer, my dear!'

The arch tone grated upon Eloise, but she merely smiled. Carefully, she picked up the note.

'Thank you; that will be all.'

She dismissed the footman and stepped away from the little group of ladies. They were all regarding her with varying degrees of curiosity. She hoped her own countenance was impassive as she opened the note and read it.

Go into the garden and look under Apollo's heel.

Eloise stared at the words, trying to work out their meaning. She realised one of the ladies was stepping towards her and hurriedly folded the note.

'So, Lady Allyngham, is it an admirer?'

She looked into the woman's bright, blatantly curious face and forced herself to laugh.

'What else?' she said lightly. 'One is pursued everywhere. Excuse me.'

Her mind was racing. Apollo. A statue, perhaps.

She remembered that the long windows of the grand salon had been thrown open, recalled seeing the ink-black sky beyond. She did not know what lay beyond the windows: she had no choice but to find out.

Eloise returned to the salon. The noise and chatter of the room was deafening and she began to make her way around the edge of the room until she reached the first of the long windows. Looking out, she could see a narrow terrace with a flight of steps at each end. Eloise took a quick look around to make sure no one was watching her and slipped out on to the terrace. From her elevated position she could see the dark outlines of the garden and in the far distance, at the perimeter of the grounds, a series of lanterns glowed between several pale figures: marble statues.

In seconds she had descended the steps and was running along the path, the gravel digging painfully into the thin soles of her blue kid slippers. The moon had not yet risen and the gardens were dark, the path only discernible as a grey ribbon. She thought she heard a noise behind her and turned, her heart beating hard against her ribs. She could see nothing behind her except the black wall of the house rearing up, pierced by the four blocks of light from the long windows.

She hurried on, past the rose garden where the late-summer blooms were still perfuming the air, and on through a tree-lined walk. The path led between two rows of clipped yews and was in almost total darkness but at the far end she could see the garden wall and hanging from it the first of the lanterns. Emerging from the yew walk, she saw the statue of a woman ahead of her, the marble gleaming ghost-like in the lamplight. She approached the statue and noted that the path turned to the right and ran past five more statues, each one illuminated by a lamp. She put her hand to her throat: the third statue was clearly male, and holding a lyre in his arms. She stepped forward: yes, it could be Apollo. She moved closer, peering at the base of the statue. One marble heel was slightly raised and tucked beneath it was a small square of folded paper.

Eloise bent to pick it up. She unfolded it, turning the writing towards the golden glow of the lantern. Her heart, thudding so heavily a moment earlier, now stopped. She had expected to find another note but this was obviously a page torn from a book. A journal, judging by the dates in the margin. It was covered with a fine, neat hand that was all too familiar. As she read the page she put a hand to her mouth, her eyes widening with horror. The sentiments, the explicit nature of the words—innermost thoughts that would cause a scandal if they were made public. A scandal that could destroy both her and Alex.

For a sickening moment Eloise thought she might faint. Then, as her brain started to work again, she quickly refolded the paper and thrust it into the bosom of her gown. Her spine began to tingle, and she had the uneasy feeling that she was being watched. She backed away from the statue, straining her eyes and ears against the surrounding darkness. The air was very still and the only sound to reach her was the faint chatter of the guests gathered in the house. Suddenly she wanted nothing more than to be standing safely in that overheated, overcrowded salon. She picked up her skirts and began to run back along the path, trying not to think of who or what might be hiding in the darkness around her. The steps to the terrace were within sight when a figure stepped out and blocked her path. She screamed and tried to turn away. Strong hands reached out and grabbed her, preventing her from falling.

'Easy, my lady. There is no need to be afraid.'

Recognising Jack Clifton's deep warm voice did nothing to calm her. The noise coming from the open windows above was such that she felt sure no one had heard her scream and no one would hear her now, if she called out for assistance. Fighting down her panic, she shrugged off his hands.

'You persist in tormenting me,' she said in a low, shaking voice.

She heard him laugh and gritted her teeth against her anger.

'You wrong me, madam. I saw you slip away, so I came outside to wait for you. I thought, perhaps, when you came back from your assignation, I might speak with you.' His teeth gleamed in the dim light.

'I did not expect you to return as if the hounds of hell were snapping at your heels.'

She peered at him, trying to read his face, but it was impossible in the gloom.

'You know why I went into the garden?'

She sensed rather than saw him shrug.

'I presumed it was to meet a gentleman.' On this occasion his opinion of her character did not arouse her anger. 'So now will you accept an apology for my behaviour this morning, madam?'

She said cautiously, 'I might do so.'

'Then I humbly beg your pardon. My conduct was not that of a gentleman.'

He was so close, so reassuringly solid, but could she trust him? She glanced nervously over her shoulder. If Major Clifton had not sent her that note, then who could it be? She looked up at him. 'Did you see anyone else in the gardens, Major?'

'No. What is it, Lady Allyngham, did not your lover keep the assignation?'

His coldly mocking tone banished all thoughts of seeking his help. She gave a little hiss of anger.

'You are quite despicable!'

'And you are hiding something.'

She drew herself up.

'That,' she said icily, 'is none of your business!'

Jack did not move as the lady turned and ran quickly up the steps and into the house. There was a mystery here: she had seemed genuinely frightened when she came running up to him. If it had been any other woman he would have done his best to reassure her, but Lady Allyngham had made it abundantly clear what she thought of him. And she could take care of herself, could she not? He thought back to that morning, when he had held her in his arms before she wrathfully fought him off. He toyed with the idea of following her and persuading her to confide in him. Then he shrugged. As the lady had said, it was none of his business.

Jack decided to leave. He had come to Clevedon House in search of Lady Allyngham, determined to deliver his apology and he had done so. There was now no reason for him to stay: he took no pleasure in being part of the laughing, chattering crush of guests gathered in the elegant salon. A discreet enquiry at the door elicited the information that Lady Allyngham had already departed and since there was no other amusement to be had, he made his way directly to his rooms in King Street. He decided not to call in at White's. He had business to conclude in the morning and needed to have a clear head. After that, he thought, he would be glad to quit London and forget the bewitching, contradictory Lady Allyngham.

Chapter Three

The following morning Jack took a cab into the City. His first meeting with his lawyer had convinced him that he was right to sell out and take charge of his inheritance, or what was left of it. Now he quickly scanned the papers that were put before him.

'Once the property in Leicestershire is sold that will give me capital to invest in the Staffordshire estates,' he decided.

His lawyer's brows went up.

'The Leicestershire estate was your father's pride and joy: he always said the hunting there was second to none.'

'I shall have precious little time for hunting for the next few years,' muttered Jack, looking at the figures the lawyer had written out for him. He pushed the papers back across the desk. 'You say you have a buyer?'

The lawyer steepled his fingers, trying to keep the note of excitement out of his voice. Years of dealing with old Mr Clifton had made him cautious.

'The owner of the neighbouring property, a Mr Tomlinson, has indicated he is interested in purchasing the house and the land. He is eager to have the matter settled. He is a manufacturer, but a very gentlemanly man.'

'As long as he can pay the price I don't care who he is.' Jack rose. 'Very well. Have the papers drawn up for me to sign tomorrow, and I'll leave the rest to you.'

Ten minutes later Jack walked out into the street, feeling that a weight had lifted from his shoulders. He had always preferred Henchard, the house in Staffordshire. It had been his mother's favourite, but sadly neglected after her death, his father preferring to live in London or Leicestershire. He had died there following a short illness eighteen months ago, but with Bonaparte gathering his army and Wellington demanding that every able soldier join him in Brussels, Jack had not had time to do more than to send to Henchard any personal effects he wanted to keep before rejoining his regiment. Now he planned to settle down. He would be able to refurbish Henchard, and in time the land might even be profitable again. Settling his hat on his head, he decided to walk back to King Street. He had reached the Strand and was approaching Coutts's bank when a heavily veiled woman stepped out of the door, escorted by a very attentive bank clerk. Despite the thick veil there was something familiar about the tall, fashionably dressed figure, her purposeful tread, the way her hands twisted together. As she pulled on her gloves he caught sight of the heavy gold ring on her right hand. Even from a distance he recognised Allyngham's signet ring. Jack smiled to himself, wondering what the lady would say if he approached her. Would she give him a cold, frosty greeting, or perhaps she might simply refuse to acknowledge him? Even as he considered the matter she swept across to a waiting cab and climbed in. Instantly the door was closed and the carriage pulled away.

'Well, Miss Elle? Is your business ended, can we go home now?'

Eloise put up her veil and gave her maid a strained smile.

'Yes, Alice, we are going back to Dover Street now.'

The maid gave a little sniff. 'I do not see why we couldn't use your own carriage, if you was only coming to the bank. It may be unusual for ladies to visit their bankers, but if they are widows, like yourself, I don't see what else is to be done.'

Eloise did not reply. Leaning back in one corner, she clutched her reticule nervously. It rested heavily on her knees but she would not put it away from her. She had never been inside a bank before, but the manager himself had taken charge once he realised her identity, and the whole process had been conducted with the utmost ease. When she had said she needed to draw a substantial amount to distribute to her staff he had given her a look which combined sympathy with mild disapproval: no doubt he thought that she really required the money for some much more trivial reason, such as to buy new gowns or to pay off her gambling debts.

She pulled a paper from her bag and unfolded it: the scrawling black letters might have been live serpents for the way they made her skin crawl. When the letter had arrived that morning and she had read it for the first time, she had felt very alone. Her first thought had been to send for Alex, but she had soon dismissed the idea. Alex was a dear friend, but he could be rash, and this matter required discretion. No, she must deal with this herself. She scanned the letter again, chewing at her lip. Her biggest problem now was how to get through the rest of the day?

Mrs Renwick was a little surprised when Eloise appeared at her card party that evening.

'I know I had sent my apologies,' said Eloise, giving her hostess a bright smile, 'but I was not in humour for dancing tonight and thought you would not object…'

'Not in the least, my dear, you are most welcome here. Come in, come in and join our little party.' Mrs Renwick drew her towards a quiet room filled with small tables, where ladies and gentleman were gathered, staring at their cards in hushed concentration. Bathed in the glow of the candles, it looked like a room full of golden statues. 'This is turning out to be an evening of pleasant surprises. Major Clifton, too, made an unexpected appearance. It seems his business in town will not now be concluded until tomorrow so we have the pleasure of his company, too—'

Eloise drew back quickly. She had spotted Jack Clifton on the far side of the room.

'No! I—I was hoping for something a little...less serious, ma'am.'

Her hostess laughed softly. 'Well if you would like to come into the morning room, some of our friends are playing looe for penny points: nothing too alarming in that, now is there?'

Resigning herself to an hour or so of tedious play, Eloise smiled and took her place between a bouncing, bubbly young lady fresh from the schoolroom and an emaciated dowager in heavy black bombazine. Concentrating on the cards proved a surprisingly effective distraction for Eloise and when the little group split up to go in search of refreshment she was relieved to note that her evening was nearly over.

She made her way downstairs to the dining room where a long table was loaded with a sumptuous array of food and drink. A little supper might help to settle the nervous anticipation that was beginning

to build within her. A group of gentlemen were help-
ing themselves to delicacies from an assortment of
silver dishes. She noted that both Major Clifton and
Sir Ronald Deforge were amongst their number so
she avoided them and made her way to the far end
of the table. She kept her eyes lowered, determined
to concentrate on the food displayed before her but
the gentlemen's light-hearted banter intruded and she
could not help but listen. The conversation turned to
gambling and she found her attention caught when
she heard the major's voice.

'You know I play the occasional game at White's
but the high stakes are not for me,' he was saying.
'You will think me very dull, I dare say, but I prefer
my funds to be invested in my land, rather than lining
some other fellow's pockets.'

'Very different from Sir Ronald, then,' laughed
Edward Graham. 'You never refuse a game of chance,
ain't that right, sir?'

'If it is cards, certainly,' Sir Ronald replied cheerfully. 'I have something of a passion for cards. I
played young Franklyn 'til dawn last week.'

'Then you have more energy for the pastime than
I do,' returned the major coolly, turning away.

'I hear that playing 'til dawn is a common occur-
rence with you, Deforge,' remarked Mr Renwick.
'By Gad, sir, your servants must be falling asleep
at their posts if they have to wait up for you every
night.'

Sir Ronald laughed.

'No, no, Renwick, I am not so cruel an employer. My household retires at a Christian hour. Only my valet waits up for me, and he snoozes in a chair in the hall until I give him the knock to let me in.'

'The pleasures of being a bachelor,' declared his host. 'A wife would certainly curtail your nocturnal activities, Deforge!'

'Oho, when have I ever prevented you doing exactly as you wish?' demanded Mrs Renwick, walking by at that moment. 'My husband would have you think his life very restricted.' She tapped the straining front of Mr Renwick's waistcoat with her fan. 'Well, gentlemen? Does he look as if he is wasting away?'

Eloise gave a little chuckle as her hostess came towards her.

'I am sure we will all find something to tempt our appetite here,' she smiled. 'A truly magnificent supper, ma'am.'

'Thank you, Lady Allyngham. Are you enjoying yourself?'

'Yes, thank you. It is a most delightful evening.'

'But, my dear, you are very quiet this evening, and a trifle pale, I think.' Mrs Renwick came closer. 'I hope you are not ill?'

'No, ma'am, a little tired, perhaps.'

Mrs Renwick gave her a warm, sympathetic smile.

'Too many engagements, ma'am?'

'I think perhaps I have had enough of town life.'

Overhearing, Mr Graham turned quickly towards her.

'My dear Lady Allyngham, you will not desert us!'

'Of course she will not,' put in Lady Parham, coming up. 'Not when there are so many diversions to be enjoyed.'

Eloise forced herself to smile. Suddenly she was tired of play-acting.

'I think I may well go back to Allyngham.'

'Ah,' nodded Lady Parham. 'Perhaps that is why you were in the Strand this morning, settling your affairs with your bankers.'

Eloise stiffened. 'No, I had no business there today.'

'Oh, I was so sure it was you!' Lady Parham gave a tinkling little laugh, glancing around at her friends. 'I had gone to Ackerman's, to look at their new prints—so amusing!—and I saw a lady coming out of Coutts's bank. But she was veiled, so perhaps I was mistaken.'

'It must have been someone else,' said Eloise firmly. 'I was not in the Strand this morning.'

She selected a little pastry and turned away, only to find Jack Clifton regarding her with a little frown in his eyes.

* * *

Now what the devil is she about?

Jack had been watching Lady Allyngham for some time. He had noted that she was nervous, her eyes constantly straying to the clock, and her vehement denial of visiting the bank aroused his suspicions. She caught his eye and moved away so fast he abandoned any thought of speaking to her, but when, a short time later, Eloise made her excuses and left the party, he followed.

The press of traffic in the streets made it an easy task for Jack to follow her carriage on foot, and when they arrived at Dover Street he was close enough to hear the lady's instructions to the coachman to come back in an hour.

Jack grinned. So she *was* up to something! He dashed back to King Street, quelling the little voice in his head that objected to the idea of spying on a lady. After all, Tony Allyngham had been a good friend and had asked him to look after his widow— well, perhaps not in so many words, but Jack was not going to admit, even to himself, that he had any personal interest in Eloise Allyngham.

Just over half an hour later he was back in Dover Street, his evening coat replaced by a dark riding jacket and with a muffler covering his snowy neck-cloth. Hidden out of sight in Dover Yard, Bob was looking after his horse and in all probability, Jack thought, animadverting bitterly on the ways of the Quality. He positioned himself opposite Lady Allyngham's door and settled down to wait. As with many of the streets in this area of London, Dover Street housed a variety of residents, from members of the *ton* to ladies who, while they would never receive an invitation from the great society hostesses, were very well known to their husbands. Courtesans such as Kitty Williams who, it was rumoured, could boast of having a royal duke amongst her many admirers. Jack was not one of their number, but Kitty's residence had been pointed out to him by his friends, and he watched with interest as an elegant town carriage pulled up at the door. A portly gentleman climbed out and was immediately admitted, as if the doorman had been looking out for him. So Lord Berrow was one of Kitty's customers. Jack grinned: the Earl professed himself to be one of Wilberforce's saints—the old hypocrite!

The sounds of another coach clattering into Dover Street caused Jack to step back further into the shadows. He nodded with satisfaction as it drew up outside Lady Allyngham's house. He saw Eloise come out, wrapped now in a dark cloak, and step up into the carriage. It drew away immediately and Jack turned and ran for his horse.

'I still think I should come with you,' grumbled Robert as Jack scrambled into the saddle.

'No, you go back now and wait for me.' Jack patted

his pocket. He had a pistol, should he need it, and besides, he forced himself to face the thought, if this should prove nothing more than a sordid little assignation with a lover, the less people who knew of it the better.

Keeping a discreet distance, Jack followed the coach as it bowled through the darkened streets. They headed north through Tottenham Court Road and soon the town was left behind and they were bowling along between open fields. It was a clear night, the rising moon giving sufficient light for the carriage to set a swift pace. The coach slowed as it climbed through the village of Hampstead. When they reached the open heath Jack drew rein and as the carriage came to a halt he guided his horse off the road into the cover of the stunted trees. He watched Eloise climb out. Silently he dismounted, secured his horse to a branch and followed her.

Eloise hesitated, glancing back at the coach drawn up behind her. The carriage lamps twinkled encouragingly and the solid shape of her coachman sitting up on the box was reassuring. She had also taken the precaution of asking Perkins to come with her. He had been her groom since she was a child and she was confident of his loyalty and discretion. Turning again to face the dark open heath, she took a deep breath and stepped forwards. She suspected it was not the autumnal chill in the night air that made her shiver as she moved along the narrow path. She felt dreadfully alone and had to remind herself that Perkins was discreetly following her. For perhaps the twentieth time since setting out she went over in her mind the instructions she had received in the letter that morning. The carriage had stopped at the fork in the road, as directed, and the path to the right between a boulder and small pond was easily found. She counted silently, thankful that the letter had stated the number of steps she would need to take rather than asking her to judge a half a mile: in her present nervous state she felt as if she had walked at least three miles already. There was sufficient light to see the path, but the trees and bushes on either side were menacingly black, and she had to force herself not to think how many malevolent creatures might be watching her from the shadows.

At one point she saw a black square on her left; a shepherd's hut, she guessed, although there were no sheep or cattle visible on the heath. Then, ahead of her, she could make out the path splitting on either side of a fallen tree. She stopped and glanced about her. Everything was silent. Shivering, she stepped up and placed a package under the exposed roots of the tree.

There, it was done. She was just heaving a sigh of relief when she heard a scuffle and crashing in the bushes behind her. She turned in time to see Perkins dragging something large and heavy out from the bushes.

'I got 'im, m'lady,' he wheezed, 'I've got yer villain!'

Eloise ran back and gazed down at the unconscious figure lying at the groom's feet.

It was Major Jack Clifton.

Chapter Four

Anger, revulsion and disappointment churned in her stomach. The major might be an odious man but she had not wanted him proved a scoundrel.

'Check his pockets,' she said crisply.

'What exactly is you looking for, m'lady?'

'A book—a small, leather-bound journal.'

'Nope,' muttered Perkins, 'Nothin' like that. But there is this!'

He pulled out a pistol and held it up so that the moonlight glinted wickedly on the barrel.

'Heavens,' exclaimed Eloise, eyeing the weapon nervously. She straightened her shoulders. 'We must tie his hands,' she declared. 'I'll not risk him getting away.'

Perkins nudged the still body with the toe of his boot.

'He's not going anywhere, m'lady.'

'Well, we cannot remain out here all night,' she retorted. 'We must take him back to town with us.'

Perkins spat.

'And just 'ow do you propose we do that? The carriage is a good half a mile hence.'

'We will carry him,' she announced. 'And don't you dare to argue with me, Perkins!'

Her groom scratched his head.

'Well, I ain't arguing, m'lady, but he's no lightweight. I'd suggest you'd be best takin' his legs but that ain't seemly…'

'Never mind seemly,' she replied, gazing dubiously at the major's unconscious form. Suddenly he seemed so much larger than she remembered. 'You cannot carry him alone, so I must help you.'

Eloise had never carried a body before. She had never even considered how it should be done. When Perkins had lifted the shoulders she took a firm grip of Jack's booted ankles and heaved. Half-carrying, half-dragging, they staggered back along the path with their burden, but they had not gone many yards before she was forced to call a halt.

'We will never carry him all the way back to the carriage,' she gasped.

'Well, I could always run back and fetch Coachman Herries.'

A cold wind had sprung up and it tugged at her cloak.

'I do not want to be standing out here any longer than necessary.' She looked around. 'There is a hut of some sort over there. Perhaps we could put him in

there until he comes around.' She sensed the groom's
hesitation and stamped her foot. 'For heaven's sake,
Perkins, do you think we should let him perish out
here?'

'Aw, 'tedn't that cold, madam, and besides I don't
see why you should worry, if he's such a villain.'

'*He* may be a villain but I am not,' declared Eloise
angrily. 'Now take his shoulders again and help me
get him into that shelter!'

It was a struggle but eventually they managed to
get their unwieldy burden into the shepherd's hut.
Perkins spotted an oil lamp hanging from the roof
and pulled out his tinder box to light it. Eloise, very
warm after her exertions, threw off her cloak before
picking up a piece of twine to bind the major's hands
behind his back. Not a moment too soon, for even
as she finished tying the knot Jack groaned.

'Quickly, now, help me to sit him up.'

'If I was you I'd leave him on the floor, where
'e belongs,' opined Perkins, but she overruled him:
she did not like to think of any creature bound and
helpless at her feet.

They propped him up against a pile of sacks in
one corner and Eloise stood back, watching as the
major slowly raised his head.

'Where am I?'

'There is no point in struggling,' she said, trying
to sound fierce. 'You are my prisoner.'

'The devil I am!'

'You keep a civil tongue when speakin' to my lady,' growled the groom.

'That is enough, Perkins.' Eloise turned back to Jack. 'Where is the journal?'

'What journal?'

'The diary. Where is it?'

'I have no idea what you mean.'

Her eyes narrowed.

'What were you doing on the heath?'

Jack looked up at her from under his black brows. The feeble lamplight threw dark shadows across his face and she could not see his eyes.

'I was following you. What were *you* doing?'

'That is nothing to do with you. I—' She stopped, her eyes widening. She turned to her groom, saying urgently, 'The package! Run back to the tree, quickly, and collect it.'

Perkins hesitated.

'I don't like to leave you alone with 'im, m'lady.'

'His hands are bound, he cannot hurt me. But leave me the pistol, if you like, only go and collect that package!'

As the groom let himself out of the hut she weighed the pistol in her hand.

'If that is mine I would advise you to keep your fingers away from the trigger, it is very light.' She glanced up to find Jack watching her. 'I would guess you had never used one of those.'

She shrugged.

'It should not be difficult, at this range.'

'Not at all, if you think you can kill a man.'

She glared at him.

'I can and will, if you give me cause!'

A derisive smile curved his mouth and she looked away.

'Who tied my hands?'

'I did.'

'And how did I get in here?'

'We carried you.'

'We?'

'Yes.' She flushed, saying angrily, 'It is you who should be answering questions, not I.'

'Then you had best ask me something.'

She was silent, and after a moment he said wearily, 'I wish you would sit down. Since I cannot stand it is very impolite of you to put me at such a disadvantage.'

Eloise was suspicious, but she could read nothing from his countenance, save a certain irritation. She glanced around. There was a small stool in one corner and she pulled it forwards, dusted it off and sat down. He smiled.

'Thank you. Now, what did you want to ask me?'

'Why were you following me?'

He leaned back, wincing a little as his head touched the sacking piled behind him.

'I saw you coming out of Coutts's this morning.

When you denied it so fiercely at the Renwicks' party I became suspicious.'

'Oh? And just what did you suspect?'

'I don't know: that you had run out of money, perhaps.'

'I am not so irresponsible!' she flashed, annoyed.

He ignored her interruption.

'I followed you through Hampstead,' he continued, watching her carefully. 'It occurred to me that perhaps someone has a hold on you. This journal that you talked of: are you trying to buy it back?'

'That is none of your business!'

'I have a cracked skull that says it is my business,' he retorted. 'By the bye, is my head bleeding?'

She looked up, alarmed.

'I don't know—does it hurt you very much?'

'Like the devil.' He winced. 'Perhaps you would take a look at it.'

Eloise slid off the stool to kneel beside him. Absently she brushed his hair out of his eyes before gently pulling his head towards her, eyes anxiously scanning the back of his head.

'Oh heavens, yes, there is blood—oh!'

Even as she realised that he had somehow freed his hands he reached out and seized her. The next moment she was imprisoned in his powerful grasp and he had twisted her around so that it was she who was pinioned against the sacks, with Jack kneeling over her.

'Some day I'll teach you how to tie knots, my lady,' he muttered, taking the pistol from her hand.

'What are you going to do to me?'

She eyed him warily. Despite the shadows she felt his eyes burning into her.

'What would you suggest? After all, you have done your best to murder me.'

'That is quite your own fault!' She struggled against him. 'You had no right to be following me, dressed all in black like a common thief! Anyone might have mistaken you!'

She glared up at him, breathing heavily. She became aware of a subtle change in the atmosphere. Everything was still, but the air was charged with energy, like the calm before a thunderstorm. Her breathing was still ragged, but not through anger. He was straddling her, kneeling on her skirts and effectively pinning her down while his hands held her wrists. She stopped struggling and lay passively beneath him, staring at his shadowed face. He released one hand and drew a finger gently along her cheek.

'I think we may have mistaken each other, Lady Allyngham.'

His voice deepened, the words wrapped about her like velvet. She did not move as he turned his hand and ran the back of his fingers over her throat. Eloise closed her eyes. His body was very close to her own and her nerves tingled. Her senses were heightened, she was aware of every movement, every noise in the small dark hut. She could smell him, a mixture of leather and wool and spices, she could feel his warm breath on her face. Eloise lifted her chin, but whether it was in defiance or whether she was inviting his lips to join hers she could not be sure. Her breasts tensed, her wayward body yearned for his touch.

It never came.

The spell was broken as the door burst open and Perkins's aggrieved voice preceded him into the hut.

'Dang me but I couldn't find it, m'lady. Looked everywhere for that danged package but it'd gone, and nothing in its place! I think it—*what the devil*!'

The groom pulled up in the doorway, his eyes popping. As he looked around for some sort of weapon Jack eased himself away from Eloise and waved the pistol.

'Perkins, isn't it? I beg you will not try to overpower me again,' he said pleasantly. 'You would not succeed, you know.'

Eloise struggled to her feet.

'I did *not* untie him,' she said, feeling the groom's accusing eyes upon her. 'But he is not our villain. The fact that the package is gone confirms it.'

'He might have an accomplice,' said Perkins, unconvinced.

'Believe me, I mean your mistress no harm,' said Jack, standing up and dropping the pistol back into his pocket. 'I want to help, but to do that I need to know just what is going on.'

He drew out his handkerchief and pressed it cautiously to the back of his head. Eloise saw the dark stain as he took it away again. She said quickly, 'Yes, but not now. First we must clean up that wound.'

'My man will do that for me when I get back to town.'

'Then let us waste no more time.'

She clutched at his sleeve and led him outside, leaving Perkins to put out the lamp and shut the door.

'Can you walk?' she asked. 'Do you need my groom to support you?'

'No, I will manage very well with you beside me.' She felt his weight on her arm. 'I am not too heavy for you?'

'I helped carry you,' she retorted. 'You were much heavier then.'

She heard him laugh and looked away so he would not see her own smile. She was not yet ready to admit to a truce. They continued in silence and soon the carriage lights were visible in the distance.

'Did you ride here?' asked Eloise.

'Yes. My horse is tethered to a bush, close to your carriage.'

'Give Perkins your direction and he will ride it back to the stable.'

'And just how is *he* to get back?' demanded the groom.

'He will travel back with me in the carriage.' Eloise bit her lip. 'I think I owe Major Clifton an explanation.'

Jack followed Eloise into the carriage and settled himself into the corner, resting the undamaged side of his head against the thickly padded squabs. The coachman had orders to go carefully, but the carriage still rocked and jolted alarmingly as they made their way back towards town. He peered through the darkness at his fellow passenger.

'Are you going to tell me the truth now, madam?'

There was silence. He thought he detected a faint sigh.

'This morning I received a letter,' she said at last, 'asking me to put one hundred guineas under the roots of a fallen tree on Hampstead Heath. The instructions were quite explicit.'

'And what did you expect to get for your money?'

'The—the return of a diary. When I went into the Clevedons' garden last night it was because I had received a note, instructing me to do so. At the base of Apollo I found a piece of paper. It was a page torn from a…a very personal diary.' There was a pause. 'I discovered it was missing last year, but with all the grief and confusion over Allyngham's death, I thought it had been destroyed.'

'I see. I take it you do not wish the contents of this journal to become public?'

'That is correct.' The words were barely audible.

'And what is it you wish to keep secret, madam?'

There was an infinitesimal pause before she said coldly, 'That you do not need to know.'

'I do if I am to help you to recover the book.'

'If you had not interfered tonight I might already have it back! Who knows but your untimely appearance frightened off the wretch?'

'He was not too frightened to take your money,' Jack retorted.

'Well…mayhap he will return the book to me tomorrow.'

'You are air-dreaming, Lady Allyngham. In my experience this type of rogue will keep on demanding money until he has bled you dry.'

'No!'

'Yes.' He leaned forwards, saying urgently, 'The only way to stop this man is to catch him.'

'Perhaps.'

'There is no perhaps about it.' The carriage slowed and began to turn.

'King Street,' she said, peering out of the window. 'We have arrived at your rooms, Major. Would you like my footman to accompany you to the door?'

'No, thank you, I can manage that short distance.' He stepped carefully down on to the flagway.

'Major Clifton!'

Jack turned back to the darkened carriage. Eloise was leaning forwards, her face pale and beautiful in the dim light.

'I am sorry you were injured,' she said. 'And I thank you, truly, for your concern.'

He grasped her outstretched hands, felt the slight pressure of her fingers against his own before she gently pulled free, the carriage door was closed and the carriage rolled off into the night.

Eloise stirred restlessly. *Such* dreams had disturbed her sleep: menacing letters, walking alone across a lonely heath, bags of guineas. An encounter with Major Jack Clifton. She sat up. *That* was no dream. As the reality crowded in upon her she put her hands to her head. She had left a packet containing a hundred guineas on Hampstead Heath. The money had gone, and the diary had not been returned. She gave a little shiver as she thought of the damage that could be done if ever its contents were made known. On top of all that she had been obliged to explain something of her plight to Jack Clifton. For a moment she forgot her own worries to wonder if his head was hurting him this morning—perhaps he had forgotten the night's events. The thought occurred only to be dismissed. Jack Clifton had not been that badly injured; witness the way he had overpowered her.

Eloise allowed herself to dwell on that scene in the shepherd's hut, Jack sitting on the floor, looking up at her with a devilish grin on his handsome face. And when she had knelt before him, fooled into concern for the cut on his head, he had not hesitated to seize her. She could still remember the sensation of being at his mercy, the shiver that had run through her when she looked up and saw the devils dancing in his eyes. It had not been fear, but excitement that had coursed through her veins, the thought of pitting herself against him, her wits against his strength. Angrily she gave herself a little shake.

'Enough,' she muttered, scrambling out of bed and tugging at the bell-pull. 'He never thought highly of you, and after last night he thinks even less. You had best forget Major Clifton.'

But it seemed that was easier said than done. As she partook of her solitary breakfast she tried to put him out of her mind but it was almost as if she had conjured him up when Noyes came to announce that she had a visitor.

'Major Clifton is here to see you, my lady. He is waiting for you in the morning room.'

For a single heartbeat she considered telling Noyes to deny her, but decided against it. After all, it was her servant who had attacked the major: the least she could do was to show a little concern.

'Thank you, I will go to him directly.' She rose, putting a hand up to her curls, and it took a conscious effort not to stop at the mirror to check her appearance before entering the morning room.

Major Clifton was standing by the window, staring out into the street. He seemed to fill the room, his tall figure and broad shoulders blocking the light, and when he turned she was disturbed to find she could not read the expression on his shadowed face. He bowed.

'Lady Allyngham.'

She hovered by the door, wishing she had asked the butler to leave it open.

'Good morning, Major. How is your head?'

'Sore, but no lasting damage, I hope.'

'I hope so, too.' She gave him a tentative smile. 'Won't you sit down, sir?'

She indicated a chair and chose for herself a sofa on the far side of the room. To her consternation the major followed and sat down beside her. Heavens, would the man never do as he was bid? She sat bolt upright and stared straight ahead of her, intensely aware of him beside her, his thigh only inches away from her own. Her heightened senses detected the scent of citrus and spice: a scent she was beginning to associate with this man. She made a conscious effort to keep still: she thought wildly it would have been more comfortable sitting next to a wolf!

'M-may I ask why you are here?' she enquired, amazed that her voice sounded quite so normal.

'I want to help you catch whoever is persecuting you.'

Her head came round at that.

'Thank you, sir, but I do not need your help.'

'Oh, I think you do. Who else is there to assist you? I presume the journal is your property, so perhaps you intend to enlist the services of a Bow Street Runner to retrieve it?'

'That is impossible.' She glared at him. 'If you had not interfered last night the matter might well have been concluded.'

'I doubt it. However, I do acknowledge that I am in some small way embroiled in this affair now…'

'Nonsense! This is nothing to do with you.'

'I would not call having my head split open nothing.'

'I should have thought *that* would be a warning to you to stay away!'

His slow smile appeared, curving his lips and warming his eyes, so that she was obliged to stand up and move away or risk falling under the spell of his charm.

'My friends would tell you that I can never resist a challenge, madam.'

'And *my* friends would tell you that I am perfectly capable of looking after myself.'

'Quite clearly that is not true, for you are in serious trouble now, are you not?' When she did not reply he said softly, 'Perhaps you intend to enlist the help of Alex Mortimer—'

'No! Mr Mortimer must know nothing of this.'

'And why not? I thought he was a close friend of yours. A very *close* friend.'

His meaning unmistakable, Eloise turned away, flushing. She said in a low voice, 'You know nothing about this. You do not understand.'

'Oh, I understand only too well, madam,' he said coldly. 'This—journal you are so concerned about: I have no doubt it contains details of your affairs. Details that you do not wish even Mortimer to know.'

She gave a brittle laugh.

'You are very wide of the mark, Major.'

'Am I? Tell me, then, what it is in this book that is so terrible?' She looked at him. There was no smile in his eyes now, only a stony determination. As if sensing her inner turmoil the hard look left his eyes. He said gently, 'Will you not trust me?'

Eloise bit her lip. She wanted to trust him. She thought at that moment she would trust him with her life, but the secrets in the journal involved others, and she could not betray them. And if he should discover the truth, she thought miserably that he would look upon her with nothing but disgust. Unconsciously her fingers toyed with Tony's heavy signet ring that she had taken to wearing on her right hand.

'I cannot,' she whispered. 'Please do not ask it of me.'

She met his gaze, her heart sinking when she saw the stony look again on his face. It was no more than she expected, but it hurt her all the same.

Jack watched her in silence. The distress he saw in her every movement tore at him. He wanted to comfort her, but she was no innocent maid: she had told him quite plainly she did not need his protection. So why did he find it so difficult to leave her to her fate? He rose, disappointed, angry with himself for being so foolish. He had wanted her to confide in him, to tell him she was an innocent victim, but it was clear now that she could not do so. Better then to go now, to walk away and forget all about the woman.

'Very well, madam. If that is all...'

'I am very sorry,' she murmured.

'So, too, am I.'

A soft knock sounded upon the door and Noyes entered.

'I beg your pardon, madam, but you asked me to bring any messages to you.'

He held out the tray bearing a single letter: she reached for it, hesitating as she recognised the untidy black scrawl.

Jack made no move to leave the room. Eloise had grown very pale and she picked up the letter as if it might burn her fingers.

'Thank you,' she said, 'That will be all.'

'Well?' Jack waited until the butler had withdrawn before speaking. 'Is it another demand? What does he say?'

She handed it to him.

'You had best read it.'

Jack ran his eyes over the paper.

'So he wants to meet with you.'

'Yes, but at Vauxhall Gardens. That will be very different from Hampstead Heath.'

'But even more dangerous. Much easier for a villain to lose himself in a crowd than on a lonely heath.'

'He does not ask for more money,' she said hopefully. 'Perhaps he means to give me back the book.'

Jack frowned. 'I think it more likely that he has other demands to make of you.' He gave her the letter. 'He does not expect an answer: the fellow is very sure of himself, damn his eyes!' He began to pace about the room. All thoughts of abandoning Eloise had disappeared. 'We will need to use your carriage, ma'am, and I think it would be useful to have your groom and my man there. We could send them on ahead of us: they will not look out of place in the crowd; one sees all sorts at Vauxhall. We have a few days to prepare…'

'We?' She raised her brows at him. 'I told you I do not want your help, Major, and I thought we had agreed I do not deserve it!'

Jack stared at her, unwilling to admit even to himself why he was so determined not to leave her to her fate.

'Allyngham saved my life,' he said curtly. 'I owe it to his memory to help you and to protect his name.'

'Whatever you may think of me?'

'Whatever I may think of you!'

Chapter Five

Eloise looked around the crowded ballroom. The plans were laid: tonight, very publicly, she was to invite Jack Clifton to escort her to Vauxhall. She experienced a sudden spurt of anger towards the unknown letter-writer: if it were not for him it would not be necessary for her to attend another glittering party. Lord Berrow was adamant that he could not sell her Ainsley Wood, so there was no reason for her to remain in London, and with Alex away she would much rather have returned to Allyngham than be walking alone into a crowded ballroom, knowing that nearly every man present would be turning lustful eyes towards her. She shivered: any one of them could be her villain.

'My dear Lady Allyngham, you are looking charming this evening, quite charming!' Lord Berrow was at her side, beaming and offering her his arm. 'And no Mr Mortimer to escort you.'

'He is gone into Hertfordshire,' she responded. 'But I expect him back very soon.'

She tried to smile, but the idea that any one of her acquaintances could have the diary had taken hold of her mind and she could not relax.

'Excellent, then you must allow me to take his place: can't have such a pretty little thing unattended.' He held up his hand as she opened her mouth to protest. 'I know what you are thinking: Lady Berrow is happily engaged with our hostess for the moment, and I know she will not begrudge me a turn about the room with a pretty woman, eh?'

She felt a tiny flicker of amusement at the Earl's behaviour. He puffed out his chest and strutted beside her, showing her off to his friends as if she was a prize he had won. However, it was not long before she began to find his rather self-centred conversation quite tedious, and it was with relief that she spotted Major Clifton. He made no effort to approach and at length she excused herself prettily from Lord Berrow, who squeezed her arm and invited her to come back and join him whenever she wished.

Eloise moved off but immediately found her way blocked by a stocky figure in an amethyst-coloured coat and white knee-breeches.

'Lady Allyngham.' Sir Ronald Deforge bowed his pomaded, iron-grey curls over her hand. 'A delightful surprise: I was afraid you had left town.'

She gave him a smooth, practised answer.

'Why should I wish to do that, when so many friends remain?'

'But you said, the other night, that you were tired of town life.'

'Did I?' She managed a laugh. 'Let us ascribe that to low spirits, Sir Ronald. I am perfectly happy now, I assure you.'

She walked away, making for the refreshment table, where she observed Major Clifton filling a cup from one of the large silver punch-bowls.

'You cannot know the happiness it gives me to hear you say that,' declared Sir Ronald, following her.

Eloise paid him no heed: she was watching Jack as he continued to fill his cup: she was sure he had seen her, but unlike every other gentleman in the room, who would have been at her side at the slightest invitation, he was studiously avoiding her eye. Stifling her irritation, she approached the table. Sir Ronald sprang forwards.

'Let me help you to a cup of punch, ma'am.'

Jack looked around, as if aware of her presence for the first time.

'Good evening, Major Clifton.'

'My lady.'

His slight bow was almost dismissive. Her eyes narrowed.

Deforge handed her a cup. 'Your punch, Lady Allyngham.'

She thanked him but turned away almost

immediately to make it plain she had no further need of his company. As Sir Ronald questioned one of the servants about the ingredients of the punchbowl, she moved a little closer to Jack.

'A delightful crush tonight, is it not, Major?' she said, smiling.

'Delightful.'

His response was polite but hardly encouraging. She reached past him to pick up the ladle and add a little more punch to her cup.

'Are you avoiding me, sir?' she asked him quietly. 'Perhaps you do not wish to continue with our plan?'

A smile tugged at the corners of his mobile mouth.

'Of course I do,' he murmured. He took the ladle from her hand, brushing her gloved fingers with his own. 'Allow me, my lady.'

She carried the refilled cup to her lips, watching him all the time. His smile grew. He turned slightly so that no one else could hear him.

'Well, madam? You must invite me to go with you to Vauxhall.'

Indignation swelled within her as she noted the wicked glint in his eye: he was enjoying this!

She raised her voice a little. 'Have you thought any more about Vauxhall, sir? I should very much like to visit the gardens on Tuesday, if you will escort me.'

He seemed to consider the matter.

'Tuesday… I *think* I could be free that evening.'

Eloise seethed. Her smile became glacial.

'If it is too much trouble for you—!'

'Did you say Vauxhall, my lady?' Sir Ronald stepped up. 'I would be more than happy—'

'Thank you, sir, but having offered to go with Major Clifton, it would be very cruel of me now to deny him.' She gave Jack a glittering smile. 'Would it not, Major?'

Her heart missed a beat as he hesitated.

'It would, of course,' he said slowly, 'but if Sir Ronald is willing…'

There could be no mistaking the venomous look that passed between the men. Sir Ronald said coldly, 'If the major is not able to escort you, madam…'

Jack put up his hand.

'And yet I do not think that will be necessary. I have not been to Vauxhall for some time, ma'am. It will be amusing to visit the gardens with you.' His eyes laughed at her. 'Shall we go by water, or the road?'

'We will take my carriage, naturally,' she replied, her calm tone quite at odds with the fury inside her.

'Naturally,' he murmured. 'So much more… intimate.'

Eloise knew her smile did not reach her eyes. She

sipped at her punch, determined not to make a hasty retort.

'Then you will not be requiring my services.' Sir Ronald's angry mutter recalled Eloise to her surroundings. She held out her hand to Sir Ronald and gave him a warm smile.

'Perhaps another time, sir.'

'Perhaps, my lady.' He bowed over her hand and walked away.

She and Jack were momentary alone at the table.

'And what was that little charade about?' she demanded icily.

'Just that, a charade.'

'You made me almost *beg* you to come with me!'

He laughed.

'You have the whole of London at your feet: there has to be some reason for the Glorious Allyngham to accept the escort of a mere major. Everyone will think I played my hand very cleverly and piqued your interest.'

She placed her cup back on the table with a little bang.

'I wish I had turned you down!'

'What, and accepted Deforge as your escort instead? You would find him a dead bore, I assure you.'

She ground her teeth in frustration.

'I do not need you! I could write to Alex: he could be back here tomorrow.'

Jack refilled her cup and handed it back to her.

'But you do not want him to know what you are about: what excuse would you give him, calling him away from his business just to escort you to Vauxhall?'

She eyed him resentfully, hating the fact that he was right. He laughed again.

'You may as well accept my help with a good grace, my lady. Now drink your punch and we will let the world see that I have fallen under your spell!'

After a solitary dinner on Tuesday night, Eloise went up to her room to prepare for her trip to Vauxhall Gardens. She chose to wear an open robe of spangled gauze over a slip of celestial blue satin. Her cap was a delicate confection of lace, feathers and diamonds that sparkled atop her golden curls. Looking in the mirror, she was pardonably pleased with the result.

'You look elegant and very stylish,' she told her reflection, adding, as thoughts of a certain tall, dark soldier entered her mind, 'and you do not look in the least fast!'

With her domino of midnight-blue velvet thrown over her arm she made her way downstairs to wait for Major Clifton. Minutes later he was shown into the drawing room, attired in a dark blue coat that seemed moulded to his figure, as did the buff-coloured pantaloons that encased his legs and disappeared into a pair of gleaming, tasselled Hessians. She put up her chin a fraction as she was subjected to his swift, hard scrutiny.

'Well, Major, do I pass muster?'

Her spirits lifted a little when she saw a flicker of admiration in his face: she had seen that look too often to be mistaken.

'I have never questioned your beauty, my lady.'

'Only my morals!' she flashed.

He put up one hand.

'Shall we call a truce, ma'am? We will need to work together if we are to succeed this evening.'

'What do you mean by that?'

'We have no idea who is writing these letters, but you may be sure that they will be watching you tonight. We must make everyone believe that I am there purely as your escort, to be easily dropped while you slip off to...where is it?'

'The Druid's Walk.'

'Yes, the Druid's Walk for your assignation.'

A smile tugged at the corners of her mouth.

'Do you really think you can act the role of a mooncalf, Major?'

He grinned back at her.

'Oh, I think I can manage that, madam.' He held out his arm. 'Shall we go?'

* * *

The journey to Vauxhall was accomplished much more quickly than they had anticipated, the traffic over the bridge being very light, and they were soon part of the line of carriages making their way to the gardens. Despite her anxiety, Eloise enjoyed Major Clifton's company far more than she had anticipated. He said nothing contentious, and treated her with such courtesy and consideration that she soon relaxed.

Jack, too, was surprised. He had heard enough of the Glorious Allyngham to expect her to be a witty and entertaining companion but he was taken off guard by the generous, unaffected nature that shone through her conversation: she was as happy to discuss the government or the plight of the poor as she was Edmund Kean's latest performance. She had little interest in gossip and confessed that she was happier living quietly at Allyngham than being ogled in the ballrooms of London. Intrigued, Jack regarded her across the dim carriage.

'This is a very different picture of you, my lady. You are not at all the Wanton Widow you are named.'

'She does not exist.'

'That is not what I have heard.'

She shrugged.

'The *ton* must gossip about someone. It may as well be me.'

'And do they not have good reason to talk of you?

You have captivated every gentleman in town, and in so doing you have made every lady jealous.'

'They have no need to be jealous of me: their menfolk may lust after me, they may talk of laying siege to the Glorious Allyngham—you see, Major, I know what is said of me!—but I have no interest in any of them.'

'If that is so, then why did you come to town?'

'Oh, for company. For the concerts, and the society.' She added pointedly, 'It is possible to enjoy a man's conversation without wanting to take him for a lover, Major.' She glanced out of the window. 'Goodness, we are at the entrance already. How fast time flies when one is talking.'

She turned to smile at him and Jack's senses reeled. The flames from the blazing torchères illuminated the interior of the carriage, glinting off the lady's lustrous curls and lighting up her countenance, giving her the appearance of a golden goddess. Desire wrenched at his gut. He wanted to reach out and pull the pins from her hair, to watch those curls tumble down her back in a glorious golden stream. He wanted to take her in his arms and lose himself

'Major? We must alight: we are holding up the traffic.'

There was a laugh in her soft voice. He snapped out of his reverie and jumped down. Damnation, he must be careful: he was enjoying her company but he had no intention of falling victim to her charms.

Jack handed her out of the carriage and waited silently while she adjusted her domino, resisting the temptation to help, knowing if he did so his hands would linger on her shoulders. What was is she had said? *It is possible to enjoy a man's conversation without wanting to take him for a lover.* Perhaps that was true: all he knew was that he wanted nothing to mar the easy camaraderie that was growing between them.

'We have an hour to spare before supper,' he told her as they walked through the Grove, the sounds of the orchestra drifting through the air towards them. 'Shall we take a stroll about the gardens?'

'Yes, if you please. Perhaps we should find the Druid's Walk, so I know where I am to go later.'

Eloise was happy to accompany Major Clifton through the tree-lined avenues illuminated by thousands of twinkling lamps. At one intersection they spotted Perkins and Jack's man, Robert, but they exchanged no more than a glance. Until that moment Eloise had been able to forget the purpose of their visit to the gardens. Now the fear came flooding back and she stole anxious glances at each person they passed.

'It is very unnerving to think that any one of these people might be our villain,' she muttered.

'We will know soon enough. Until then let us try

to pass the time without worrying. Perhaps you could tell me something of your history.'

She looked up at him, surprised.

'It is not very interesting. I have done little, and travelled less.'

'I understand there was some opposition to your marriage to Lord Allyngham?'

'Strong opposition,' she told him. 'My parents died when I was a baby and I was sent to Allyngham to be brought up with the family. Lady Allyngham had no daughter, you see, and she brought me up with the intention that I would be something in the nature of a companion to her.'

'Did they treat you well?'

'Yes, very well. Tony and I grew up together—and Alex, of course, who lived on the neighbouring estate. We were all close friends, inseparable until the boys went away to school, and even then we were always together when they came home for the holidays.'

'If that was the case then the Allynghams might have expected Tony to fall in love with you.'

She sighed. 'I do not believe the thought occurred to them. He was their second son and it was expected that he would make an advantageous match. It is not surprising that they were mortified when he decided to marry me, a penniless orphan.'

'That must have been very unpleasant for you.'

'It was, a little. Oh, they did nothing so very bad;

they loved Tony far too much to disinherit him or anything of that nature, but there was always a certain—coolness. It lasted until they died five years ago.'

'If you had given Allyngham an heir...'

She flinched a little at that.

'Perhaps that might have helped, but it was not to be.'

He glanced down at her, concerned, and she gave him a strained little smile.

'You are not to be thinking my life is empty, Major. I have plenty to occupy me, looking after the Allyngham estates.'

'That must be a heavy burden for you.'

'Not really, I enjoy it. I took charge initially because Tony was away in the army. He trusted me to look after everything for him and we have an excellent steward, too. And Alex is always there to advise me.'

'Ah, Mortimer.' She heard the harsh note creep into his voice. 'And was he also *always there* while your husband was away?'

She stopped. Suddenly it was important that she make him understand. She turned towards him, fixing her eyes upon his face.

'Alex and I are very close, we share many of the same interests, but we have never been more than friends. Tony knew that: it gave him some comfort to know that when he was away we could look after each other.' Impulsively she put her hands on his chest. 'I may flirt a little, Major, but I have never played my husband false, and I never intend to do so. I want you to believe that.'

They stared at one another, oblivious of the raucous laughter and exclamations of the crowds around them. Jack's hand came up and covered her fingers.

'I do believe it,' he said slowly. 'The more I know of you, the more I am intrigued. I think you are more innocent that you would have me believe.'

Eloise stepped back. Warning bells were clamouring in her head: he was far too close to the truth! She gave a little laugh.

'Do not put me on a pedestal, Major, I pray you.' She tucked her hand in his arm. 'Shall we find our supper box now?'

However, when they were seated in their box, Eloise gave Jack a smiling apology.

'I am afraid my appetite has quite deserted me. We are so exposed here, with all the world and his wife walking by.'

'Then let us give them a performance,' murmured Jack, bringing his chair a little closer. 'You need to eat, so I shall feed you titbits.'

'No, I should not—'

He speared a tiny piece of the wafer-thin ham with his fork and held it out to her.

'Yes, you should.'

'But everyone is watching!'

'Exactly. If our man is out there he will be reassured. And as for the rest, well, they will think I am the luckiest dog alive!'

Looking into his smiling eyes, Eloise capitulated. She opened her lips to take the proffered morsel. It was delicious, which seemed to heighten the decadence of the action, and she did not protest when Jack offered her another. She felt he was tempting her with so much more than a mouthful of food. Eloise put down her wine cup. The arrack punch was very strong and it was already making her senses swim.

'You are flirting with me, Major.'

'Very much so. And if I bring my head closer to yours while I pour the wine…'

'No more for me, thank you! I need to keep a clear head for later. Do you really think we are being watched?'

'I do. We must show him that I am truly enamoured of you.'

'Oh, how?'

He took her hand.

'Like this.'

Her toes tingled with excitement when she saw the wicked gleam in his eye. She watched as he slowly pulled off her glove, holding her hand like a delicate piece of porcelain. Gently he turned it over and lowered his head to press a kiss on the inside of her wrist. She gasped. He continued to drop kisses on the soft skin of her arm. Little arrows of fire were shooting through her; it was all she could do to keep still.

'I—um—I think we should stop now.'

He ran the tip of his tongue lightly across the hinge of her elbow. Unspeakably pleasurable sensations curled around inside her, so intense she was afraid she might slide off her chair. She gazed at his head as he bent over her: she wanted to reach out and caress the raven's gloss of his hair. She clenched her free hand to prevent herself from trying such a thing.

'Major. *Jack*!' She hissed his name, almost squirming now under his touch. 'People are staring.'

He raised his head, fixing her with a devilish grin.

'That is exactly what we want,' he murmured. 'It is almost time for you to keep your appointment in Druid's Walk.'

Immediately the pleasant lassitude she had been feeling disappeared. She swallowed nervously.

'It is?'

He nodded, slipping one arm around her waist.

'So I am going to try to kiss you, then you will slap my face and leave me. Can you do that?'

Swallowing again, she nodded. Smiling, Jack gently pulled her into his arms. It was like coming home. Eloise gazed up into his eyes, black and fathomless as night. His face was only inches from her own. Her lips parted instinctively, her eyelids drooped. She ached for him to kiss her but his mouth remained tantalizingly just out of reach.

'Now you have to slap me.' Jack's voice was no more than a croak. He said curtly, 'Do it!'

Eloise dragged her wandering thoughts back. She knew what was expected of her. Pulling herself out of his grasp, she slapped him with her bare hand. Then, snatching up her glove and her domino, she marched off.

The gardens were much more frightening for an unescorted lady. Eloise pulled the hood of her domino over her head and hurried along the paths, trying to ignore the rowdy laughter coming from the darker walks. She kept her head down. Someone knocked her shoulder.

'I beg yer pardon, lady.'

She heard Perkins's familiar voice and felt a rush of gratitude, glancing up in time to see him tugging at his forelock before he turned and sauntered away. It was reassuring to know she was not quite alone.

She had memorised the instructions. The second arbour off Druid's Walk. Now as she turned into the famous avenue she began to worry. What if someone was already there? What if the writer wanted to harm her? She shook her head and tried to think rationally. If her tormentor had the journal then most likely he would want some extortionate payment. She

would pay it, too, if it was the only way to get the
book back.

She reached the second arbour and slowed down.
Cautiously she approached the dark space. A canopy
of leaves blotted out almost all the light, but as her
eyes adjusted to the darkness she could see an empty
bench at the back of the enclosure. Her heart beating, she walked to the bench and sat down to wait.
Almost immediately a voice sounded to her right.

'You keep good time, madam. I congratulate
you.'

Eloise jumped up. A black shape detached itself
from the shadows. It was a man, wrapped in a dull
black cloak and hat, his face hidden beneath a black
mask. As he moved forwards the light glittered eerily
on the eyes peering through the slits in his mask. She
cleared her throat.

'What do you want of me?'

He held out his hand and she saw the grey oblong
held between his fingers. It was too dark to read it
but she knew from its shape and size that it was another page from the diary. As her hand reached out
he snatched it back.

'How much?'

He laughed.

'You are very sensible, ma'am. No tears, no
hysterics.'

'Would they do me any good?'

'Not at all.'

'Then I will ask you again, how much?'

'This page I will give you in exchange for a kiss.'

'And the rest of the book?'

She heard him chuckle. It sent a shiver of revulsion running through her.

'That depends upon the kiss.'

He reached out and pulled her to him, pressing his lips hard against her mouth. She froze, fighting against an impulse to push him away.

When he let her go she gasped and instinctively dragged the back of her hand across her mouth.

'Who are you?'

'You will discover soon enough. Here.' He held out the grey oblong. 'Take it. I shall let you know the price for the rest.'

She twitched the paper from his fingers.

'How...how did you come by the book?'

'You do not need to know that.'

She put up her chin.

'It could be a forgery.'

He laughed softly in the darkness.

'And would you have left me a hundred guineas on Hampstead Heath if it had not been genuine?'

She bit her lip, regretting that first, rash action. She said, coldly, 'What if I refuse to continue with this?'

'But you won't.' His voice was low, just above a whisper, and it sent unpleasant shivers through her.

'Neither will you leave town. Do you think if you bury yourself in the country you can escape the scandal? You know that is not true.'

She put up her head.

'If you publish I shall go abroad—'

'And what of the Allyngham name? Such an illustrious history—are you content to see it tainted?'

Eloise peered into the darkness. It was impossible to tell much about her tormentor: the hat and cloak concealed his body as effectively as he had disguised his voice.

'What is it you want from me?'

'You will continue with your engagements. I understand a party will be going to Renwick Hall at the end of the month. You will be invited.'

'How can you be so sure?'

'Mrs Renwick likes you. I have heard her say she would like you to be there.'

She turned away, shaking her head.

'No. I have had enough of your games—'

'If I publish that book your name will be disgraced.'

'Allyngham is dead,' she said dully. 'It will make no odds.'

'But others are very much alive, and they will suffer, will they not? Are you willing to risk their disgrace, perhaps even to risk their lives, Lady Allyngham?'

She stopped. He was right, of course. Slowly she turned back.

'How much do you want?' she asked again.

'I shall let you know that in due course. For now you will continue to adorn the London salons and ballrooms while you await my instructions.'

He stepped back into the shadows. There was a rustle of leaves, then silence. She could see nothing. She put her hands out and stepped towards the back of the arbour. Branches and leaves met her fingers; there was no sign of the cloaked man. Eloise backed away. As she moved closer to the main path she held up the paper, still clutched in her fingers. Even in the dim light she recognised the writing. It was another page from that damning journal. Turning the page to catch the best of the light spilling in from the walk, she read it quickly then, with a sob and a shudder, she turned and ran out on to the path.

Chapter Six

After the darkness of the arbour the lamps strung amongst the trees of the Druid's Walk were positively dazzling. Eloise looked around wildly. Perkins and Robert came running up as she emerged on to the path.

'Did you see him?' she cried. 'He was in there. Did you see him?'

'Wasn't no one in that nook when we got 'ere,' said Perkins. 'We've bin watching all the time and no one's appeared.'

Hasty footsteps scrunched on the gravel and she looked around as Jack approached. He went to put his arm about her but she held him off.

'Where were you?' she demanded. 'You said you would follow me.'

'I did. I set off shortly after you. I admit the crowds in the main walks impeded my progress but I was no more than five minutes behind you.'

Eloise shivered. Had she been in there such a short time?

Jack took her arm. 'You are trembling. Come away from here.'

'No, I must know how he got into the arbour and how he left it again without being seen. There must be a back way.'

Robert reached up and unhooked one of the lanterns from a nearby tree.

'Well, then, madam, perhaps we should take a look.'

With Jack beside her, she followed Robert and Perkins back into the arbour. The lamplight flickered over the closely woven branches that formed the walls. She pointed behind the bench.

'He disappeared through there.'

Robert moved closer, holding the lantern aloft.

'Aha.'

Jack's grip on her arm tightened. 'What is it, Bob?'

'Two of the uprights have been sawn through. A man could squeeze through there.'

Perkins stepped up.

'Shall I go after 'im, m'lady?'

'No,' said Jack. 'He will be long gone by now. We must take Lady Allyngham home. Run ahead, Perkins, and summon the carriage.' He looked down at her. 'What happened, did he demand more money?'

Beneath her cloak Eloise crumpled the paper in

her hand and slipped it into her reticule. She was not about to let Jack read it.

'He said he will let me know his demands later.'

'And did you get a look at him, ma'am?' asked Robert. 'Was he taller than you, fatter—'

She shook her head.

'I could not see. It was very dark, and he was disguised.' She cast a quick glance up at Jack. 'I am sure it is someone who was at the Renwicks' party earlier this week—he knew I was thinking of leaving town. I wondered for a moment if it might *be* Mr Renwick, but he is such a short, round, jolly gentleman his size would have been difficult to disguise.'

'But why should you think of Charles?'

'Because the man said I would be invited to join the Renwicks at their house party, and I was to accept.'

'So our villain is not a stranger to society.' He put his hand over hers. 'I should not have let you meet with this man alone.'

Eloise said nothing. She found herself listening to his voice, trying to match it to the breathy tones of her tormentor. After all, Jack had been at the Renwicks' and standing near to her when she had said she might leave London. And he had been nowhere in sight when she had emerged from the arbour. Had he been discarding his disguise?

She tried to dismiss the idea as they walked back through the gardens. Her instinct was to trust him, but what did she know about this man? He was a soldier, but that might not make him any less a villain. Every nerve was stretched to breaking point and she could not relax, even when they were seated in her comfortable travelling chaise and on their way back to town. She was not at ease, being so close to Jack Clifton. She remembered that night on the Heath. Was he really as innocent as he claimed? He might well have had an accomplice, who had taken the money from the tree roots. She cast a swift, furtive glance at the black shadowed figure beside her. Had the man in the arbour been taller or shorter than Jack, had he been fat, or thin? It was so difficult to tell; the enveloping cloak and tall hat had been a very effective disguise. She thought perhaps he had been more her own height, but everything had happened so quickly she could not be sure.

She turned to stare out of the window at the dark, shadowy fields and the houses flying by. Jack had kissed her once. It should be possible to compare that to her experience in the arbour. Both kisses had been swift and rough, but could they have been from the same man? She tried to think back to Major Clifton's first visit to Dover Street. She remembered her surprise when he had pulled her into his arms, she could even recall the excitement that had flared within her, the dizzying pleasure that for a brief moment had kept her motionless in his arms. But she could not remember the *detail*.

The carriage jolted over the uneven road and she was briefly thrown against her companion. Instead of shrinking away, she held her position, her face only inches from his shoulder. She breathed in, trying to detect any scent that might remind her of the man in the arbour. She leaned closer, desperately searching her memory for any little point that might identify the man. It had been very dark in that leafy bower, and she had seen very little, but she had felt the man's hands gripping her arms—that certainly had been very similar to Jack's savage embrace!—and she had been aware of his mouth pressing her lips, and his rough cheek rubbing against hers. If it was the man sitting beside her in the carriage, there was one way to find out. Aware of her proximity, Jack turned towards her.

'What is it?' he asked her, concern in his voice. 'Madam, are you afraid still?'

Amazed at her own daring, Eloise edged a little closer.

'I vow I *am* a little nervous, sir.'

Jack put his arm about her shoulders.

'There is nothing to be nervous of now, Lady Allyngham. I shall not let anything happen to you.'

She leaned against him with a little sigh.

'You are very good,' she murmured, looking up towards the paler shadow that was his face. She felt his arm tighten around her. There was a momentary hesitation before he bent his head, blocking out the light. Her face upturned, Eloise closed her eyes and waited for his kiss.

The feel of his lips, soft and warm against her own, almost robbed her of her senses but she battled against the mind-numbing sensations he was arousing within her. She must remain calm and make her comparisons. The man in the arbour had smelled of leather and snuff and wine. Now her head was filled with much more refreshing aromas of citrus and spices. The rogue had been content to press his lips hard against hers but Jack's mobile mouth was working gently upon her lips, encouraging them to part. She almost swooned as his tongue explored her mouth, playing havoc with her already disordered senses. She had peeled off her gloves, now with a little moan her hand came up to his cheek. It was smooth and cool beneath her fingers, not rough and pitted. Suddenly it was all too clear; Major Jack Clifton was *not* the villain.

Having established this fact, Eloise knew she should now draw back, but her body would not obey her. Instead of pressing her hands against his chest and pushing him off, they crept up around his neck. In one sudden, swift movement he caught her about the waist and dragged her on to his lap, all the time his mouth locked on hers and his tongue darting and teasing, robbing her of any ability to think.

At last he raised his head and gave a long, ragged

sigh but he kept his arms tightly about her, and she could not find the strength to disengage herself from his hold. Instead her fingers clung to his jacket and she buried her face in his shoulder.

'Oh, what must you think of me?' she murmured into the folds of his beautifully starched neckcloth.

He rested his cheek on the top of her head.

'You were in need of comfort,' he murmured.

She could feel the words reverberating in his chest.

'I was, of course, but I should not have imposed upon you.'

His laugh rumbled against her cheek.

'That was no imposition, my dear, it was sheer delight. In fact, I think we should do it again.'

Eloise was filled with horror. She had behaved quite as wantonly as her reputation had led him to expect and suddenly it was very important that he should not think ill of her. She raised her head and tried to slide off his lap, but strong hands held her firm. She blushed in the darkness, aware of his body pressed against her. The heat from his powerful thighs seemed to be transmitting itself to her own limbs and she had to make a determined effort not to wriggle. She said quietly, 'Please, Major, let me go.'

Immediately he released her and she eased herself back on to the padded seat of the chaise.

'It—it is not as is seems,' she began. How

much should she tell him? How much *could* she tell him?

They were rattling into London now and when she looked up the light from the streetlamps showed her that her companion was smiling.

'How is it, then?' he said. 'Tell me.'

Jack waited, watching as she clasped her hands in her lap, searching around in her mind for words to explain herself. She was such an intriguing mixture of shy innocence and searing passion. It was almost possible to believe she was a virtuous woman. Almost.

'I am afraid I have given you a very false impression, Major Clifton. I am nothing like the Wanton Widow society has christened me. In fact, I—'

She broke off as the carriage slowed. Jack glanced out of the window.

'Dover Street. You are home, my lady.' He opened the door and jumped down, turning to hold out his hand to her. 'We will continue this conversation inside.'

'Oh, no!' She shrank back. 'No, I do not think we should to that. It is so very late…'

He grinned.

'After the events of the past few days I do not think we need to stand upon ceremony, ma'am. Come, we will be more comfortable inside. Besides, your nerves are still disordered and I want to see you take a cup of wine before I leave. It will help you to sleep.'

Jack helped her down from the carriage, but even as they trod up the steps into the house she was suggesting that they should continue their discussions on the morrow. Jack ignored her protests. He was reluctant to leave her: the anger he had felt when he realised the blackguard had escaped them was nothing compared to the cold, gut-wrenching fear he had experienced, knowing that Eloise had been alone with the villain. Lady Allyngham might consider herself a woman of the world, she might enjoy her flirtations with gentlemen of the *ton*, but for a brief time tonight she had been at the mercy of an unscrupulous villain, and Jack's blood ran cold when he thought of what might have happened to her. With one hand possessively around her waist he swept her into the house and guided her towards the morning room, where a thin strip of candlelight glowed beneath the door.

'Major Clifton, I assure you I am perfectly composed now.' She continued to protest as the wooden-faced lackey threw open the door of the morning room. 'There really is no need for you to stay.'

Jack opened his mouth to reply as he followed her into the room but the words remained unspoken. They were not alone. Alex Mortimer was sitting in a chair beside the fire, a glass of brandy on the table beside him and his booted legs stretched out towards the hearth.

'Alex!'

The lady's unfeigned pleasure at the sight of her visitor had Jack grinding his teeth. Mortimer, too, looked particularly at his ease. Damn him. He rose as Eloise went forwards, her hands held out towards him.

'I did not expect you back in town for days yet.'

'My business was concluded early.' Mortimer took her hands and planted a kiss on her cheek. 'Noyes told me you had gone to Vauxhall, so I thought I would wait for you.' He looked across at Jack and raised his brows. 'Am I *de trop*?'

'No, of course not,' said Eloise quickly. Jack noticed she had the grace to blush. 'You know Major Clifton?'

'We have met.' Alex nodded towards Jack, his eyes wary. 'Is it the usual practice to bring gentlemen home now, Elle?'

Jack's chin jutted belligerently. 'Is it the usual practice to treat a lady's house as if it was your own?'

Eloise stepped between them.

'Major Clifton escorted me back from Vauxhall.'

Alex's brows rose higher. 'I trust you had a pleasant evening.'

Jack was about to retort that pleasure had not been the object of attending the gardens when he realised Eloise was looking at him, such a look of entreaty in her blue eyes that he could not ignore it. He allowed himself a faint, mocking smile.

'How could it be otherwise,' he drawled, 'with Lady Allyngham at my side? And now that you are safely home, madam, and have no further need of my...services, I shall take my leave.'

There was some bitter satisfaction in the way her cheeks flamed at the inference. Mortimer frowned and took a step forwards. Jack braced himself for the challenge but it never came. Eloise put out her hand, palm down, saying coolly,

'Yes, thank you, Major, for escorting me tonight. I am very grateful.'

The shadow of reproach he saw in her eyes flayed his lacerated spirits. He cursed silently. They find Mortimer making himself at home in her house and she expects *him* to act like a gentleman. Clenching his jaw against further unwary comments, he gave a stiff little bow and retired, reminding himself that the widow's behaviour really was no concern of his. But this comforting thought did nothing to alleviate the black mood that enveloped him as he strode back to King Street.

Eloise watched the door close with a snap behind the major and let her breath go in a long and very audible sigh. She untied her cloak and threw it over a chair.

'I am sorry if I have frightened off your lover,' murmured Alex.

Eloise swung round.

'Major Clifton is *not* my lover!' she retorted, knowing the heat was flooding back into her cheeks.

'Well, I think he would like to be,' mused Alex, pressing her down into a chair. 'The look on his face when he saw me here was one of severe disappointment.'

'It was?' She looked up hopefully.

Alex grinned.

'Oh, yes. I think he could happily have murdered me. He looked most disapproving.'

'Well, that is no surprise,' she retorted. 'It was a shock for *me* to find you here at this time of night.'

'This time in the morning, actually,' Alex corrected her, sitting down. 'I was concerned about you. It is not like you to go off to Vauxhall with only Clifton for company. Unless, of course, you have decided to live up to your wicked reputation.'

'I would never do that!' she retorted.

She clasped her hands tightly in her lap, thinking back over the events of the evening. She did not know what to do. About the journal. About Jack. He had been angry when he left, and with good reason. To find Alex waiting for them had been a shock. She was so accustomed to having Alex around that she had thought nothing of it, but a moment's reflection had shown her how it must look to Jack. It confirmed all the disgraceful things he had already heard about her. She gave an inward shrug. It was too late now to worry about that. She turned her mind instead to the problem of the missing journal. She glanced at Alex. Perhaps, after all, she should take him into her confidence. He had always been her friend and she knew she could trust him. Besides, this matter involved him. It was only right that he should know what was happening. She said slowly, 'You will remember, after Tony died, we searched for the journal and could not find it?'

'Yes, but I thought Tony had destroyed it.'

'No. It was stolen.' Eloise looked up. 'And now someone is using it against me.'

Alex sat up straight. 'The devil they are!'

Briefly, Eloise told him all that had happened since he had left town. When it came to explaining Major Clifton's role in the affair she said only that he wanted to keep Tony's name free from scandal and to help her to catch the culprit. When she had finished her recital she reached into her reticule and pulled out the crumpled paper. 'When I met with the villain he gave me this tonight.' She shuddered as she handed it to him. 'Burn it, please, once you have read it.'

Alex took it, rubbing his chin as he frowned over the writing.

'You will see that you are only mentioned there as "M",' she said, 'but if anyone begins to put together the dates and the places, your identity must be known.'

He looked up.

'Why did you not tell me?' he asked. 'Why did you not write to me? I would have come back to town immediately.'

She spread her hands, saying miserably, 'I thought I could deal with this myself. And then...and then Major Clifton became involved.'

Alex tossed the paper into the fire, a look of distaste marring his fair features. He said, 'Tony mentioned Clifton to me in one or two of his letters. Thought quite highly of him, so I suppose we can trust him.' He shot a glance at her. 'How much does he know, Elle?'

'Only that I am desperate to recover the diary.' A knot of unhappiness was twisting itself in her stomach. 'He knows nothing of its contents.'

She lowered her eyes, unwilling to meet Alex's keen glance.

'He thinks it is a scandalous record of your affairs,' he stated baldly.

Eloise shrugged. 'Better that than the truth.'

'And you don't mind that?'

'Of course not. Major Clifton is nothing to me!' She looked away from his searching gaze. 'And there is no need for you to look at me like that. You know I have no wish for another husband.' She managed a scornful laugh. 'Certainly not the major!'

Eloise did not think she sounded very convincing, but Alex seemed satisfied. He said, 'Well, I am here now, and I will help you recover that damned book. You can tell Major Clifton that we no longer require his help.'

Eloise could not understand herself: she had thought she wanted nothing more than to be free for ever of Jack's disturbing presence, but Alex's words gave her pause.

'I am not sure he will be that easy to put off,' said Eloise slowly. 'He is very anxious to protect the Allyngham name.'

'Is that all he wishes to protect?'

Her cheeks grew warm again as she remembered her behaviour in the carriage. She stifled a sigh.

'He has no reason to think well of me.'

'No, it is most likely that Clifton thinks to take you for his mistress.'

'No!' cried Eloise, tears starting to her eyes. 'He must know I would never agree to that!'

'Are you sure? When you go off alone with him to Vauxhall, and invite him into your house in the middle of the night?'

Eloise bit her lip. She had been about to tell Jack the truth, but had he understood that, or had he thought she was offering to take him to her bed?

'Much as I hate to admit it, Jack Clifton could be useful to us,' mused Alex, rubbing his chin. 'After all, we cannot involve too many people in this affair.

And if we are careful, there is no reason why he should ever discover that the journal is anything other than an account of the Wanton Widow's scandalous past, is there?'

Eloise stared into the fire. A short while ago she had been on the verge of telling the major everything. Now she must continue with her role, and abandon any hope of Jack Clifton ever regarding her with respect.

'No,' she said dully. 'No reason at all.'

Chapter Seven

Lady Chastleton's rout promised to be a huge success: the elegant salons were so full that it was impossible to move freely and even though the tall windows to the garden had been thrown open, the noise and heat had increased to an uncomfortable level.

Catching sight of her reflection in the gilded mirror, Eloise thought that no one watching the Glorious Allyngham would think her anything other than a wicked flirt.

She was in Lady Chastleton's elegant salon, at the centre of a group of attentive gentlemen. One young buck was gazing at her adoringly, another had taken her fan and was gently waving it to and fro; Sir Ronald Deforge was offering her a glass of champagne while a red-faced gentleman in a powdered wig was bending to take snuff from her upturned wrist.

Her eyes travelled to where Alex was standing, paying court to a shy ingénue who blushed prettily whenever he addressed her. She sighed. They were both playing out their charade and she knew Alex was as sick of it as she. If only they could retire again to their respective country acres. But it could not be, not yet. Not while the threat of exposure hung over them.

'You must take care not to allow the snuff to stain your fair skin, my lady.' Sir Ronald's voice broke into her reverie. 'Allow me to brush it off.'

He caught her hand and rubbed his thumb over her wrist. It was an effort for her not to pull her hand away with a little shudder of revulsion. Instead she gave him a roguish smile as he bent to touch his lips to the soft whiteness of her inner wrist. Some instinct made her look up at that moment and her smile slipped a little when she saw Major Clifton glowering at her from across the room. Her head went up and she hunched one white shoulder at him. She had heard nothing from him since Vauxhall and it did not matter what he thought, he was nothing to her. When she looked again he had disappeared into the crowd and Eloise tried to convince herself that she did not care, but her dissatisfaction with the evening was intensified.

With soft smiles and caressing words she retrieved her fan, disengaged herself from her entourage and moved away. Lord Berrow was smiling and nodding to her from across the room but she pretended she had not seen him: he might still be persuaded to sell her Ainsley Wood but she had laughed and flirted enough for one night. She would find Alex and ask him to take her home.

'You are frowning, madam. It does not become you.'

Major Clifton's voice at her shoulder brought her to a halt. She looked round to find him beside her. Glancing up, she saw no sympathy in his face, only a cool, considering look in his hard eyes.

'I have the headache,' she said shortly.

'A little air will revive you.' He held out his arm. 'Let me escort you outside.'

She hesitated but the sight of Sir Ronald Deforge standing a short distance away decided her: if she turned from Major Clifton she knew Sir Ronald would be at her side, offering to escort her, enveloping her with his suffocating attentions. She laid her fingers on Jack's sleeve and allowed him to lead her to the nearest of the tall windows. His arm was reassuringly solid beneath the soft wool of his evening coat and it was tempting to lean upon him. It was very odd that she should feel so safe with Jack Clifton beside her, despite his obvious disapproval.

As they stepped outside the night air was cool on her face and the exposed skin of her arms. After the cloying heat of the salon it was refreshing. There were several couples already on the wide balcony, and Eloise made no protest as her partner led her away from them.

'I have not seen you since Vauxhall, Major,' she began. 'I wanted to thank you.'

'For what?' His voice was harsh. 'The kiss we shared in the carriage, or for not knocking Mortimer's teeth down his throat?'

'Neither! For escorting me to the Gardens. For your protection.'

'Little enough protection, since the rogue was able to approach you.'

'Nevertheless, I was very grateful that you were there.' Eloise released his arm and busied herself with arranging her fine lace shawl over her shoulders. 'After…after you had gone, the other night, I decided to tell Alex about the letters. He is involved, you see.'

'I had guessed as much. Well, he will be able to deal with this.'

She paused. She had promised Alex she would seek the major's assistance in recovering the journal. This was her opportunity. She drew a breath.

'Actually, I—*we* would appreciate your continued help, Major. This is a very delicate matter, and there is no one else we can confide in.'

He turned away from her, staring out across the vast expanse of Green Park that stretched away beyond the moonlit gardens. Eloise looked at him. There was something very reassuring about his strong, uncompromising profile, his upright bearing. He looked honourable, incorruptible. Suddenly it was very important to her to have his support. She reached out and touched his arm.

'Please, Major Clifton.'

'Give me one reason why I should help you.'

'You called Tony your friend. I thought you wanted to protect his good name.'

'I did, I do, but why should I concern myself with keeping the name of Allyngham free from scandal when *you* are so determined to sully it?'

Her hand dropped.

'Because I flirt a little—'

He swung round to face her, his countenance as hard as stone in the moonlight.

'A little? You are the talk of the town, madam. The betting books are filled with wagers about you!'

She stiffened.

'I allow no man to go beyond friendly dalliance.'

He gave a bark of mirthless laughter.

'Oh? I was watching you tonight, surrounded by your admirers! Why, you even allowed that fop to take his snuff from your hand!'

'But that is all. It goes no further than that!'

'Does it not?' *I* have kissed you twice, madam. Was that mere dalliance? And what of Mortimer? You consider it *friendly dalliance* to allow him into your house at all hours of the night?'

'No one but you knows he called upon me.'

'Oh, so as long as he visits you in secret it does not matter?'

She bit her lip.

'Alex is an old family friend, nothing more. I told you that.'

'Aye, you did, and I wanted to believe you, but the more I see and hear of you—' He shook his head and said bitterly '—I fear our standards are not the same. Standards—hah! I have known alley cats with better morals than you.'

'How dare you!' Eloise brought her hand up swiftly but he was even quicker. He caught her wrist, his fingers biting into her flesh.

Jack stared at the angry face turned up towards him. The moonlight glinted on her eyes, sending daggers of light towards him. She was radiating fury, her lips parted as if she was about to hiss and spit at him. And with good reason; he had been very uncivil— but what had he said that was not true? It angered him that he threw such accusations at her and she did nothing to deny them. He admitted to himself that he was jealous, too. Jealous that she should bestow her smiles and honeyed words on other men.

They were standing very close and as her breast rose indignantly the flowers of her corsage brushed his waistcoat and filled his senses with a heady perfume. It was distracting, intoxicating. His fingers tightened on her slender wrist, pulling her even closer. Suddenly he wanted to sweep her into his arms and kiss her, transforming her rage into the passion he sensed was just beneath the surface. He saw the anger leave her face. Her eyes widened, as though she was reading his thoughts. He could take her now, he knew it. They were standing breast to breast; he would only have to move a little to bring his mouth down to hers. It was like holding a taper close to a tinderbox, knowing that the slightest touch would ignite a blaze.

She swallowed hard and his eyes were drawn to the convulsive movement in the slender column of her throat. He would like to kiss her there, he thought distractedly. He would like to trail his mouth over her skin to the base of her throat where a pulse was beating so rapidly, and carry on until his lips reached the soft swell of her breasts. Then…

She gave a little sob.

'Let me go, you monster!'

His head jerked up and he came to his senses. She was struggling to free herself from his vice-like grip. Jack released her and she stepped away from him, her left hand cradling her wrist. He hardened himself against her look of anger and reproach to say coldly, 'I am not one of your fawning admirers, Lady Allyngham. You will not strike me for telling the truth.'

Eloise glared up at him, rubbing her sore wrist. She was still furious, but beneath her anger was a lurking fear for the disturbing emotions he aroused in her. The blaze she had seen in his eyes when they had been standing so close had very nearly overset her: she had wanted to throw herself at him, kicking, biting and scratching until he responded. For one dizzying moment she had imagined him pinning her against the wall, subduing her anger with a savage kiss before carrying her off to ravage her in ways that she had heard other women talk of, but had never experienced for herself. Even now, standing before this big, disturbing brute of a man, she did not know whether she was most glad or sorry that he had let her go. She struggled to regain some form of dignity and managed to say in glacial accents, 'We have nothing more to say to each other, Major Clifton. We will consider our acquaintance at an end.'

He clipped his heels together and made her a stiff little bow.

'As you wish, madam.'

She drew herself up, blinking away the tears that threatened to spill over.

'I *wish*,' she said in a low, trembling voice, 'that it was you and not Tony who had perished at Waterloo!'

Turning on her heel, she marched back into the ball-room and did not stop until she had found Alex.

He was playing cards, but as soon as he saw her he excused himself and came to meet her.

'Well, well,' he said, taking her arm, 'now what has occurred to ruffle your feathers?'

'Nothing. I merely want you to take me home.'

He grinned.

'Then I shall do so, of course, but you cannot storm into the card room with the colours flying in your cheeks and tell me nothing is wrong.'

She almost ground her teeth.

'Major Clifton has insulted me.'

Alex raised his brows.

'Oh? Do you want me to call him out?'

'Yes,' she said savagely. 'I want you to challenge him to a duel and then run him through. I want him to die very painfully!'

'Well, I would, of course, my dear, but Clifton is a soldier, so he is bound to be a much better swordsman than I. Then, of course, he might choose pistols, and you know what a terrible shot I am…'

Even through her rage she could not but laugh at his nonsense. Alex patted her arm.

'That's better. Come along then, I will take you home.'

They said nothing more until they were bowling along in the elegant Allyngham town chaise. As they rattled over the cobbles, Alex demanded to know just what had occurred.

'I was going to tell Major Clifton that I had received my invitation to Renwick Hall. I thought he might help us.' She rubbed her sore wrist.

'And what happened?'

'He told me I had the morals of an alley cat.' She

hunted for her handkerchief. 'And I c-could not deny it, especially after he found you in my house when we got back from Vauxhall.'

'He hasn't spread that about, has he?'

'No, of course not.' She blew her nose defiantly. 'But he thinks me quite *sunk* in depravity.'

'As well he might,' remarked Alex with what she thought was heartless candour. 'I think he might be jealous.'

'No, he is not.' She wiped her eyes. 'He is merely the most odious man that ever lived. I hate him!'

'If that is the case, then why are you so upset?'

'Because I am quite *sick* of this charade! I hate everyone thinking ill of me.'

'You mean you hate Jack Clifton thinking ill of you.'

She stamped her foot on the carriage floor.

'That is not it at all,' she said crossly.

'If it's your reputation you are concerned for, I could always marry you.'

'Alex!'

'Well, it is one solution.'

'But you do not want to marry.'

'No, and I do not think it would make you happy, Elle. But if it puts paid to a scandal…'

She shook her head.

'It will not do that, we both know it.' She sighed. Putting away her handkerchief, she reached across the carriage to pat his hand. 'It is very good of you,

Alex, but we neither of us want to marry. I am sorry; I should not have let the hateful Major Clifton upset me so. I think I must be very tired tonight.'

'I think so, too. It is not like you to be so disheartened. If you are truly worried about that journal, Elle, why not come abroad with me and forget about England? It matters little to me now where I live.'

'No, I am resolved not to run away because some, some insignificant little *worm* dares to threaten us!' She drew herself up, saying in a much stronger voice, 'But I am determined we will not ask for Major Clifton's help again. You and I will go to Renwick Hall, we will find a way to recover this wretched book and then I can go back to Allyngham, build my foundling hospital in Tony's memory and, and become a recluse!'

Eloise found herself looking forward to the Renwicks' house party. At least it would mean that she need no longer parade herself in the fashionable salons of the town. During her period of mourning she had missed the society, but the role she had set herself was proving to be very wearing. When Tony had introduced her to the *ton* she had enjoyed the parties and the company, but then the admiration of the gentlemen for Lord Allyngham's wife had always been tempered by her husband's protective presence. Even when Tony was fighting in the Peninsula and she had come to town with only Alex as her escort, somehow Lord Allyngham's shadow hovered over her and no man dared to go too far. However, all that was now changed. As a widow—and a rich one at that—she seemed to attract the predatory males of the town. They circled about her like a pack of wolves and it was only the fact that they considered her to be under Alex's protection that kept them from pouncing. She was aware of her precarious position: her wealth and status gave her entrée to all the grand houses of the *ton*, but if she allowed the flirtations to get out of hand, if she caused too much of a scandal, then society's hostesses would close their doors to her. She would be consigned to the ranks of the *demi-monde* and the proud name of Allyngham would no longer be revered. Her husband would no longer be remembered as a valiant soldier—she might even be obliged to remove the memorial stone from the wall of Allyngham church. That was why it was so important to recover the journal: if its contents ever became known, she and Alex would not only be ostracised by the *ton*, they would be obliged to fly the country.

These sobering thoughts occupied her mind as she journeyed to Renwick Hall. Eloise became even more acutely aware of how society viewed her when she joined her hostess in the drawing room before dinner that evening.

'My dear, how prompt you are,' declared Mrs

Renwick, coming forwards to meet her. 'Everyone else is still at their *toilette*.'

'Oh dear, if I am too early...'

'By no means. I am glad of the company. Come and sit here beside the fire and tell me how you like your room.'

'It is very comfortable, ma'am, and has a lovely view of the lake,' said Eloise, disposing her skirts about her on the satin-covered sofa.

'I knew you would like the blue bedchamber,' smiled Mrs Renwick. 'I regret that we could not find an adjoining room for Mr Mortimer. He sent me word that he will be joining us in the morning. We have had to put him in the bachelor wing, on the far side of the house. With such a house full of guests, I am sure you will appreciate that we have to allocate all the bedchambers in the main building to our married guests.'

Looking into her hostess's kind face, Eloise's heart sank at this tacit acceptance that Alex was her lover. She took a deep breath.

'That is as it should be, ma'am. As a matter of fact, I wanted to ask your advice. I have been thinking for some time that I should have a companion when I am in London. I thought I might ask Allyngham's cousin, Margaret Cromer. We have lost touch a little in recent years but I hope she will consider my request. I have always been a little in awe of her, but I know she is a good friend of yours, ma'am, and wanted to ask you what you thought of the idea before I write to her: do I presume too much, do you think she would accept?'

'Meg Cromer? Oh. I had thought you preferred *not* to have a chaperon! That is, I mean...'

'A widow has a great deal more freedom than a single woman,' said Eloise, taking pity on her hostess's confusion. 'I am aware that there is already a great deal of talk about me, although I hope you will believe me when I say that it is all unfounded. And Mr Mortimer...Mr Mortimer is a good friend, but I have imposed upon him long enough. I think I should go on more comfortably now if I had some female company.'

'You do not think...' Her hostess looked down at her hands. 'Have you considered that marriage would give you a great deal more protection, Lady Allyngham? I am sure there can be no shortage of eligible suitors...'

Eloise shook her head.

'You are very kind to say so, but I have no wish to marry again.'

'No, of course,' replied Mrs Renwick quickly. 'It is very early days, and I believe Lord Allyngham to have been the very best of men. It would be difficult to find his equal.'

'I would not even attempt it,' replied Eloise. 'I am resigned to a single life, but that does not mean I need be bored or lonely. I have a large estate at Allyngham.

That brings its own responsibilities, and I intend to travel, now the Continent is safe again, but for the present I need to make a life for myself, and that necessitates spending some little time in London and I find I am growing tired of being labelled the Wanton Widow.'

Mrs Renwick nodded.

'You are very right, Lady Allyngham, you would be subjected to much less comment if you had Meg as your companion. And you have no need to write to her because she is staying here with me at the moment. So, you may ask her as soon as you wish. She is a stickler for convention, of course: her reputation and character are of such high standing that I feel sure her presence would be an advantage to you.'

'That is why I thought I might invite Cousin Margaret to come with me when I leave here and return to London.'

'Very wise, my dear. Talk to her while you are here. As a widow of several years' standing she is a very independent person, but I am sure she would be happy to stay with you for a few months. But I hope that does not mean you intend to cut short your visit here. I am looking forward to such a happy time, for we have invited only close acquaintances on this occasion—and here is one of Mr Renwick's oldest friends, now. Major Clifton, you are in good time, sir!'

Chapter Eight

Eloise's head snapped around. She watched Jack
Clifton walk into the room, tall and elegant in his
black swallow-tailed coat and buff pantaloons. He
looked relaxed and at his ease, and she schooled her
own features into a look of bland indifference as she
rose to her feet. More people were coming into the
room and Mrs Renwick hurried away to greet them,
leaving Eloise with the major.

'What are you doing here?' she demanded as he
bowed to her.

He raised his brows.

'Renwick invited me. Do you think I should remove
myself because you do not want me here? I am a
guest, madam, as you are. You will have to make the
best of it.' He bared his teeth. 'Smile, madam, we
are in company; you do not want anyone to suspect
an intrigue, do you? Or perhaps, considering your
reputation, it is of no matter to you.'

'Your being here is no matter to me, Major,' Eloise

flashed back at him. She gave him a smile as false as his own and swept away to meet the other guests.

With the exception of Alex Mortimer, the party was complete, and when Eloise sat down to dinner it was with the almost certain knowledge that her tormentor from Vauxhall Gardens was amongst the guests. She glanced around the table as the servants came in with the first course. She discounted Mr and Mrs Renwick from her list of suspects and, reluctantly, Major Clifton. Lord and Lady Parham were inveterate gossipmongers, but she did not think either of them capable of such subterfuge. Sitting near her were two other couples, both related to Mrs Renwick, plus Sir Ronald Deforge. Then there was a gentleman called Graham with an unfortunate taste in florid waistcoats and her late-husband's cousin, Mrs Margaret Cromer, an iron-haired lady whose forbidding countenance was relieved by a decided twinkle in her grey eyes. At the far end of the table was Mr Renwick's sister, her clergyman husband and two pretty daughters. Eloise knew them slightly, but since Mr Briggate and his family had travelled from Dorset to join the party at Renwick Hall she hoped she might discount them.

With a sigh she turned her attention to her dinner. In truth, she had no idea whom she should suspect. She must not relax, even for a moment. She pushed a piece of chicken across her plate, sadly aware that her appetite had disappeared.

After dinner the ladies withdrew to the long gallery, where fires blazed in the two fireplaces. They disposed themselves gracefully on the elegant sofas while they talked and gossiped, and during a lull in the conversation Eloise wandered off to look at the numerous pictures that covered the walls.

'We have some very fine paintings here, Lady Allyngham,' said Mr Renwick, leading the gentlemen into the room at that moment. 'However, they don't show to advantage in the candlelight: you are best looking at them during the day.'

'I should like to do so,' she replied.

'And I should be delighted to escort you,' replied her host, smiling. 'Or let Clifton be your guide; he knows as much as I about the pictures here at the Hall.'

'You flatter me, Charles,' said Jack. 'I do not claim to be an expert.'

'But you have an eye for a beautiful work of art,' returned Mr Renwick.

'And for a pretty woman,' added Mr Graham, walking by.

'And that,' Jack replied gravely.

He was about to turn away. Eloise said quickly, 'You consider yourself a connoisseur, perhaps?'

'Of art, madam, or women?'

'Oh, Clifton is decidedly a connoisseur of women!' laughed Mr Renwick, clapping his friend on the shoulder.

'I take leave to question that,' muttered Eloise, so quietly that only Jack could hear her. She found his dark, unsmiling gaze resting on her.

'I have enough experience to know when beauty is merely a sham, a bright veneer to cover a tarnished character.'

Colour flamed through Eloise's cheek. She turned away, furious with herself for challenging him. It was a game she could not win. She fixed her eyes on a large portrait, pretending to study it while she struggled to regain her composure.

'What—' Jack was standing at her shoulder, his words quiet in her ear, '—has the Glorious Allyngham no laughing riposte for me?'

She drew herself up and turned to him, masking her anger with a glittering smile.

'I am amazed, sir, that you claim any expertise at all when it comes to our sex. In my experience you show no aptitude at all and see only what you want to see!'

With no more than a small inclination of her head Eloise moved away, back to the relative safety of the crowd.

It was still early so it came as no surprise when one of the younger members of the group suggested dancing. The party moved to one end of the room where the fine pianoforte was situated and footmen were called to roll away the carpet. With her nerves at full stretch, Eloise could not share in the general high spirits so she stepped up to her hostess and offered to play for the dancers. Mr Graham, overhearing her, immediately cried out at this, saying with a laugh, 'Would you deprive us of the pleasure of watching you dance, Lady Allyngham?'

'Would you deprive us of the pleasure of partnering you?' added Sir Ronald Deforge.

She shook her head.

'Thank you, but I am very happy to play tonight.'

Mr Graham was inclined to argue.

'But, my lady—'

'Someone else may take a turn at the pianoforte later,' declared Mrs Renwick, the peacemaker. 'I know Lady Allyngham to be an excellent pianist and it would be an honour to have her play for our little party.'

Major Clifton carried a branched candlestick across to the pianoforte.

'Out of sorts, Lady Allyngham?'

She gave him a frosty look and turned her attention to leafing through the music piled on a nearby table.

'I am not always so flighty as you think me, Major.'

'Perhaps you are missing Alex Mortimer.'

'Oh, do go away!'

She ground her teeth as he sauntered off, laughing.

Seating herself at the instrument, Eloise began to play. Her fingers flew over the keys, her lively playing accompanied by the happy laughter of the dancers.

After an hour even the most energetic of the young people was glad to take a break and while they refreshed themselves with cups of wine, lemonade or ratafia, Mrs Renwick and her husband were persuaded to sing a duet. This was so successful that their audience clapped and cheered and demanded more. Mrs Renwick beckoned to Mrs Cromer.

'Meg, my dear, come and join us to sing the trio from *Così fan tutte*. Do you remember, we saw it together at the Haymarket in the year Eleven and immediately purchased the music so we could learn it.?'

Margaret Cromer stepped up.

'I remember it well and will sing it, with pleasure, if Cousin Eloise can play it?'

'I can,' said Eloise, waving her hand towards the side-table. 'If I can find the music.'

Before she could get up Jack picked up a large book and carried it across to the piano.

'You will need someone to turn the pages for you, my lady.'

'That is not necessary, Major Clifton, I shall manage.'

'Do not be so stubborn,' he murmured, placing the music before her. 'Would you have the performance ruined because you will not accept a little help?'

Knowing he was right, she set her jaw and began to play. The soft, haunting notes soothed away her anger. *Soave sia il vento*, 'May the wind be gentle'. She knew the song well, a beautiful, sad farewell sung by two sisters to their soldier sweethearts. The ladies' voices blended beautifully, with Mr Renwick's rich baritone adding depth to the gentle, lilting melody. Eloise concentrated on the accompaniment, trying to ignore Jack standing so close, his arm stretching past her as he turned the pages. She was calmed by the music, and by the singers' sweeping cadences rising and falling, imitating the gentle breeze of the Italian lyrics. She was almost disappointed when the last notes died away and the applause began. While everyone was praising the singers for their splendid performance, Eloise remained very still, enjoying the sinful sensation of Jack Clifton's presence beside her, his lean body so close she could feel his heat. Energy emanated from him, making her skin tingle with anticipation. She jumped when he reached out to pick up the book.

'Mr Mozart's opera is clearly a favourite,' he re-marked, flicking through the pages. 'Let me find you something...here it is.' He replaced the open book on the piano and she looked at the aria he had chosen. '"*Donne mie, la fate a tanti e tanti*",' he read the title. 'Perhaps you would like me to translate if for you: "my dear ladies, you deceive so many men..."'

Abruptly Eloise stood up.

'I can translate it very well for myself,' she muttered, turning away from him.

She forced her lips into a smile as Margaret Cromer approached her.

'You play most beautifully, Cousin, but you have a delightful singing voice, too. Will you not let us hear it?'

'Thank you Meg, but I do not think—'

'Oh, my dear ma'am, do say you will sing for us,' declared Lady Parham, beaming at her. 'Mrs Cromer has been telling me that you were used to sing regularly for the guests at Allyngham.'

Eloise tried to decline, but other guests came up, adding their persuasion. Mrs Renwick took her hand and led her back towards the pianoforte.

'Come along, my dear, you have played so well for us it is your turn now to shine—Mrs Cromer will accompany you, will you not, Meg?'

'Of course, I should be delighted to play for Eloise—such a beautiful voice you have, Cousin! Now, what will you sing for us, my dear?'

Eloise hesitated, looking around at the happy, expectant faces. To decline would be impolite. She smiled.

'Something else from Mr Mozart, I think. *The Marriage of Figaro.*'

'We have it!' cried Mrs Renwick, pulling another book from the pile.

Eloise nodded and looked at her cousin.

'Can you play "*Porgi, amor*," Meg?'

'Oh heavens, my favourite aria!' declared Lady Parham. 'Do be quiet, everyone, and listen!'

An expectant silence settled over the room as Mrs Cromer played the short introduction. Eloise ran her tongue over her dry lips and composed herself. Many of the guests had pulled their chairs into a semi-circle to watch. Her eyes strayed around the room, noticing tiny details such as Sir Ronald leaning forwards, hands on his knees, Mr Graham sitting at the back of the group, picking his teeth, Mr and Mrs Renwick sitting shoulder to shoulder. And Jack Clifton, standing a little apart, his face in shadow. She must forget them all.

Eloise began to sing the Countess's heartbreaking aria about the pain of losing her husband's love. She had chosen to sing the English translation, but it was still beautiful and she closed her eyes, allowing herself to be swept away by the evocative words and music.

Jack stood in the shadows and listened, entranced. He was familiar with the opera but it had never before had such power to move him. Eloise sang the countess's role with dignity and restraint, her full, rich voice filling the long gallery. There was such longing in her voice, such sadness in her blue eyes that he could almost believe her sincere. Almost. As the last, lingering notes died away he found himself swallowing hard to clear some constriction in his throat. There was a moment's silence, then the room erupted into cheers and applause. Lady Allyngham was blushing, accepting their praise with modestly downcast eyes. Jack scowled as Sir Ronald stepped up to take her hand and kiss it. Damnation, the woman had bewitched them all!

There was a few moments' stir and confusion. Renwick's young nieces came up for their turn to perform and the mood lightened considerably as they sang a selection of folk songs. Jack watched Eloise move away from the crowd and he stepped quickly up to her.

'So you identify yourself with the wronged countess, my lady.' His tone was harder than he had intended. She cast one brief look up at him and he was taken aback to see her eyes glistening with tears.

She hurried past him without speaking and slipped out of the room while the company's attention was fixed upon the young performers. In two strides Jack was at the door and following her along the cold stone corridor.

'Lady Allyngham—Eloise!'

She stopped at his words but did not turn.

'Will you not leave me alone?' she muttered as he came up to her. She was hunting for her handkerchief. Jack handed her his own.

'I beg your pardon. I did not mean to upset you.'

'Did you not? I think you delight in upsetting me.'

He heard the bitter note in her voice. There was a sudden upsurge of sound as the door to the long gallery opened again. Eloise looked up, startled. Jack caught her arm and pulled her to one side, into an unlit corridor. There was a half-glazed door at the far end, through which pale moonlight gleamed and fell in silvery squares upon the tiled floor of the passage. They stood silently in the semi-darkness, listening to the soft sound of footsteps hurrying past. When the silence settled again Eloise realised that he was still holding her arm and tried to shake him off.

'Let me go. We have nothing to say to each other!'

'I think we do.' Instead of obeying her demands, Jack caught her other arm. Her struggles to free herself were half-hearted. 'Will you not hear me, madam? Please.'

She grew still suddenly, but did not raise her eyes. Jack breathed out in a long sigh and looked up at the blackness above him. 'I don't know why it is, but you bring out the worst in me.'

'I have done nothing to warrant your cruel jibes.'

'That is just it! To have spent the whole evening in

your company and received not one warm look, one real smile. I confess I wanted to provoke you, to make you respond to me, even if it was with anger.'

'Then it is better that we should not meet—'

'No! At least, you must allow me to apologise—to say how sorry I am that Allyngham is dead. Your words when we last parted—that you wish I had perished on the battlefield instead of Tony—I had never before considered what you have lost, what you must have suffered. Watching you in there, hearing you sing, I realised how much you miss him.' Jack looked at the still figure before him. She was trying very hard not to cry, her bottom lip caught between her teeth to stop it trembling. He said gently, 'I do not pretend to understand your behaviour, madam, and if I have misjudged you, I pray you will forgive me.'

Even in the dim light he could make out the long lashes fanned out on her pale cheeks. Now those lashes fluttered and lifted slightly. Jack put two fingers under her chin and gently pushed her head up. He said softly, 'My lady, will you not cry friends with me?'

She met his eyes for a moment, her own so dark and liquid he thought he might drown in them.

'Not friends,' she said quietly. 'Too many harsh words have been exchanged for that. But it would be better for our hosts if we were not always arguing,'

He smiled, his spirits lifting a little.

'A truce, then. And if I can help you discover who is sending those letters—'

'No.' She was withdrawing from him again. 'I would not have you concern yourself with that.'

Jack was tempted to argue but he resisted: if she was not willing to confide in him then he would not force her. With time and patience he would win her round, he was sure of it. His instinct was to protect her. He wanted to carry her off, to shelter her from every ill wind. She was, after all, the widow of a valued comrade. With a little nod he stepped back.

'Very well. But if you need my assistance, you only have to ask.' He lifted his head, listening to the quiet strains of the pianoforte drifting from the long gallery. 'They are dancing again. Do you wish to return?' She gave a little shake of her head and his mouth twisted into a rueful smile. 'No, nor I.' Jack held out his arm to her. 'Perhaps a stroll through the gardens, until you are more composed? There is a full moon tonight.'

Eloise opened her mouth to refuse, but it was as if someone else was controlling her voice.

'Thank you, I would like that.'

Moments earlier she had been wishing Jack Clifton at Jericho, now she was taking his arm and accompanying him outside. The passage door opened on to a small cobbled yard at the far side of which a narrow gate in the low wall led the way into the rose garden. The bushes were overgrown with only a few late-summer blooms hanging on, but even so it looked beautiful in the moonlight. The only sound was the occasional cry of a fox from the park and the soft crunch of the gravel beneath their feet. Eloise felt her tension draining away. Despite their differences, Jack Clifton was the one man at Renwick Hall she was sure she could trust.

'You seem to know your way about the house very well, Major.'

'Renwick and I are old friends. I have stayed here many times before when I have been on leave.'

'I understand you have quit the army now. What will you do?'

'Yes, I have sold out. I have no family, My father died just a year ago, leaving me a pretty little property in Staffordshire, Henchard. It needs some work but it is a snug little house and the land could be very profitable, I think. Did I not tell you I shall become a gentleman farmer?'

She smiled at that.

'Yes, I remember, but somehow I cannot imagine it!'

'Oh? How do you see me?'

She thought for a moment.

'As an adventurer.'

It was Jack's turn to laugh. Eloise liked the sound, it was deep and rich and dangerously attractive. Just like the man.

'I have had enough of adventure. It is time I settled down.'

She nodded. He was a man of means, it would be very sensible to settle down, marry and have children. Her head jerked up. The thought of Jack taking a wife hit her with such force she felt as if someone had thrown a bucket of cold water over her.

He stopped.

'Is something wrong? Are you cold, do you want to go indoors?'

'N-no, a sudden chill, nothing more,' she said quickly. 'Do let us continue, the gardens have a different kind of beauty in the moonlight.'

'Very well, but I cannot have you catching cold.'

He shrugged himself out of his coat and placed it around her, his hands resting on her shoulders for a moment. The action was so personal, so intimate that Eloise was obliged to set her jaw hard to stifle a gasp. The air, so calm a moment ago, now seemed charged with expectation. She knew a brief disappointment when he stepped back and waited for her to stroll on. She stole a glance at him. An exquisitely tailored waistcoat hugged his body, accentuating the broad shoulders. She was dazzled by the whiteness of his billowing shirtsleeves and the tumbling folds of his neckcloth. She found her eyes wandering down the tapering form. The slim hips and flat abdomen drew her attention, as did the strongly muscled thighs outlined by the pantaloons. Swallowing, she dragged her gaze back to his face, but the sight of his clean, chiselled jaw and raven-black hair gave her no relief from the sudden fire that was engulfing her. She realised Jack was watching her, a faint, glinting smile in his eyes. Heavens, had she considered him an adventurer? He was far more dangerous than that! She looked away and began to walk again, this time at a much quicker pace.

'We should not linger, sir, or it is you who might catch a chill. I see a balustrade directly ahead of us. Is that the end of the garden?'

'Yes, it runs along a high ridge. There is a fine view of the park from that point.'

Eloise walked on. The scrunch of the gravel beneath her firm step was reassuringly crisp and business-like. The major had fallen in beside her, his long legs allowing him to take a much more leisurely stride.

'I understand Mortimer will be joining us tomorrow.' His voice was perfectly calm. 'Renwick tells me you particularly asked that he should be invited.'

'Yes.' Had she told him the real reason for coming here? She could not recall. 'I did not wish to find myself here without any good friends to keep me company. Of course, I did not know then that *you* would be here.'

Eloise winced: that was just such a flirtatious remark as he might expect from her. She glanced up. Jack's smile had disappeared, and he was looking directly ahead, his lips pressed firmly together. She sighed and huddled beneath his coat. She turned her head to rub her cheek against the lapel. The fine wool was soft on her skin and she breathed in the faint slightly spicy scent that she now associated with Jack Clifton.

The balustrade was soon reached and she gazed out in genuine admiration at the park stretching out before her, bathed in moonlight. They were standing on a ridge with the land falling away on all sides. The full moon sailing high above cast a silvery sheen over the landscape.

'It is beautiful,' she breathed.

'Yes. Renwick's grandfather planned it all and planted the trees.' He pointed. 'Down there to the south, just beyond the lake, is the deer park.'

Eloise looked around. 'And what is that building on the promontory over there?'

'That is the Temple of Diana. The family used to hold dinner parties there, but now I think it is employed mainly by the ladies of the house for their sketching. The path between the temple and the house is thickly wooded, but the views on the other three sides are magnificent. Would you like to walk there now?'

The temptation to accept was very great, to prolong this magical time together, but she knew she must not. She shook her head.

'Thank you, but no. I think it is time we returned to the house. They will be serving tea soon.'

She took one final look at the little Temple of Diana with its elegant cupola outlined against the night sky. The shallow steps and graceful columns looked most romantic, and the idea of being there in the moonlight with Jack sent a little shiver of excitement down her spine. All the more reason to return to the safety of the house, she thought, setting off back along the path. Without a word Jack fell into step beside her and they walked in silence back through the gardens. She laughed to herself: if she had been alone with any other man he would have taken the opportunity to make love to her, at least to flirt—here she was in the moonlight with the most attractive man she had ever known and he was behaving with perfect propriety.

And she hated it.

They slipped back into the house by the little glazed door and Eloise handed Jack his coat.

'You will need this before you rejoin the others, Major.'

She helped him into it, telling herself it was necessary for her hands to smooth the coat over his broad shoulders, to brush a speck of dust from one lapel, but it was such an intimate gesture that her mouth went dry and her fingers trembled. Jack caught her hand and carried to his lips. She was immobilised by the tenderness of the gesture. She looked up and did not move as he lowered his head towards her.

'We…should…not…' she breathed, still looking up at him.

'Why not?' he murmured. 'Moonlight is the time for stolen kisses.'

'You cannot steal what I give you freely.'

A fierce gleam lit his eyes: elation, triumph, she could not be sure. She dropped her own gaze, and gave a remorseful little sigh.

'I should not be here with you. It was very wrong of me to go outside—what must you think of me?'

He pushed up her chin and gently brushed her lips with his own.

'I think you an enigma, but I hope one day you will explain yourself.'

'If only that were possible.'

'It *is* possible. You have only to trust me.'

For the space of a heartbeat she was tempted.

'If it was just my secret—'

'Yes?'

She gave her head a little shake, put her hands against his chest to hold him off.

'Perhaps, one day, I might be able to tell you more, but not yet.'

'Then I shall not press you. When you are ready, you may come to me and tell me everything.'

Eloise bit her lip and blinked to drive back the tears. The more she knew of Jack Clifton, the more honourable she thought him. And the more impossible it was that he would ever understand. She said, with a masterly effort to keep her voice from shaking, 'Mrs Renwick will be preparing tea soon. We should go back now, I think.'

'As you wish, my lady.' Jack pulled her hand on to his sleeve and walked her through the dark corridor.

They reached the hall just as the butler appeared, carrying the tea tray.

'I have no doubt our absence will have been noted,' murmured Jack as they followed him into the long gallery.

'Then it will be best if we move apart, Major Clifton.' She pulled her arm from his sleeve, saying nervously, 'Pray do not speak to me again tonight, sir. I fear we may set tongues wagging.'

'Not for the first time, Lady Allyngham,' he said drily.

A little tut of exasperation escaped her. 'I had hoped to repair my reputation with this visit.'

'There is time yet. And Mortimer will be here tomorrow: you will have your guard dog to protect you.'

With a last, fleeting smile he walked away and she joined the crowd around her hostess. It was only when she was preparing for bed that she realised Jack's handkerchief was still in her pocket. She took it out and held it for a moment, pressed against her mouth. She should of course give it to Alice to have it laundered and returned to the Major. Instead she turned and tucked it quickly under her pillow.

Chapter Nine

'So Mortimer is arrived. The Glorious Allyngham's lapdog.'

Jack heard Deforge's words as he walked into the library. Sir Ronald was standing by the window, gazing out at the post chaise and its four sweating horses that had just pulled up at the door of Renwick Hall.

'Ah, but has he lost his place as the lady's favourite?' Edward Graham threw down the newspaper he had been reading and grinned at Jack. 'Well, Clifton, you and the widow were missing for some considerable time last night: is she well and truly won?'

'Lady Allyngham required a little air. I accompanied her,' returned Jack evenly.

Sir Ronald shot a piercing look at him. 'So you obliged her with a stroll in the moonlight. Are you sure it was nothing more?'

Jack made an effort to keep his countenance impassive.

'Nothing.'

'Then you wasted your opportunity, Major.'

'I do not consider it so,' said Jack, shrugging. 'Forcing a woman is not *my* style, Deforge.'

Sir Ronald's heavy features darkened angrily.

'Are you saying it is mine?'

'I have heard so.' Jack's lip curled. 'I have heard that even your wife tried to run away from you.'

'Blast your eyes, Clifton, you will unsay that!'

'You will have to make me, Deforge.'

Jack met his look steadily, facing down the blustering challenge in the other man's eyes. At length Sir Ronald shrugged.

'Of course you would like to believe that, would you not, Major? It must be galling to know that pretty little Clara chose me over a penniless soldier. I can see how it would be some comfort to think she was unhappy, but she was not.' He stepped closer. 'I served her very well, Clifton, remember that when you are lying awake at night!'

Sir Ronald turned on his heel and walked away. He picked up the newspaper and carried it over to the far corner of the room. Mr Graham gave Jack a knowing look.

'Well,' he said, rising, 'I'm off to change for dinner. How about you, Clifton?'

The two men left the room together and as the door closed behind them Graham said softly, 'A word of warning, Major. Be wary of Deforge. He's a nasty piece of work.'

'I am aware,' muttered Jack grimly, 'but he won't call me out, no matter how hard I try.'

'Not his style,' Graham retorted. 'You are more likely to be found in a dark alley with a knife in your back.'

Jack gave an angry snort. 'I am surprised Renwick invited him.'

'No choice, old boy. It appears he's some sort of distant cousin to Mrs Renwick, and he almost invited himself. She of course is far too kind-hearted to turn anyone away, especially family—' He broke off as they reached the hall, where they found their host greeting Alex Mortimer, who was divesting himself of his greatcoat. 'Mortimer, how do you do! Good journey?'

Alex Mortimer looked up, a ready smile on his fair, handsome features.

'The last stage was tiresome. One of the wheelers was lame. Couldn't make any pace at all.'

'Well, you are in good time for dinner,' declared Mr Renwick. 'I'll have Grassington show you to your room—'

'No need,' cried Mr Graham, stepping forwards. 'He's in the room next to me, is he not? Clifton and I will take him up with us. Come along, Mortimer. Grassington can follow on with the bags!'

Linking arms with Jack and Alex, Edward Graham

set off up the wide, shallow staircase, chatting merrily. Looking up, Jack realised that Mortimer was regarding him with a very thoughtful expression. No wonder, if Lady Allyngham had told him of their stormy meeting in London. Well, that was past now, and he hoped that after last night he and the lady could at least meet as friends. And once Eloise had explained matters to Mortimer, perhaps they could even work together to help the lady out of her predicament.

When the party gathered in the drawing room before dinner that evening, Eloise greeted Alex with unaffected pleasure, and she was happy to find that most of the party shared her delight. To have another handsome and eligible bachelor staying at Renwick Hall could not be considered anything other than an advantage, and she was amused to watch Mrs Briggate taking every opportunity to bring her daughters to his attention.

Seeing Lady Allyngham was alone, Jack crossed the room to join her. At first she did not notice him, for her eyes were on Alex Mortimer, who was standing on the far side of the room, surrounded by ladies.

'Mortimer is very patient,' he murmured. 'I was not half so polite when the Briggate woman forced her chits under my nose. He will find himself leg-shackled if he doesn't take care.'

She smiled.

'Not he! Alex is too good-natured to snub anyone, but he will not allow the situation to get out of hand. Nor will he let either of those silly girls lose their hearts to him. He is far too kind for that.'

'Perhaps his interests lie in another direction.'

She looked up at him, a startled look in her eyes.

'I—I don't understand you, Major.'

He gave her a rueful smile.

'I thought his heart lay at your feet.'

'Oh.' The colour rushed back into her cheeks. 'Oh, well, yes, I suppose that is true.'

He leaned a little closer.

'Perhaps, when you talk to him, you will tell him that I am no longer your enemy. He has behaved like a dog with his hackles up ever since he arrived here. You may also tell him, if you please, that I am no rival. He has nothing to fear from me.'

He turned on his heel and walked away. Eloise stared after him, but she had no time to consider his words, for no sooner had he moved off than Sir Ronald Deforge was at her side and she forced herself to listen to his pleasantries and respond with a smile. There was no opportunity to speak to Alex until they were going into dinner, when he offered her his arm as they processed from the drawing room across the hall and into the dining room.

'Well, my dear, you have all the men enchanted, as usual. And judging by the number of times I heard you laugh I suppose you must be enjoying yourself.'

'You are mistaken!' Eloise glanced around to make sure no one was close enough to overhear them. 'Until I know who has been writing those dreadful letters to me I cannot relax for a moment. Oh, Alex, it is so unsettling! With the exception of yourself and Mr Renwick, not one of the gentlemen can come near me without I have to suppress a shudder.'

'Not even Major Clifton? I thought we had agreed he was above suspicion.'

Eloise spread her hands.

'He is, but that does not mean I can bear to have him by me.' She was not going to admit to Alex that the shaking she experienced when Jack Clifton was near was for a very different reason. 'However, we are not enemies any more.'

'You are not?'

'No. We—um—we understand each other now.'

'Is that since he took you into the garden last night?' He grinned at her horrified look. 'Graham took great delight in telling me that Clifton had cut me out.'

They were entering the dining room and Eloise was obliged to swallow the infelicitous remark that rose to her lips.

'It was no such thing,' she hissed. 'We merely… talked, and he apologised for misjudging me.' After a brief pause she added, 'He said to tell you that he is not our enemy. And that he is not your rival.'

Alex handed her to her seat, saying, 'Generous of him to tell me he has no interest in you.'

'Yes,' she said bleakly. 'Isn't it?'

The following morning Mr Renwick took the gentlemen off shooting and the ladies were left to amuse themselves. The more energetic of the ladies, including Eloise, joined their hostess for a tour of the grounds, ending with refreshments served at the Temple of Diana. As they approached the pavilion, Eloise could see that it was a perfect cube with shallow steps on four sides leading to columned porticos. It was a bright, sunny day and Mrs Renwick had ordered the wide doors of the pavilion to be opened and the chairs moved out under the porticos so that the ladies could all sit and enjoy the magnificent views. The occasional gunshot could be heard, carried on the light breeze. Miss Briggate and her sister whiled away the time by staring at the woods on the far horizon, trying to spot the gentlemen. Eloise took a chair beside her cousin and they sat in companionable silence, gazing out across the park. The autumn colours were beginning to show themselves and Eloise could not help comparing the cheerful riot of green, red and gold with the silver-blue landscape she had seen the previous night.

'Such a sad sigh, Cousin,' remarked Mrs Cromer. 'I hope you are not unhappy?'

Eloise started.

'Did I sigh? Oh dear, I was not aware of it. I beg your pardon. How could one be unhappy in this beautiful place?'

'I could not, certainly, and when you were younger I remember how much you enjoyed being in the country,' returned Meg, smiling. 'But I have not seen you for a long time, Cousin, you may have changed. We have seen little of each other since you and Tony were married. Understandable, of course.'

'No, it was very remiss of me,' declared Eloise. 'I should have made more effort to invite you to stay—'

Meg threw up her hands and laughed at that.

'No, no, you young people were far too busy with your own concerns. Besides, I had my girls to look after, and they were a handful, always wanting to be gadding about the town.' She threw a smiling glance at Eloise. 'That is why I thought you might be missing the delights of London.'

Eloise quickly disclaimed, 'Not at all, Meg, why should you think that of me?'

'Gossip travels, my dear.'

'Ah.' Eloise turned in her chair to regard her cousin. 'Gossip about me, I suppose. I know some people think I am behaving disgracefully.'

Meg leaned across and took her hand. 'Cousin, it is

only natural that you should want to enjoy yourself, after a year in mourning, but perhaps you have let your high spirits run away with you. And it is not only your behaviour in town: I am well aware that you and Major Clifton were missing for more than an hour last night. A reputation is far more easily lost than won, you know.'

Eloise bowed her head.

'I know it. Did—did anyone else notice?'

'I am sure they did! Mrs Renwick made some passing comment, but only to the effect that she was glad to see the major taking an interest in women again.'

'Oh.' Eloise began to rearrange her skirts, saying casually, 'Our hostess knows the major well?'

'Her husband does, certainly,' replied Meg, turning her face up to the sun. 'I understand Major Clifton suffered some disappointment in his youth. He was in love with a maid but she married someone else. Seems she was such a paragon that he has not looked at a woman since—not at women of his own class, that is,' she amended with a knowing smile. 'I have heard that he has had any number of mistresses.'

Eloise stared across the park in silence as she digested this. She could well imagine the upright, incorruptible Major Clifton falling in love with a model of propriety. In comparison, her own reputation would seem bad indeed, but he was clearly attracted to her. Perhaps he saw her only as mistress material. Suddenly the day did not seem quite so bright.

'I think perhaps I have been a little careless,' she said quietly. 'Some may even call me fast—but I intend to change that.' She paused. Everything depended upon her recovery of the journal, but she could not tell Meg that. She told herself fiercely that she would not countenance failure. She said decisively, 'When I leave here I have to return to London for a few weeks, to wind up my affairs before going back to Allyngham for the winter. Once in Norfolk the management of the estate will take up most of my time, but I wanted to ask if you would come back to town with me.'

'To lend you countenance?' asked Meg, giving her a quizzical look.

'Yes, if you like,' said Eloise, smiling. 'To make me respectable!'

'Oh, my dear, you know I would love to come with you, but my daughter is lying in next month and I must go to Shropshire to be with her. I am so sorry. But next Season, if you go to town, it would be my pleasure to come and live with you.'

'Yes, of course, Meg. Thank you.'

'And until then I am sure we can find some other respectable lady to keep you company in town—'

'No, no, I would not wish to take on a stranger for a mere few weeks.' Eloise shook her head. 'And once I retire to Allyngham, there is so much to do that I shall not have time to be lonely.' She smiled reassuringly at her cousin. 'I am sure I can manage to keep out of trouble for a few more weeks!'

'Then let us start with this evening,' retorted Meg, a twinkle in her sharp eyes. 'There must be no moonlight walks tonight, no matter how handsome the gentleman!'

No one could have been more decorous than Lady Allyngham at dinner that evening. She was gracious and charming, but she could not be persuaded to leave her hostess's side until the card tables were set up and even then she would only play a friendly game of whist. Jack observed it all. He made no move to approach her, and watched with a detached amusement as the other single gentlemen tried unsuccessfully to draw her away from the group. Mortimer, he noticed, was unconcerned, and he guessed that whatever game the widow was playing, her guard dog knew of it. He was even more convinced when Mortimer agreed to join him for a game of billiards.

'You would not rather play at cards with us, Mortimer?' cried Edward Graham, looking up.

Alex grinned and shook his head.

'If Sir Ronald has only half his usual luck I would be handing over my shirt to him. I shall enjoy a quiet game of billiards with Clifton instead.'

'On leave from your sentry duty?' Jack murmured as the two men made their way to the billiard room.

Alex did not pretend to misunderstand him.

'My lady has turned over a new leaf,' he replied evenly, selecting a cue from the rack. 'She wants her cousin to live with her, to protect her reputation.'

'That sounds very much like shutting the stable door after the horse has bolted.' Mortimer said nothing, but Jack observed the heavy frown that flitted across his face. He said, 'Have I offended you?'

Alex shrugged.

'Not at all. Shall we play?'

'I would rather you told me about Lady Allyngham.'

'What is there to tell?' Alex responded lightly. 'She is a beautiful woman.'

'And you have known her a long time?'

'Almost all my life. We grew up together, as neighbours. She is a very loyal friend.'

'Then perhaps you know what it is that she is hiding from me.'

Alex did not reply until he had made his first shot.

'All women have their secrets, Major Clifton.' His derisory grin flickered. 'As a man of the world you must know that. Now...' he nodded towards the billiard table '...I have made my play; it is time to see what you can do!'

* * *

By the time they returned to the drawing room the card tables were packed away and the party was gathered about the crackling fire, drinking tea. There was a burst of laughter as they entered: Mr Renwick was entertaining his guests with stories of his childhood at Renwick Hall.

'Always falling into some fix or another,' he chuckled, shaking his head. 'The woods were our favourite playground. The poor gamekeeper came pretty close to peppering us with shot on more than one occasion.'

'Ah, but boys will be boys,' murmured Mr Briggate, steepling his fingers.

'And not only boys,' put in Mrs Cromer with a laughing glance at Eloise, sitting beside her on the sofa. 'My cousin here was for ever in trouble with Lord and Lady Allyngham.'

'Meg, please, you will put me to blush!' Eloise protested laughingly.

'No, please, do go on, Mrs Cromer,' Sir Ronald begged. 'We can never hear enough of Lady Allyngham.'

'She and my cousin grew up together,' explained Meg. 'Anthony treated her more like a boy than a girl, and as often as not when I came to call they would be out together clambering over the rocks or climbing trees,' She nodded towards Alex. 'And that young man was usually with them. Three scamps they were, but inseparable, until the boys went off to school and Eloise was sent to Bath, where she learned to be a lady.'

'Ah, so your youthful companions were lost to you after that,' remarked the eldest Miss Briggate, sighing.

'Not at all,' replied Eloise, smiling. 'We were together in the holidays and once my schooling was over I returned to Allyngham and saw them often and often.'

'And you were all as wild as ever,' laughed Meg. 'The number of times I called and found that Eloise was in disgrace and had been confined to her room! My poor Aunt Allyngham was in despair, wondering how to deal with such a hoyden!'

'I think I must defend my lady,' put in Alex, smiling. 'She was loyal to a fault and often took the blame for our pranks.' He walked across and stood behind the sofa. 'Of the three of us, Lady Allyngham was the sensible one. She spent most of her time rescuing Tony and me from our more outlandish scrapes.'

There was general laughter, Mrs Renwick began to refill the teacups and Jack wondered if anyone else had noticed Alex's hand rest briefly on Eloise's white shoulder. His eyes made a quick sweep of the room. Most of the guests were chattering but Sir Ronald was silent, staring intently at Eloise, his fingers tapping on the arm of his chair and a sly smile on his face. Jack frowned. He misliked that smile.

The man was dangerous, and if Lady Allyngham had somehow offended him, perhaps rejected his advances…

He broke off from his reflections as Miss Briggate brought him a dish of tea, but even as he joined in the general conversation he made a mental note to keep an eye on Deforge.

It was gone midnight when the party broke up and Eloise accompanied her cousin up the stairs to the main guestrooms. She was very sleepy and was tempted to remark that remaining virtuous all day was extremely tiring, but she did not think Meg would appreciate the joke. They parted on the landing and Eloise retired to the cosy silence of her bedchamber. Several candles were burning and the draught as she shut her door set the shadows dancing on the painted panels of the room. There was no sign of her maid, and she tugged on the embroidered bell-pull, impatient now to get out of her gown. Something on the bed caught her eye, a small, pale square on the near-black of the covers. A letter.

A sudden chill swept through her bones. Her fingers were not quite steady as she picked up the paper and unfolded it. The heavy black writing danced before her eyes and she turned the paper towards the light, blinking until her vision cleared.

'I beg yer pardon, my lady, I wasn't expectin' you quite so soon.'

Eloise pressed the paper to her chest as Alice bounced into the room. She must think, and quickly.

'Alice, I need you to run an errand for me.'

'At this time o' night, m'lady?'

'Yes, I am afraid so.' She turned and tried to give her maid a confident smile. 'I need you to carry a message to Mr Mortimer for me.'

Alice's eyes grew round.

'Mr—but 'e's in the east wing, with all the gentlemen!'

'I know, Alice, and I am sorry to ask it of you but it is very important, and I cannot trust anyone else.' She added coaxingly, 'You have known me since we were little girls together at Allyngham: you know I would not ask if it was not very important.'

She could see the maid mentally girding her loins as she digested this.

'Very well, Miss Elle.' Alice drew herself up, looking very resolute. 'What is it you want me to do?'

Eloise stood by the little gate into the rose garden, clutching her cloak around her. She prayed that Alice had carried her message faithfully. A sudden movement to her left made her jump: someone was approaching. She relaxed a little as she recognised Alex's familiar form.

'Now, Elle, what is all this?' he whispered.

'He has written.' She held up the note. 'It is too

dark for you to read it, but he wants me to meet him, tonight, at the Temple of Diana.'

'Does he, by thunder! Then I'll go back and fetch my pistol—'

She gripped his arm.

'No, no violence! But I want you to come with me, Alex, and hide in the woods. The letter says I am to come alone but I do not think I am brave enough to do that.'

'Of course I will come with you, I would not let you go unattended to meet the villain.'

'Good. We will set off now, if you please. I expect him to be watching out for me, so we must go separately. You must take the path through the woods, I will follow the lower track beside the lake.'

'It could be dangerous.' Alex caught her arm. 'You do not have to do this, Elle.'

'I do,' she replied softly. 'You know that until we destroy the journal we cannot be safe.'

'There is a way out of this that does not involve paying the blackguard!'

'Go abroad, you mean? The Allyngham name would still be tarnished, and I will not do that to Tony's memory.' She squeezed his arm. 'Wait for me in the woods, but be ready to come if I call.'

They hurried through the rose garden and Alex set off up the hill. Eloise watched him disappear into the trees and felt a slight moment of panic. Giving herself a mental shake, she pulled her cloak more tightly about her and set off along the lakeside path. Black clouds were scudding across the sky, occasionally blocking out the moon and making it difficult to see the ground in front of her. The sudden cry of a fox made her jump and at one point an owl flew silently overhead like a sinister dark angel. Eloise walked on, keeping her eyes fixed on the solid shape of the temple in the distance. A slight breeze blew across the lake, rippling its calm surface. The trees sighed and a tingle ran the length of her spine: unseen eyes were watching her, she knew it. She left the lakeside and made her way up the slope towards the temple. The steps and the portico gleamed white in the moonlight, but deep shadows filled the interior. Taking a deep breath, she climbed the steps and entered.

The square temple had a glazed door and large windows on each of the four sides, casting a silver-grey light into the centre. Eloise was immediately aware of a figure standing in one of the shadowed corners. His face was a ghostly pale disc against the blackness around him.

'I have come,' she said, steeling herself to keep still. 'What is it you want of me?'

'Well, that depends.' The grating whisper jarred on her stretched nerves. 'How badly do you want the return of that book?'

She shrugged. 'It is worth something to me,

I admit, but not much. There are no names in it, after all.'

He laughed softly.

'Oh, come now, Lady Allyngham. A full year's reminiscences: dates, places. It would not take a vast intelligence to work out the identities of those mentioned. I have not yet decided if I should publish it in book form—look how popular Caro Lamb's *Glenarvon* has become in just a few months!—or perhaps I should release it to the newspapers, little by little…'

'How much do you want?' she interrupted him sharply.

'Everything.'

'Now you are ridiculous!'

'Am I? To prevent your ruin, and that of your friends?'

Anger surged through her.

'Step out of the shadows,' she challenged him. 'I am tired of talking to nothing. I want to see the villain who dares to threaten me!'

Again that soft laugh.

'Villain, madam? I am your most ardent admirer.'

He stepped forwards and as the cloak of darkness fell away she recognised Sir Ronald Deforge. Eloise knew a momentary insane desire to laugh. The fear, shock and horror she should have felt was outweighed by relief. Relief that it was not Jack Clifton. Despite everything she had been afraid her judgement had let her down where Major Clifton was concerned. She stared haughtily at Sir Ronald as he stood before her, one white hand resting negligently on his silver-topped cane. With his tight-waisted frockcoat and tasselled Hessians he looked as if he had just strolled in from Bond Street.

'An admirer who would stoop to threats,' she said, her lip curling. 'Tell me, how did you obtain the diary?'

'A stroke of great good fortune, nothing more. Some time ago I was travelling back to town on the Great North Road and when we stopped to change horses a ragged wretch approached me. He wanted the fare to London and offered to sell me the journal.'

'So you bought it.'

'Of course not. I do not deal with thieves. He had no idea what it contained, I doubt if he could read well enough to know its true value. No, I had him flogged, and told him I would return the book to its rightful owner.' He grinned. 'Of course, I did not then know what a pleasant task that would be.' He moved closer. 'I admit when I first read that journal I thought only to sell it. After all, I guessed it must be worth something to protect the revered Allyngham name. But then you came to town and I was captivated. The more I see you, the more you inflame me.'

She suppressed a shudder and stepped away from him.

'And you disgust me.'

'Now that is a pity, my lady, because there is only one way I will give up the journal to you.' He waited until she had turned again to face him. 'You must marry me.'

Eloise laughed at that.

'The full moon has affected your wits, Sir Ronald! I would never do that.'

'Oh, I think you will, madam, when you consider the consequences of *not* becoming my wife. I can tell by your look that you are not convinced. Perhaps you think to wrest the book from me. You will not succeed. It is with my lawyer in London, in a sealed box. He has instructions to make its contents public if anything should happen to me. Anything at all,' he added softly, 'so you should pray no ill befalls me!' He moved towards her. It took all Eloise's will-power not to back away. He reached out to touch her face. 'Do not look so shocked, my dear, you might even enjoy being my wife.'

She brushed his hand aside.

'It astonishes me that you should wish to marry someone you do not know.'

He bared his teeth in a leering smile that made her feel physically sick.

'Oh, I know you, Lady Allyngham. I have seen you in the salons and ballrooms, throwing out lures to every man in the room. And remember I have read that journal. You are a woman of experience, not averse to the more...unusual demands of the male.'

His hand shot out and grabbed her wrist as she began to back away.

With a cry she tried to pull free. A shadow fell upon them and she heard Alex's curt voice from the open doorway.

'Let her go, Deforge!'

Sir Ronald's brows rose.

'So you did not come alone as I instructed.'

'Did you think I would be that foolish?' she retorted, struggling against his grasp.

'I thought you had more concern for your friends.'

Even as Sir Ronald was speaking Alex launched himself forwards. Deforge released Eloise and leapt back, putting his hand to the top of his cane and unsheathing a lethal-looking blade.

'Alex, be careful, he has a sword-stick!'

Her warning came too late. Deforge lunged and the blade pierced Alex's shoulder. He staggered back. Eloise tried to grab Deforge's arm but he shook her off so violently that she fell to the floor. In horror she watched him advance upon Alex, who retreated to the door. Moonlight glinted on the sword as Deforge slashed Alex across the thigh and following up with a kick that sent him tumbling down the steps and on to the grass.

Eloise was still struggling to rise when another shadowy figure flew past the window. She saw Sir Ronald turn but before he could defend himself his head was snapped back by a swift, hard punch to the jaw and he crashed to the ground.

'Attacking an unarmed man is not worthy of you, Deforge.'

Jack Clifton bent to pick up the sword-stick. For a moment a look of pure hatred transformed Sir Ronald's face.

'What are you doing here?'

'Taking a stroll in the moonlight. It appears to be a very popular pastime.' Jack stepped into the little room and held out his hand to Eloise. She allowed him to help her up, aware of the tension within him. Despite his casual words he was taught as a bow-string, alert and ready for action.

'So she has caught you in her web, too, Clifton.' Sir Ronald was climbing to his feet, one hand feeling his jaw.

'We will leave the lady out of this, if you please.'

Sir Ronald laughed.

'Your concern for the lady's reputation is touching, Major, but misplaced, believe me.'

With a growl of anger Jack stepped towards him, fists raised. Eloise gripped his arm.

'No, Major, please!

'She is right to stop you, Clifton. If you lay an-other finger on me I shall cause a scandal that will destroy what remains of Lady Allyngham's reputa-tion, and that of her...friends.' He straightened his coat and made a play of smoothing out the creases of his sleeve. 'I am going back to bed. I leave you to explain it how you will, Major Clifton. You may try what you can to keep the lady's name out of this. Oh—my cane, if you please?'

Jack picked up the discarded cane and sheathed the wicked blade.

'Here.' He tossed it to Sir Ronald. 'You had best keep out of my way, Deforge. I would like nothing better than an excuse to kill you.'

Sir Ronald bared his teeth.

'Oh, I am well aware of that, Major. I rely upon Lady Allyngham to dissuade you from doing anything foolish.' He turned to Eloise. 'Consider my offer, madam. It is all that stands between you and disaster.' Then, with an airy salute of his cane, he walked down the steps and strolled away, walking past Alex's body without even a glance.

Chapter Ten

As if released from a spell, Eloise ran down the steps and fell to her knees beside Alex.

'He breathes,' she muttered thankfully.

Jack gently turned him on to his back and Eloise bit back a cry. One leg of his buff-coloured pantaloons was black and wet with blood and another dark stain was spreading over the left shoulder of his coat

'The first thing we must do is to stop the bleeding from his thigh,' said Jack, pulling off his neckcloth and wrapping it tightly around the wound. Alex groaned.

'Keep still,' muttered Eloise, her fingers scrabbling at his throat. 'I am going to use your cravat to staunch the blood from your shoulder wound.'

'Damned villain. If only you had let me bring a pistol—'

Eloise choked back a sob.

'I know, Alex, I am very sorry. It is all my fault—'

'Recriminations can come later,' Jack interrupted her. 'We must get you back to the house, Mortimer. If I help you to stand, do you think you can walk?'

Alex closed his eyes, his brow contracting.

'I do not know…'

'Well, we must try. I do not want to send to the house for assistance. The less people who know of this escapade the better.'

'I can help,' said Eloise. She blushed, knowing that Jack's eyes were upon her and added fiercely, 'I *can*. I carried you over the heath, and Alex is much slighter.'

'I am also conscious,' muttered Alex as Jack helped him to his feet. 'If you let me put my weight on you, Clifton, I think we can manage.'

With Alex's arm about his shoulders, Jack set off for the house, half-carrying, half-dragging the wounded man. Eloise walked along beside them, keeping the pad firmly pressed over the injured shoulder. It was clumsy and uncomfortable and her heart went out to Alex as he gritted his teeth to prevent himself crying out in pain.

'Hold on, my dear Alex,' she muttered, her voice breaking, 'hold on and we will soon have you safe.'

Jack heard the affection in her voice and blotted out any angry thoughts as he struggled back towards the house with his burden. He must think of Mortimer as a wounded colleague, not a rival, but it was hard to ignore the lady's concern as she kept pace with them, her whole attention locked upon Mortimer. Jack had left the house by a side door and he was relieved to find that it was still unlocked. By this time Alex had lost consciousness and it took Jack and Eloise's combined efforts to carry him up the stairs to his room.

When they struggled into the bedchamber Mortimer's valet fell back, a look of profound shock upon his face. Eloise gave him no time to ask questions.

'Your master has been wounded, Farrell. Pray run downstairs and fetch hot water and bandages while we get him into bed. Immediately, if you please.'

The valet dashed away. Jack carried Mortimer to the bed and laid him upon the patterned bedcover.

'You command and Farrell obeys.'

She did not look at him, but threw aside her cloak and made her way around the room, lighting every candle.

'Alex and I have been acquainted since childhood. Farrell knows I am a friend.'

But how good a friend?

Jack dared not ask the question, afraid he might not like the answer. He stripped off his coat and turned his attention back to the unconscious man lying on the bed. Eloise came up to stand beside him, her hands clasped as if in prayer.

'Can you bind him up?'

'You need not look so anxious, madam. I dealt with much worse than this in the army. These are two clean cuts: there is no reason that they should not heal perfectly well. Help me get him out of his clothes.'

Sensing her hesitation, he glanced down at her, his brows raised. She swallowed and nodded.

'Of course.'

Silently they set to work. Eloise was already un-buttoning the coat and waistcoat so Jack pulled off Alex's boots and began to unfasten his pantaloons. By the time Farrell returned with a jug of hot water and an armful of clean linen, the bed had been stripped back to its bottom sheet and Mortimer was lying naked in the centre.

Farrell took one horrified look at the bloodied body of his master and turned an anguished glance towards Eloise.

'Madam, you should not—'

'Enough, Farrell!' she interrupted him swiftly and bent a frowning look upon the valet. 'We can involve no one else in this,' she said crisply. 'Major, what do you want me to do next?'

'Keep the pad pressed to that hole in his shoulder,' he told her. 'I'll deal with the cut on his leg first.'

He was pleased at the way she responded. No tears or vapours and with her hands shaking only a little she folded a pad of clean pad and held it against the wound. 'Very good,' he murmured, giving her the glimmer of a smile. 'We'll make a soldier of you yet, madam.'

They worked quietly together, Farrell tearing the linen into bandages while Jack cleaned and bound up the cut on Alex's thigh.

'Should we not call a doctor?' suggested Farrell. 'Perhaps we should bleed him.'

'After all the blood he has already lost?' Jack shook his head. 'No. The slash on his thigh looks bad but it is not that deep. I am hopeful that with rest the leg will be as good as new, except for a scar.'

'And the shoulder?' asked Eloise. 'It is not bleeding so very much now.'

She was still pressing one white hand to the wound; the other was tenderly brushing Alex's fair hair from his brow. A memory slammed into Jack. He recalled how she had brushed his hair from his eyes when they had been alone together in the shepherd's hut. Just before he had overpowered her, grabbing those slim white wrists and turning her until she was trapped beneath him. How those blue eyes had glared up at him, her breast heaving with indignation, her soft mouth so close to his, just asking to be kissed. His body stirred at the very thought of it. He dragged his eyes and his mind away from her and back to Alex Mortimer.

'He may find it painful to use his arm for a few days, but that should soon pass.'

Some of the anxiety left her face.

'Perhaps a little laudanum would help,' she suggested.

'Yes, if there is some in the house. He will be in pain when he wakes up.'

She nodded.

'The housekeeper will have some. Farrell must fetch it. Of the three of us, it will cause less comment if he is seen abroad at this time of night.'

'I'll go at once, my lady.'

'But you will tell no one that Lady Allyngham is here,' ordered Jack. 'You had best tell the housekeeper that Mr Mortimer was attacked in the woods. By poachers.'

The valet slipped out of the room and a silence descended. Jack tied the final knot around Alex's thigh.

She said quietly, 'Thank you, Major Clifton.'

'For what?'

'For coming to our aid. For being here.'

Jack nodded. He poured water on to a fresh cloth and began to wipe the blood from Alex's shoulder.

'I assume it is Deforge who is threatening you?'

'Yes. He sent me a note to meet him tonight. Alex came with me, for protection.' She looked up. 'But what were you doing there?'

'I followed Deforge.' He observed her look of surprise and shrugged. 'I have my own reasons for hating the man. And I saw the way he looked at you tonight. I thought he might be dangerous, so I had my man watch him. When he told me Sir Ronald had slipped out of the house I went after him. I saw you go into the temple and guessed he had sent for you, but it was not until I realised Mortimer was hiding in the woods that I was sure. What did he want this time?'

She hesitated, as if debating with herself how much to tell him.

'More money. Alex was angry and thought he could stop him.' She gave a little sob. 'It almost cost him his life. If you had not been there…'

'I should have run Deforge through with his own sword-stick!' muttered Jack savagely.

'Then all would have been lost. He—he says he has left the journal with his lawyer, with instructions to publish if anything happens to him.'

'Very clever.' Jack gave a little huff of frustration. 'And you plan to settle with him?'

'The alternative is to have the Allyngham name disgraced. Our private affairs would be discussed in every coffee house, reported in the newspapers for everyone to read, even lampooned like the Prince Regent! No, I will not risk that.'

'So you will allow a man like Deforge to impose upon you.'

'While he has the journal, yes. I see from your frown that you do not approve, Major.'

'No. It galls me to see you under any obligation to that man.'

She took the bloodstained cloth from his hand and handed him a clean one.

'You said you hate Sir Ronald. Will you tell me why?'

Jack's jaw set hard: she dared to ask, yet she refused to tell him her own secrets! He said lightly, 'Would you have me bare my soul to you, lady?'

His barb went wide. She merely met his mocking glance with a gentle smile.

'They say confession is good for the soul, Major. I feel there is some great bitterness in you when you think of Deforge, as if he has done you a great wrong. It cannot be good for you to keep such a thing to yourself.'

Jack did not reply immediately. At last he shrugged.

'Perhaps you are right,' he said at last. 'I will share it, since Deforge is our common enemy.' He placed a clean wad of cloth against the wound in Alex's shoulder and concentrated on strapping it into place with the bandages. 'It goes back a long time—five years or more—and concerns Lady Deforge.'

'His wife? She died three years ago, did she not?'

'Deforge killed her.'

Eloise gasped.

'Do you have evidence for that?'

'I do not, but knowing the man, and the lady, I believe it to be true. Oh, I know he was not at Redlands at the time of her death, but if he did not actually commit the deed I believe he drove her to it. Clara and I were childhood friends—more than friends, I thought. I believed she loved me as I loved her. True, she was a little wilful, but who could wonder at it if her parents spoiled her, for she was such a beautiful, delightful girl. Her father was against our marrying. I thought at the time it was because we were so young. She was her father's only child and I was a lowly captain, but later…' He paused, conscious that in his anger he was pulling the binding far too tight about Alex's shoulder.

Eloise reached across him and gently took the bandage from his hand.

'Here, let me.'

He watched her for a moment, part of his mind noting how deftly she readjusted the dressing. He walked to the fireplace and stared down at the hearth.

'Five years ago Clara's father died and I came home thinking that there would be no impediment now to our marriage, but when I arrived in London I found she was already betrothed. To Sir Ronald Deforge.' The story had been locked inside him for years, but now he had started he knew he must finish it. He said, 'I think, I believe, that when I first joined the army she intended to wait for me. We had agreed that there was no possibility of our marriage until I had achieved some promotion and could afford to keep a wife. She was far too good, too innocent to deliberately mislead me. When her father died she became the target of any number of men looking for a wife, and I suppose I was just too far away.' He shrugged. 'By the time I returned to London Clara had been swept off her feet by Sir Ronald. He was a wealthy, fashionable man of the town; by comparison I must have seemed a very callow youth of four-and-twenty, and how could I compete with a baronetcy? When I met her in London she seemed very happy with her choice.' His face darkened. 'I knew nothing of Deforge, save that he was a gambler, and that is a common enough trait. So I wished her well and went back to the Peninsula, where I tried to forget her.' He exhaled slowly. 'Wine, women and war—I survived them all. I fared better than my poor Clara. Two years later she was dead, drowned in the lake at Redlands, her family home. There was talk that she was not happy, that Deforge had married her only for her fortune. I do not know, but I can well believe it. After that one meeting in London I never heard from her again.'

'It is common knowledge that Sir Ronald's wife died soon after giving birth to a stillborn son,' said Eloise slowly. 'If the poor woman was unhappy, that would be cause enough, I think.'

'Of course, but I cannot believe he ever really

cared for her. What I do know is that when Deforge married Clara he had already run through his own fortune and within two years most of Clara's money was gone. Since her death he has been selling off his properties and is almost at a stand. I have no doubt he is now looking for another rich wife.'

Eloise thought of her meetings with Sir Ronald Deforge and a cold chill ran through her. He was a cruel man: he would certainly publish the journal if she refused to marry him, but if she gave herself into his power, what then? Would he make her life so miserable that she would be willing to end it? She looked down at her shaking hands.

'Perhaps you could finish binding up Alex's shoulder,' she said, moving aside.

Jack returned to the bedside and she watched his strong, capable fingers take up the bandage. She screwed up her courage. It would be better to tell Jack Clifton the whole truth, to let him deal with Deforge. Even as she searched for the words to begin, the valet returned and the opportunity was lost.

Jack tied the final knot in the bandage around Alex's shoulder and straightened, easing his tense shoulders. 'There,' he said. 'I have finished.'

He wiped his hands on a cloth and dropped it on to the pile of bloodied rags on the floor.

'You may leave him to me now, Major.' Farrell tenderly pulled the covers over his master. 'I will clear up here and watch him until morning. I was obliged to explain to the housekeeper why I needed to disturb her, so I did as you suggested and told her my master had been attacked by poachers. I took the liberty of saying that it was you who found Mr Mortimer in the gardens and brought him upstairs, Major. No one need know of Lady Allyngham's part in any of this.'

'Thank you, Farrell.' Jack looked at Eloise, who was hovering beside the bed.

'I think it is time you returned to your own room, madam. Come, I will escort you.'

She hesitated, smoothing the sheet and straightening the covers until Farrell said quietly, 'You should leave now, my lady. Our situation will be much worse if you are discovered here.'

'Yes, yes, of course.'

With a final look at Alex she turned and accompanied Jack out of the room. The lamps burning in the corridors made it unnecessary to carry a bedroom candle but their low light threw black, wavering shadows against the walls. He sensed rather than saw her step falter and put his hand under her arm.

'No need to be afraid, ma'am, you are safe enough here.'

'I am not afraid. It is just—after all the excitement, I feel a little...'

She collapsed against him. Jack caught her up as she fainted. For a moment he stopped, staring down at the lifeless figure in his arms. Her head was thrown back, the dark lashes fanned out across her pale cheeks, the fine line of her jaw accentuated by the flickering light. What the devil was he to do now? They were in the part of the house known as the bachelor wing. The main reception rooms lay between here and the other guest rooms. To carry her all the way to her bedchamber would be to court disaster, for there were at least two flights of uncarpeted stairs to negotiate as well as a number of long passages. It would only take one light sleeper to open a door and look out…

With sudden decision he turned and carried her to his own bedchamber at the end of the corridor. It was similar to Mortimer's room, a square, panelled chamber with a fireplace in one wall, a window in another and a large canopied bed taking up most of the floor. He laid Eloise gently on the covers and turned to throw a couple of logs on the smouldering fire. He lit a candle from the glowing embers and placed it beside the bed.

She was lying as he had left her, pale and still against the dark coverlet, her hair in wild disorder and gleaming in the soft light. She was still wearing the blue gown she had put on for dinner but the embroidered skirts were in disarray and displaying her shapely legs in their fine silk stockings. As he reached out to straighten the skirts he noted that her shoes were stained and wet. His mouth twisted as he looked at the elegant satin slippers. They were designed for dancing 'til dawn on polished floors, not walking at night through wet grass. He began to untie the ribbons, his fingers shaking a little when they brushed her slender ankles. As he eased the wet satin from her feet Eloise stirred.

'What are you doing?'

'Your shoes are wet through so I have removed them.'

'Where am I?'

She put up one hand and he caught it in his own.

'You are in my room—do not be alarmed. You fainted, and I did not want to risk being seen with you in my arms.'

She sat up, but made no attempt to release his hand. If anything, her grip tightened.

'I am sorry; I do not know why I should suddenly have become so weak.'

He smiled at that.

'A reaction to the excitement of the night.'

'Where is your valet?'

'Gone to bed. When I went out I told him not to wait up for me.' Jack leaned a little closer. 'You are very pale. Shall I fetch you a glass of wine? I have a decanter here.'

'Yes, thank you.'

As Jack turned away Eloise glanced around the room. Everywhere there was evidence of the major's presence, illuminated in the golden glow of the fire-light. His shaving kit spread out on the wash stand, silver-backed hair brushes lying on the dressing table. Even here on the bed beside her was the garishly coloured silk banyan he would wear over his night-shirt. Her fingers reached out and touched it. The silk was cool and smooth beneath her fingers. She imagined Jack wearing the banyan, the thin silk fitting snug across his broad shoulders—directly against his skin perhaps, since she knew some men did not wear nightshirts. Eloise snatched her hand back, quickly pulling her mind away from the sensations such thoughts aroused in her. Nervously she slid off the bed and stepped across to sit in an armchair drawn up beside the fire. She perched nervously on the edge of the chair. She should not be here. Everything in this room was alien to her. Masculine. She and her husband had always had their separate apartments, and she had never entered Tony's bedchamber when he was there. She swallowed hard. Jack Clifton was not Tony: he was very much more dangerous.

She should leave, now. Slip out of the door while Jack was pouring the wine, but her wayward body would not move. She realised with a shock that she felt secure in this man's room, where the air was redolent with wine and wood smoke, with spices, soap and leather. And, knowing that Sir Ronald Deforge was still a guest in the house, she did not want to be alone.

Jack carried two glasses of wine across the room and offered one to her. He was not surprised to see that she had moved from the bed to a chair by the fire. She was sitting bolt upright, rigid with tension. Pity stirred within him when he saw the anxious look on her face. She took the glass and held it in both hands, staring down at the dark liquid.

Jack hooked his toe around the leg of a footstool and dragged it across so that he could sit at her feet.

'Drink it,' he urged her. 'It is not drugged. I have no evil designs upon you.'

She looked at him, a faint smile breaking the rigidity of her countenance.

'I would not think that of you. I left my cloak in Alex's room.'

Jack indicated his shirt sleeves, billowing out from the tight-fitting waistcoat.

'My frockcoat is there, too. We must trust Farrell to return them to us in the morning.'

'So there is nothing to worry about.'

He met her eyes, hoping his smile would reassure her.

'No, madam, there is nothing to worry about.'

As she sipped at the wine Jack sensed the tension draining out of her. After a little while she leaned back in the chair and they sat in a comfortable silence. Jack stared into the fire, his elbows resting on his knees as he cradled the glass between his hands. He was very aware of the woman sitting in the chair. If he leaned slightly towards her, his arm would be touching her thigh. By turning just a little more he could rest his head in her lap. How pleasant that would be! How pleasant to be able to sit like this every evening. He glanced down at her dainty ankles and little feet. Her stockings were stained with mud and grass, reminding him of what had occurred that night. He would make no progress with her while she was in danger. If only he could extricate her from this mess, then perhaps she might consider his suit.

His suit?

Jack caught himself up. What was he thinking of? Not marriage, surely. It had always been his intention to settle down one day and this had included some vague plan to find himself a wife, but he had envisaged proposing to someone like his childhood sweetheart, Clara, an innocent maid of good family, not a widow whose past was so dubious that it was ripe for extortion. He glanced again at the woman before him. All at once her past seemed unimportant: he was certain in his own mind that whatever she had done it could not be so very bad. If she had had a string of lovers—well, who was he to criticise that?

Eloise stirred in her chair. She finished her wine and put down her glass upon the hearth.

'Thank you. I should go now.'

'Stay a little longer.'

'I—um—my feet are wet. I should dry them.'

Her blue eyes flickered over his face. There was nothing of the coquette in the look she gave him, only uncertainty, and a shy wistfulness. Suddenly his heart was hammering against his ribs. *Why not?* whispered the voice in his head. *If the lady is willing.*

'You can do that here,' he murmured. 'If you will allow me.'

Eloise gripped the arms of the chair as he put out one hand and gently pushed her skirts up to expose her knee. One word, one tiny gesture would stop him, she knew that, but she said nothing. She remained motionless as he untied her garter. An aching excitement pooled low in her body, her skin tingling in anticipation of his touch. She watched him roll the silk stocking down her calf and gently pull it away from her toes.

'There, that's better. Now, shall I remove the other one?'

No! She knew she should be running from this room, screaming. He was undressing her, carrying out a task that no one other than a husband should be permitted to perform. It was wrong. Immoral. Indecent. She should stop him. She looked at him, opening her mouth to object, but Jack was smiling at her and she felt the last remnants of her resistance melting away. Her mouth closed again and she was aware that she was nodding.

'Yes, please.'

The lightness of his touch was an almost unbearable pleasure and when his hand cupped her heel as he removed the second stocking she gave a little moan.

Jack glanced up.

'Is anything wrong?'

He was still holding her foot, his thumb idly stroking her ankle and inducing a wonderfully soothing lassitude throughout her body. It was an effort to speak.

'I did not realise how chilled I had become.'

She bit her lip to prevent herself protesting as he released her foot and turned away.

He picked up the poker and began to stir up the fire.

'Stay here, then, until you are warm again.'

Relief suffused her, and a warm rush of gratitude for this man. She smiled and stretched, luxuriating in the warmth of the fire and the calm, soothing atmosphere of the room.

'I should like to stay here for ever,' she murmured. 'To sit by this fire, warm and comfortable and not worry about anything—it is my idea of paradise! But it cannot be. I must get back to my room before anyone begins to wake.'

'It is still dark,' said Jack. 'The servants will not

be abroad for another hour or so yet.' He reached for her hands and pulled her to her feet. 'Stay here and let me show you my idea of paradise.'

Eloise gazed up into his face, mesmerised by the glow of the firelight reflected in his dark eyes. She trembled as his hands ran lightly over her arms and on to her shoulders. Her lips parted in a tiny gasp of expectation when he bent his head towards her. Her last, conscious thought was that he was going to kiss her—that she *wanted* him to kiss her, but the sensation of his mouth sliding across hers drove everything from her mind, save a desire to kiss him back. She threw her arms around his neck, leaning against his hard body while his tongue explored her mouth and played havoc with her senses. She felt as if she was floating and realised that indeed her feet were no longer on the floor, for Jack's arms were crushing her against him, lifting her as easily as a rag doll.

Desire consumed her. She returned Jack's kisses with a passion that was both exciting and confusing. She followed his lead, and if her kisses were inexpert he did not seem to mind, but held her even more closely. There was a crash as he kicked the footstool aside and carried her to the bed where he placed her down, all the time covering her face and neck with warm, heady kisses. When he raised his head she reached out and pulled him back towards her, intoxicated by his presence. He lay down with her, measuring his length against her, and she gasped as his hand came up to cup her breast. His thumb slipped beneath the lacy edge of her bodice and stroked gently over her nipple. She pushed against his touch, her skin tightening as the excitement built within her. She fumbled with the buttons of his waistcoat, eager for him to remove it yet sighing with frustration when Jack broke away from her. He gave a soft laugh.

'Patience, my lady. There is time to undress: I'll not tumble you like some cheap straw damsel.'

He shrugged himself out of his waistcoat and as he pulled his shirt over his head Eloise sat up and slipped her arms around his waist. She laid her face against the flat plain of his stomach, caressing him with her cheek. He groaned and fell back on the bed, drawing her to him again and as his mouth captured hers he tugged on the drawstring fastenings of her bodice. Between frantic kisses they discarded their clothes until they were lying naked together on the bed, their bodies illuminated only by the residual light of the dying fire and a single, flickering candle.

Jack pushed himself up on one elbow and stared down at her. Eloise did not make any effort to cover herself. She basked in the admiration of his glance, revelling in the novel sensation of truly enjoying a man's attentions.

'You are beautiful,' he murmured, resting one hand on her naked thigh.

She smiled up at him, putting her hand to his cheek and gently drawing his face down to hers. His kiss was slow and thorough and she never wanted it to stop. The hand on her thigh slid up and inwards. Her body responded instinctively, pushing against his fingers while a heady excitement grew inside her, spreading through her body. She arched her back, gasping, only vaguely aware of Jack's body shifting on top of her. She dug her fingers into his back and cried out as they were united. There was an exhilarating, joyful satisfaction in knowing they were as physically close as any man and woman could be but even that was not the end. Their bodies were moving together, the blood singing in her veins as the dizzying excitement rose higher and higher until there was no more conscious thought. She cried out and clung on tightly as she felt herself tumbling and crashing into oblivion.

Jack lay with Eloise in his arms. He was breathing heavily, dazed and exhausted by the physical and emotional ferocity of their union. It had never happened before, even after battle when he had taken comfort in the arms of a woman; he had never experienced such an all-consuming passion. His arms tightened possessively. Whatever secrets the lady's past might hold he did not care. She stirred in his arms.

'Awake, sweetheart?' He nibbled gently at her ear. 'Did you enjoy that?'

'I—yes.' Her voice was hardly above a whisper. 'I never knew.'

The wonder in her voice made him smile.

'You have been alone for a long time. Perhaps you have forgotten.'

'No, not forgotten. I…that was the first time.'

He nuzzled her neck.

'Then I am very honoured, although I am sorry for it if all your other lovers failed to give you such pleasure.'

'No, you misunderstand,' she murmured. 'I am… *was* a maid. Until tonight.'

Jack grew still.

'A maid? But Allyngham…'

'Our union was never consummated.'

In one swift movement he rolled over and sat up on the side of the bed.

'A maid!' He was still intoxicated with her, his mind in turmoil. Nothing made sense. 'But you were married to Tony Allyngham for seven years! And in London, all those men—'

'Nothing more than flirtation.'

'Then by God, madam, you played your part well!' he retorted, more sharply than he intended.

She said in a small voice, 'I am sorry if I have deceived you.'

'Deceived me! Aye, you deceived me!' He put his hands to his head. It had always been a point of honour with him to avoid innocent maids. She had been so willing, so eager for his kisses, how could it be that he did not know? Confusion swirled within him. 'By heaven, madam, I do not know what to say. Why in hell's name should you wish to act in such a manner if you were not...?'

She gave a little sob and scrambled away from him, dropping off the bed on the far side.

'Now you think me the very worst type of flirt,' she muttered. He watched her scrabbling around for her clothes. His brain was still reeling, trying to make sense of everything. He had been so bewitched that he had allowed his desire for her to overwhelm him. He shook his head, trying to clear his thoughts.

'A *flirt*, yes, but— Oh my God, I would never have taken you to bed if I had known you were a virgin!' He dropped his head in his hands again. 'I thought you a woman of experience, one who played by society's rules. A discreet little affair while it amused us, then we could both walk away...'

'Well, you need not be afraid. You can still walk away.'

He looked up. 'That is not what I meant.'

He watched, bemused, as she made an attempt to find a way into her gown, but the flimsy material

seemed to defeat her. Impatiently she threw it aside
and pulled his banyan from the bed. The silk wrap
was much too big and it pooled around her feet. She
looked absurdly young and vulnerable.

'I know exactly what you meant, Major Clifton.'
She threw the words at him as she tied the belt around
her with angry, jerking movements. 'It was never my
intention to entrap you. I am only sorry that I con-
fided the truth to you, although no doubt you would
have realised it soon enough. The evidence on the
sheets will be all too plain in the daylight!' She ran
to the door.

'No—Eloise—wait!'

But she was gone.

Chapter Eleven

Eloise sped through the dim corridors and down the stairs, scarcely aware of the cold boards beneath her bare feet. She dared not cry and held back her tears until she was safely inside her own room with the door locked, then she threw herself on to the bed and gave way to harsh, gasping sobs that racked her body.

She had been a fool to give herself to Jack Clifton. It was mere weakness to blame the excitement of the night and her anxiety over Alex for her inability to keep the man at arm's length. He had despised her when he had thought her wanton, and he thought even less of her now he knew it was all a charade. It was very lowering to know that he had thought her easy prey, someone to tumble into bed for a few nights' amusement, but his reaction when she had told him she was a virgin was even more upsetting. He was outraged, as if she had deceived him on purpose. She beat her fists against the covers. Did he think she wanted to trick him into marriage? Hah! She would show him! He was nothing but a rake, a low rascal, and she would have nothing more to do with him.

At length her sobs abated and she lay exhausted on the covers, only the occasional hiccup interrupting her misery. She had felt so comfortable in his arms, so *right*. She had spent years listening to her married friends, smiling and nodding as if she quite understood when they complained of how tiresome it was to have to pleasure one's husband, or giggled over the attributes of their latest lover, but until today she had never known just how exciting and enjoyable it was to be swept up by a man, to be kissed and caressed and...and *loved* until one's whole being was convulsed with pleasure. More tears squeezed themselves between her closed eyelids. If only it had been someone other than Major Clifton!

Eloise pulled the banyan around her. The silk was cool against her skin, and in its folds she could smell the distinctive fragrance that was Jack Clifton. It was like being in his arms again. With a petulant cry she threw off the wrap and slid naked between the cold sheets of her bed. She had told Alice not to wait up for her, and the hot brick her maid had placed in the bottom of the bed was now a cool, hard lump and no comfort at all. Eloise reached out for the banyan and pulled it into the bed with her. Tomorrow she would be cold and distant when dealing with Major

Clifton, but for the few hours that were left of the night she hugged the silk to her, curling her body around it. As sleep closed in and her acute unhappiness mellowed into a dull and aching despair, she found herself thinking that there was one tiny crumb of comfort to be found in all this: even if she was forced to marry Sir Ronald Deforge to secure the return of the journal, at least she would not be giving him her virginity.

A soft scuffling at the door roused Eloise. She lay, tense and alert beneath the covers, listening. Her straining ears detected the slight sound of footsteps padding away along the corridor. It was still dark, but the shutters of her window had not been closed and the faint glimmer of moonlight penetrated the room, leaving only the far corners in deep shadow. For the first time she noticed the pale shape of her nightgown spread out across the bottom of the bed and she quickly pulled it on, shivering a little as the cold cotton slid over her skin. Then she reached for her tinderbox. Once her bedside candle was alight she slipped out of bed and went to the door. It opened almost silently and she peeped out into the empty corridor. Looking down, she saw a grey bundle lying at her feet. She scooped it up, carrying it into the room. It was her cloak, still muddy and a little damp from her nocturnal ramblings. Wrapped inside it she found the rest of her clothes—shoes, stockings, her chemise and stays, the thin muslin gown with its muddy hem and traces of Alex's blood on the front. It was all there, except the embroidered ribbon garters. She chewed her lip. It was possible that Major Clifton had overlooked them, but she doubted it. She thought of his handkerchief, lying hidden at the bottom of her drawer. Perhaps it was a fair exchange.

The talk the next day was all about the poachers who had so savagely attacked Mr Mortimer. Alice informed her mistress of the news when she brought in her hot chocolate that morning.

'I have no idea what you and Mr Alex got up to last night and I don't want to know,' the maid told her mendaciously, 'but when Mr Farrell announced this morning that poor Mr Alex was at death's door it was as much as I could do to keep my lips sealed— and if I hadn't peeped in and seen you sleeping so peacefully before I went down to the kitchen I think I should have run straight back upstairs to make sure you was in your bed! And now I finds *this*.' The maid picked up the crumpled gown and held it out. 'Don't you try to tell me that's mud on your skirts, Miss Elle, because I know very well it's bloodstains.'

'Well, it is not all blood,' put in Eloise, sipping at her chocolate. 'There are grass stains as well, where I fell on my knees beside Mr Mortimer.'

Alice gave a gusty sigh and shook her head.

'Oh, my dear lady, I knew I should have waited up for you last night—'

'And you know I ordered you to go to bed,' retorted Eloise. 'You would have been very much in the way. Now do stop scolding me, Alice, and tell me instead how Mr Mortimer goes on. Has Farrell sent for the doctor?'

'No, ma'am: it seems Major Clifton bound up his wounds.' The maid shot a fierce, searching look at her mistress. 'Just what happened last night, Miss Elle? You told me you and Mr Mortimer was going out to put an end to those horrible letters that have been upsetting you.'

'And so we were, Alice.' Eloise hesitated, regarding her maid over the rim of her cup. Alice had been with her since she was a child, and it was impossible to snub her. Eloise never doubted her loyalty, but she dare not take her fully into her confidence. 'Unfortunately the man attacked Mr Alex. He drew a sword upon him, although Alex was unarmed.'

'Oh, mercy me, the villain!'

'Quite. Thankfully Major Clifton was in the gardens and helped me to carry Mr Alex back into the house.'

'Then we should inform the magistrate, my lady, and set up a hue and cry for the culprit!'

'That would cause far too much of a scandal, Alice, you must see that.'

The maid sniffed.

'There would certainly be a scandal if anyone was to know that you had been running around the country at night with Mr Alex!' She looked again at the gown, then picked up her muddy slippers. 'And what am I suppose to do with these? Ruined, just like your gown and your stockings! And all left on the floor for me to fall over! You should not have had to undress yourself, madam: if I had been here when you came in last night I could have taken these away and cleaned them, but now the dirt is so dried on there will be no getting it out.'

'No, I think you should dispose of the gown and the slippers,' said Eloise. 'But do it discreetly, Alice.'

The maid snorted. 'Do you think I would take these things down to the servants' hall and announce to all and sundry that my mistress was gallivanting the night away?'

Despite her heavy heart, Eloise smiled. 'No, of course not. I am very sorry to be so troublesome, truly I am. There is something else.' She pulled the silk wrap from under the bedclothes and held it out, saying airily, 'This needs to be returned to Major Clifton.' She observed Alice's shocked countenance and looked away, her cheeks growing hot. 'I was very chilled when we came back last night…'

Alice reached out and took the banyan, holding it at arm's length as if it was some contaminated rag instead of a very costly and fashionable item of a gentleman's wardrobe.

'Well, I never did!' exclaimed the maid. 'So you put this on over your gown? Ooh, Miss Elle, if anyone had seen you!'

'Well, they did not see me,' replied Eloise, her cheeks very hot. 'So see that it is returned to Major Clifton, if you please, and leave me to drink my chocolate in peace!'

Later, when she helped her mistress to dress, Alice was still muttering about the heathenish ways of the Quality. Eloise made no attempt to stop her, knowing her handmaid would talk herself back into a good mood all the sooner if she was allowed to have her say.

Thus Eloise was prepared for the talk and consternation of the party when she joined everyone in the breakfast room later that morning and she was able to assume a suitable expression of shock when Mr Renwick's sister greeted her with the news of the attack.

'Poachers,' exclaimed Mrs Briggate, 'and in the park, too! I do hope, brother, that you will take precautions to secure the house.'

'I have already done so, sister.'

Mr Renwick's response was calm and reassuring.

'How is Mr Mortimer?' asked Eloise as she took her seat at the table.

'Very poorly, but Major Clifton says his life is not in danger,' replied Mrs Renwick. 'It was Major

Clifton who found Mr Mortimer and he has been looking after him.'

'He is with him now,' added her husband, 'I have told him he has only to say the word and a man shall ride for the doctor immediately, but he does not seem to think it necessary at present.'

Sir Ronald had sauntered into the room and he said softly, 'The question is, what took Mortimer into the grounds at night in the first place?'

Eloise wrapped her hands around her coffee cup and tried to ignore his sly look.

'Perhaps he likes those horrid little cigarillos that are so popular with the gentlemen today,' said Mrs Renwick.

'That would certainly explain what Clifton was doing in the gardens,' put in Edward Graham. 'Doubtless he picked up the habit while he was in the army.'

'Don't know what these young fellows should want with those things,' barked Mr Briggate. 'What's wrong with snuff, I should like to know? Good enough for m'father.'

Eloise glanced at the brown stains around his nostrils and suppressed a shudder.

'Or a pipe,' put in Mrs Renwick. 'I remember my father enjoyed a pipe of tobacco of an evening. I always thought it smelled quite delicious.'

'Yes, yes, this is all very well, but we are straying from the point,' put in Mrs Briggate with a nervous glance around the table. 'What is to be done about the poachers?'

'We will do what we have always done, sister.' Mr Renwick smiled at her. 'I shall put extra men into the grounds today, and tonight we will let the dogs loose, so I would warn all of you to remain indoors after dark.'

'We are shooting today, are we not, Renwick?' asked Edward Graham. 'Perhaps we can bag a few of the rascals for ourselves.'

There was general laughter at this, and the gentlemen soon went off to prepare for their day's sport. Mrs Renwick carried the ladies off to the morning room and Eloise slipped away. She was anxious to see Alex and since the back stairs were deserted she quickly ran up to the bachelor wing and scratched upon the door.

'My lady! You cannot come in here!'

Eloise pushed past Farrell, ignoring his half-hearted attempts to deny her.

'It is my fault your master is injured and I must know how he is,' she said, walking into the room.

Alex was propped up in his bed, looking very pale. He raised his brows when he saw her.

'Go away, Elle. You should not be here. What if the servants see you?'

'They will not, for I am very careful. Besides, it does not matter if they do,' she said bitterly. 'It will merely add to my reputation. I had to find out how you go on.'

'I feel devilish,' he muttered. 'I have a neat hole in my shoulder which is a little sore but the cut on my leg will keep in bed for a week at least. I suppose I should be thankful it is no worse.' He frowned suddenly. 'Farrell tells me you and Clifton put me to bed.'

She flushed.

'Yes.'

'Damnation, Eloise, there was no need for that!'

'Yes, there was. It needed two of us to undress you and Farrell had to fetch the bandages.'

'You should have made some excuse and left the room.'

She had been thinking much the same thing, but at the time she had wanted to stay, and Jack's calm assumption that she would not be shocked by the sight of a man's body had allowed her to override her scruples. She realised now that it had only added to his conviction that she was a woman of the world.

She said quietly, 'I wanted to help.'

'But, good heavens, Elle, what will Clifton think?'

'I neither know nor care what the major thinks,' she retorted. 'He is an odious man.'

She looked away from Alex's searching gaze.

'Quarrelled again, have you?'

'Of course not. But I beg you will not confide in

him. Do not tell him anything more about us. I do not trust him.'

'Well, I think you should. Jack is sound enough, my dear.'

Eloise pressed her lips together and hoped she was not scowling. So it was Jack now, was it? Alex put a hand to his shoulder.

'He made a capital job of binding me up, and he was here first thing this morning, checking the bandages. You've no need to worry about Clifton.'

'Did I hear my name?'

Eloise whipped round as Major Clifton came into the room. Her face flamed but he gave her no more than a nod as he walked towards the bed.

As if we were no more than acquaintances, she thought. *As if he had forgotten what happened last night.*

She bit her lip, knowing that she was being uncharitable. Perhaps he was trying to spare her blushes.

'Aye, we were talking of you.' Alex held out his hand to him, grinning. 'I was telling my lady what a good sawbones you would make.'

'One picks up a little knowledge in the army.' Jack gave Eloise a half-smile but she turned away, determined not to respond. 'Lady Allyngham nursed you, too, you know.'

'And I am very grateful to you both. But, Elle, now you can see that I am getting better I do wish you would go away: we are not related, my dear, and there will be the devil to pay if you are found here.'

'You should have thought that way last night before you went off together to meet Deforge,' growled Jack.

'That was different.' Alex shifted uncomfortably. 'No one was meant to know about that.' He glanced at Eloise. 'What are they saying downstairs?'

'That it was poachers. I saw Sir Ronald this morning.' She shuddered. 'I could hardly bear to sit still at the breakfast table, for he was smiling in the slyest manner.'

'The devil he was! When I am back on my feet I shall take a pistol to the villain!'

'When you are back on your feet you may of course do what you wish,' replied Jack. 'But for now you must rest. I've sent your man down to fetch you some breakfast.'

Even as he spoke, Jack was very aware of the lady standing silently beside the bed. She looked so pale and forlorn that guilt wrenched at his insides. If only he could go back and unsay his hasty words of last night. He was furious with himself for his outburst. From the little he had overheard when he walked into the room he was sure she had not told Mortimer what had occurred, so he would follow her lead and say nothing, at least when they were in company.

He needed to talk to her, to explain his behaviour, but that was not possible here, with Alex Mortimer looking on. He was not at all sure that it was possible under any conditions. How could he make her understand just how he had felt, after the most glorious, the most fulfilling lovemaking he had ever known, to discover that she was still a maid? He had been shocked, mortified to think he had not known. True, she had responded to him, matched his passion with her own but that was no excuse. He was not inexperienced and he was horrified to think he had been so insensitive to her. She had thought his annoyance was directed towards her and by the time he had collected his dazed wits she had gone, fled back to her room. Unable to rest he had collected her cloak, wrapped up her discarded clothes and deposited them at her door. He hoped she would know from that gesture that he intended to be discreet, that he meant her no harm. Until he could find a way to talk to her privately, it was all he could do.

Mortimer was pulling angrily at the bedcovers.

'Breakfast! I had rather you sent Farrell with a challenge to Deforge!' He glowered. 'He has gone too far this time. I won't have it, Elle. I say let him publish and be damned to him, we'll fight!'

Jack looked up quickly. 'Why, what is Sir Ronald demanding?'

As Alex opened his mouth to speak, Eloise put up her hand, saying icily, 'Major Clifton is no longer party to our plans, Alex.'

'Gammon! If Jack had not rescued us last night we

would have been in the devil of a fix!' Alex turned his angry eyes towards him. 'Deforge wants Eloise for his wife.'

'The devil he does!' Jack could not prevent the exclamation, nor the sudden, intense surge of possessiveness. No wonder she had looked so frightened when he had told her of his suspicions about Deforge. He wanted to gather her up in his arms but he knew that if he made any move towards her she would run away from him. Despite the fear he could see in her eyes, she bravely put up her chin.

'That is nonsense, of course. I told him so last night.'

'He must think his hold upon you very secure to suggest such a thing,' Jack said slowly.

The lady was silent, but something in her countenance caused Alex to sit up.

'Thunder and turf, you are not to think of giving in to that villain, Eloise!'

Jack saw a shadow cross her face but it was gone in an instant. Smiling, she reached out to push Alex gently back against his pillows.

'No, of course not. Now lie still or you will set your shoulder bleeding.'

'You are not to do anything until I am on my feet again.' Alex grabbed her wrist. 'Promise me, Elle! Clifton—you must look after her, make sure Deforge has no opportunity to bully her.'

'By all means.'

She flushed.

'That will not be necessary. I am going back to London in the morning. I shall tell Mrs Renwick that I have business to attend to.'

'I would rather you remained here, under my eye,' declared Alex.

She smiled at that.

'A poor chaperon you would be, confined here in your room!'

Alex sighed. 'I am sorry, love: I had thought for once I should be able to help *you* out of a scrape, but it seems I have only succeeded in causing you more problems.'

She squeezed his hand and smiled fondly at him.

'You must not worry over me, Alex. We will deal with everything once you are well again.'

'But you are determined to leave?'

'Yes. There is plenty to occupy me in London. You know, I still have hopes that I might persuade Lord Berrow to sell me his land.'

Jack watched them, beating down the little demon of jealousy that gnawed at his insides. They were not lovers—he knew that now—but they were very close and they shared secrets that he was not privy to. His frown deepened as he realised how much he wanted Eloise to trust him as she trusted Mortimer. She kissed Alex's cheek and moved towards the door.

'Wait,' said Jack. 'Let me go first, to make sure there is no one to see you.'

Silently he checked that the passage was empty and preceded her down the stairs. When they reached the great hall the faint sound of voices could be heard coming from the drawing room. Jack stopped.

'Will you join them?'

Eloise shook her head.

'I would rather not. I would like to be alone. I think I shall go to my bedchamber.'

Even as she uttered the words the door of the drawing room opened and Lady Parham's shrill voice could be heard. It could only be a matter of moments before they were spotted and Jack knew that the lady would insist upon carrying Eloise away with her. The hunted look in his companion's blue eyes decided him. They were standing by the entrance to the long gallery. It was the work of an instant to whisk Eloise inside and shut the door.

He said, by way of explanation, 'I thought perhaps you might prefer to avoid them.'

On the other side of the door he could hear Lady Parham talking with her hostess, their voices echoing through the marbled hall. Eloise moved away from him.

'Thank you. I can find my way from here.' She nodded dismissively and when he made no move she added sharply. 'Please, you may leave me now.'

Jack smiled, his eyes flicking towards the door.

'Would you throw me out? Lady Parham would be

sure to pounce upon me and drag me in to tell them all how Mortimer goes on.'

A reluctant smile lurked in her eyes.

'Surely you are not afraid of a group of ladies, Major.'

'Terrified,' he replied cheerfully. 'I shall have to remain in here until I know it is safe to venture out.' He moved further into the room. 'Renwick has some fine paintings here; will you not take a few moments to look at them?'

She had been walking away from him but now she stopped, uncertain, and he added quickly, 'If you are leaving in the morning you may not have another opportunity of seeing them in daylight.'

It was clear from her expression that she was torn between a desire to look at the pictures and a disinclination to be alone with him. At least she had not refused to stay. He pointed to the nearest painting and said in a matter-of-fact voice, 'This Cuyp landscape is highly prized and this next is thought to be a Rembrandt, although there is some doubt about that: what do you think?'

She moved a little closer.

'I cannot tell,' she said slowly. 'It is certainly very good, if it is a copy.'

'But what of the colours, and the brushstrokes, are they not a little fine for Rembrandt?'

'Not necessarily. I think his style changed when he

grew older. And the subject matter, a biblical scene: this is typical of his later work.'

He regarded her with admiration.

'And you say you are no connoisseur? I believe you misled us, my lady.'

'My husband was very interested in the old masters. I picked up a little from following him around Florence and Rome.'

'You would enjoy the Louvre, I think. Now Paris is free once more you might like to see it.'

'Perhaps. One day.'

He smiled to himself, thinking how much he would like to escort her there. His previous visit had been in the company of his fellow officers: how much more enjoyable to be with someone who really appreciated art.

'And who is this?' Her soft, musical voice recalled him with a jolt. He cleared his throat.

'This next is a portrait of one of Renwick's ancestors—can you see the family resemblance?'

Jack moved slowly along the gallery, drawing her attention to various pictures, asking her opinion, searching his brain to drag up long-forgotten snippets of information about the artists. His patience was rewarded: gradually she relaxed and gave her attention to the paintings. He stood beside her, close but never touching, enjoying her company and amused by her forthright opinions. By the time they were halfway down the long gallery she was chattering away quite naturally. She even turned to him at one point, laughing at something he said. Jack found himself wishing the gallery were twice as long. He drew her attention to a small pen-and-ink drawing.

'There is an interesting picture here of the house painted about sixty years ago, before it was remodelled into its present state.'

She stepped forwards for a closer look.

'The formal gardens are much smaller, and there looks to be a village where the park is now.'

'Yes, it was demolished by Renwick's grandfather, to improve the view.'

'Oh dear, and the villagers?'

'You need not worry; he built houses for all his tenants on the far side of the Home Wood. They were delighted to have new, weatherproof houses. I hope my own people will feel the same.'

She turned to look at him, her blue eyes wide with surprise.

'Are you evicting your tenants?'

He laughed at that.

'No, no, but I plan to build better houses for them as and when the funds will allow.'

'This is at Henchard, your estate in Staffordshire?'

He smiled, inordinately pleased that she had remembered.

'Yes. I have a very good agent, who has been looking after matters while I have been away, but there is much to do and I plan to spend more time there in the future.'

'And will you be content with such a quiet life, sir?'

'Quiet? It will be hard work, improving my land and the lot of my tenants. The house needs to be enlarged, new kitchens built—do you think I cannot be happy unless I have a sword in my hand?'

'No, of course not. I suppose I had not considered. I know so little about you, Major Clifton.'

'There is a great deal we do not know about each other, my lady.'

A shy smile lit her eyes and Jack's spirits soared. This was progress indeed: perhaps now he could talk to her about last night. As if reading his thoughts her cheeks flushed and she turned quickly back towards the paintings.

'This is by Ricciardelli.' She leaned forwards to read the label on the frame.

'Yes.' Jack nodded. 'It is a particularly fine view of Naples—do you agree? I remember Tony telling me you visited Naples on your honeymoon.'

Jack clamped his mouth shut, cursing himself. Eloise's face flamed. She turned to go and he reached out for her.

'I beg your pardon. I did not mean to remind you of your marriage, if it was not happy.'

He was holding her arm and she stood perfectly still, keeping her face averted.

'Tony and I *were* happy.' Her voice was so quiet he could hardly hear her. 'Despite what you now know of me, we were very fond of one another. Excuse me, I must go.'

He released her and she hurried towards the door. He followed, saying, 'And you are determined to leave for London in the morning?'

'I am.'

'Then first let me talk to you—let me apologise—for last night.'

'There is nothing more to say.'

She reached for the door handle but he stepped past her, putting his hand against the door to prevent her from escaping.

'Oh, but there is! At least let me tell you that I know now how much I had misjudged you—you were not what I thought.'

She turned to look at him, fixing him with eyes as dark and troubled as a stormy evening sky.

'You thought me wanton, which is the impression I have been at some pains to give. I cannot blame you for that.' She looked away. 'We enjoyed a night together and that is all there is to it. Now I would be obliged if you would forget all about me.' Her chin lifted: he thought he detected the faintest wobble in her voice. 'I am sure I am not the first woman to have enjoyed your attentions for a single night. There will be no regrets, no recriminations and if we are obliged to meet in company, I hope we can do so like civilised beings. As far as I am concerned the matter is over.'

Jack stared at her. His instinct was to drag her into his arms, to melt her icy resolve with a savage kiss, but he was haunted by the memory of her distress that morning. Despite her brave words she had been a virgin when he had taken her to his bed and he was ashamed that he had not realised it. That she had not told him, that their lovemaking had been as passionate and intense as any he had ever experienced, was no excuse for his lack of control. More than that, he was confused by his feelings for her. She did not trust him, she certainly did not confide in him—it seemed now that she did not even *want* him, so why could he not just do as she asked and leave her to her fate?

'My lady. Eloise—'

She closed her eyes and lifted her hand as if to defend herself.

'Please, let me go!'

Her impassioned whisper cut him like a knife. She did not want him near her. He removed his hand from the door and stood back.

'As you wish, madam.'

Chapter Twelve

'My lady, are you going downstairs for dinner?'

Alice's voice roused Eloise from her sleep. She blinked and gazed around the room. As her mind cleared she remembered with a sinking heart the events that had resulted in her spending the entire afternoon curled up on her bed.

Alice was bustling around the room, pulling clothes from the linen press and chattering all the while.

'I made sure everyone thought you had the migraine, my lady: even fetched up a tisane for you, which I drank myself since you was asleep. Didn't want anyone connecting your malaise with Mr Mortimer's antics last night. Mrs Renwick sends her compliments and says that if you wish she will arrange for you to have dinner in your room, so I said I would come and find out how you are.'

Eloise sat up and rubbed her eyes.

'No, I must put in an appearance, I think.'

Alice gave an approving nod.

'I have brought you up some hot water. Shall I lay out your new gown for you?'

She allowed Alice to dress her in the white silk with its exquisite silver embroidery. She pulled out the diamonds Tony had given her for a wedding present and as her maid fastened the necklace she gazed at her reflection in the mirror, feeling very much as if she was putting on her armour to go into battle.

When Eloise walked into the drawing room some time later she had the impression that there was a sudden lull in the conversation, that all eyes were turned upon her. She kept her smile in place and walked towards her hostess: not even by the flicker of an eyelid would she betray her inner trepidation.

'My dear Lady Allyngham, I am so glad you could join us: migraine can be most debilitating.' Mrs Renwick leaned forwards and peered into her face. 'But, my dear, you are still a little pale, are sure you are quite well?'

'Yes, ma'am, thank you. You must not worry about me, especially when we have a much more serious invalid in the house. Is there any news of Mr Mortimer?'

'I think Major Clifton can answer that for you,' said Mrs Renwick, beckoning to Jack. 'He has been most solicitous of poor Mr Mortimer and can tell us if there is any change, can you not, Major?'

Eloise berated herself for her stupidity. She should

have realised that any enquiries about Alex would be directed to Major Clifton. Unable to escape, she fixed her eyes upon the floor as Jack approached. He did not look at her, but addressed himself to his hostess.

'I called in upon Mortimer on my way downstairs, ma'am, and I am pleased to tell you that he is looking much better.'

'So we have no need to summon Dr Bellamy?' asked Mr Renwick, coming up.

'Not in the least. In fact I expect to see him out of bed in a few days, once his leg has begun to heal.'

'That is excellent news,' declared Edward Graham. 'Poor Mortimer, he will be sorry when he hears what a good day's shooting he missed today. And you too, Clifton. Pity you didn't come out with us, but I take it you'll be able to join us tomorrow?'

'Yes, if the weather holds.'

The conversation turned to sport and Mrs Renwick went off to greet Meg Cromer, who had just come in. Eloise moved towards the fire to warm her hands. She did not know whether to be most relieved or disappointed by the cool reception she had received from Jack, yet what did she expect, after the way she had repulsed him that morning? Her mind strayed back to their walk through the long gallery. For a short time she had been able to forget her troubles and lose herself in discussing art and the paintings on the walls. It was as if they had been old friends, until his chance remark had reminded her that she was not free to indulge in such luxury. She and Jack Clifton could never be friends. After last night he knew too much about her—for him to learn more might endanger everything she had worked so hard to conceal.

She allowed her eyes to stray towards the little group of gentlemen: Jack Clifton's powerful figure immediately claimed her attention. His broad shoulders filled the black evening coat without the need for padding and his long legs encased in biscuit-coloured pantaloons gave him the height to stand out amongst his companions. Some called him saturnine, with his raven-black hair and hard, unsmiling features, but she had seen the kindness in his eyes, experienced the warmth of his smile and found more jovial countenances insipid by comparison.

I love him.

The revelation shocked her. She turned away quickly, afraid that someone might look into her face and discover her secret. It could never be, of course. Witness his reaction when she had revealed that she was a maid—surely he would never have reacted in such a way if he cared for her at all. If he loved her.

Aye, there was the rub: she was being foolishly romantic. Jack Clifton was a kind man, an honourable man, but he did not love her. He had told her himself that he had loved Clara Deforge and she had been a sweet, innocent young maid, a paragon of virtue compared with the disgraceful Lady Allyngham, who flirted and teased and kept all manner of secrets! Jack could never love such a woman. He wanted to help her because she was Tony's widow. Lying on her bed that afternoon, she had relived the moment when she had told him she wanted nothing more to do with him, only in her silly, foolish, fairy-tale imagination he did not let her walk away from him. An unhappy lump settled in her throat. If only Jack had held her then, told her he would not let her go, that she was his and he would keep her no matter what happened. But he had said nothing. He had stood back and let her walk out, probably relieved to be free of her toils.

'A penny for your thoughts, Lady Allyngham.'

Sir Ronald Deforge's soft words brought an abrupt end to her reverie. This man had the power to ruin her, he had tried to kill her best friend, but she dare not denounce him. Instead she assumed the brittle, society manner that served her so well.

'They are not worth even a groat, Sir Ronald.'

He leaned closer and it was all she could do not to back away.

'I thought you might be thinking over my... proposal.'

'That requires a great deal of consideration, sir. It is not something to be undertaken lightly.'

'Very true, but I am not a patient man, and I want

your answer.' He took out his snuffbox and flicked it open. 'Our hostess tells me you intend to leave us.'

'Yes. I am going back to town.'

'This is very sudden, is it not?'

She was silent while he took a delicate pinch of snuff.

'I made my decision last night,' she said at last. 'I informed Mrs Renwick earlier today that I have business in London requiring my attention.'

His puffy, pock-marked face pushed even closer, so that she could feel his breath on her skin.

'I hope you do not plan to run away from me, madam.'

She raised her head, her lip curling disdainfully.

'Of course not. But I need time to think.'

'So you are leaving your lapdog Mortimer behind you? Do you think that is wise? Will he be quite safe, do you think?'

Her head came up at that. She fixed him with a steady gaze.

'Let us understand one thing, Sir Ronald. I shall not make any decision until Alex Mortimer is quite well again. It is in *your* interests to make sure he comes to no more harm.'

His look of surprise gave her some small satisfaction

'Perhaps you think Major Clifton will protect you,' he muttered. 'Let me warn you, madam, that I shall not be caught unawares again. Any attempt by the major to interfere in this affair will have disastrous results, for you both.' He added silkily, 'I shall not hesitate to kill him, my lady, do not be in any doubt about that.'

'Oh, I believe you capable of any base act,' she retorted haughtily. She turned on her heel and walked away, head held high, yet a deadly depression was already seeping into her bones: if she was to protect everything she held most dear, she could see no alternative. She would have to marry Sir Ronald Deforge.

London was cold. Eloise ordered fires to be lit in every room of her house in Dover Street but the chill never seemed to leave her. She told herself she was anxious for news of Alex, but even when his letters arrived, and she knew he was recovering well, still something was missing. She found herself re-reading the letters, searching for any mention of Jack Clifton, but Alex told her very little, save that Jack intended to accompany him back to town, as soon as he was well enough to travel, and with that crumb she had to be satisfied.

Everyone welcomed Lady Allyngham back to town and she threw herself into the round of breakfasts, parties, routs and balls that filled the days and nights of any society lady, but although she was relieved to be away from Sir Ronald's presence she could not relax. At one particularly tiresome party she

began to think of going to Allyngham until Alex
returned. She was idly making plans for this when
Lord Berrow sought her out and invited her to tell
him more about the foundling hospital she intended
to build. He hinted that he might be persuaded to
sell her the land she needed at Ainsley Wood, and
it occurred to her that she should make sure that
her plans for the hospital were well under way, and
a trust set up for its support as soon as possible: she
was all too aware that if she was forced to marry Sir
Ronald she would lose all control of the Allyngham
fortune.

Alex came in to London sooner than she expected.
Eloise returned from the Green Park one afternoon
to find a hastily scrawled note awaiting her.

'When did this arrive, Noyes?'

'It was delivered shortly after you left the house,
my lady.'

She looked up, smiling.

'Mr Mortimer is back in town. Since I am dressed
for walking I shall go and see him immediately.'

'I will summon your maid, madam.'

'No, I will not wait for that.'

'But, my lady!'

She waved an impatient hand at him.

'It is only a few doors away and not yet dark. Open
the door, Noyes. I shall not be long.'

Ignoring the butler's tut of disapproval she hurried

along the street, holding her skirts up to avoid the dirty pavement.

If Alex's butler was shocked to find an unescorted lady at his master's door he was too well trained to reveal it and merely ushered her to the drawing room. Alex was stretched out on a day-bed, one arm in a sling and a brightly coloured rug thrown over his legs. Eloise ran forwards and bent to hug him.

'Oh, my dear, I am so pleased that you are back! I am sorry I did not come earlier, but I was out walking with Lord Berrow when your note arrived. How was your journey, was it terribly painful for you?'

'Not as bad as I feared. Jack brought me in his new carriage, which is very well sprung. I scarcely noticed the bumpy road.'

'Oh, I beg your pardon. I did not realise you had company.'

She straightened and turned to see Major Clifton standing by the window. As he walked forwards she observed the warm look in his eyes and heat seared her cheeks. He was not deceived by the cool, polite smile she was giving him, and she scolded herself for allowing that first, initial burst of irrational pleasure to show. Jack bowed to her.

'You will want to talk alone,' he said. 'I shall leave you—'

'The devil you will!' retorted Alex. 'You promised to keep me company at dinner, Clifton, and I will hold you to that.'

'Then I should go,' said Eloise quickly. 'I wanted only to assure myself that you had survived your journey.'

Alex reached out and gripped her hand.

'No, there is no need for you to rush off, Elle. We three know each other well enough to take a glass of wine together, do we not? My dear, ring the bell for me. Then you must sit down. A gentleman should not lounge around in a lady's presence, but you know very well that I cannot get up.'

'Allow me,' said Jack, pulling up a chair for her.

She did not look at him but sank into it with a murmur of thanks.

'Have you seen Deforge?' Alex's question brought her eyes to his face and he said impatiently, 'For heaven's sake, Elle, there's no need to look daggers at me. It is not as though Clifton does not know what is going on.'

'But Lady Allyngham would prefer not to discuss the matter while I am here…'

She put up her hand.

'No,' she said carefully. 'I have no objection to you being here, Major. After all, you saved Alex's life.'

Alex nodded. 'I am glad you are being sensible at last, my dear.'

'Sir Ronald left Renwick Hall two days before us,' explained Jack. 'He said he was calling upon friends, but I thought he might try to steal a march by coming straight to town.'

'I have not seen him,' said Eloise. 'I have no doubt he will seek me out when he is ready.'

'Then we must decide what is to be done,' declared Alex.

'You will do nothing, my dear,' she said quickly. 'At least, not until you are well again.'

'Then perhaps Jack—'

'No!' She sat up very straight. 'Major Clifton need not involve himself further in our affairs.'

'But I should like to help,' said Jack mildly.

She glanced across at him. Her heart lurched at the sight of his smiling face and she squeezed her hands together in her lap, reminding herself of her resolution.

'That is very kind of you, Major, but there really is nothing to be done at the present time.'

She was relieved that the entry of a footman carrying the wine caused a diversion.

'Yes, yes, that will do,' said Alex, impatiently waving away the servant. 'Clifton, will you pour? I am weak as a cat.'

'Hardly surprising after a long journey,' said Jack. 'You will feel better when you have had a good night's sleep.'

He held out a glass of wine to Eloise, saying with a faint smile, 'I insisted he send for his doctor to call upon him in the morning.'

'I am glad of it, thank you.'

She was very aware of her fingers brushing Jack's

as she took the wine. She remembered the feel of them on her skin and experienced a little *frisson* of pleasure at the memory. Giving herself a mental shake, Eloise put both hands around the wine glass. Heavens, she must curb such thoughts!

Jack had turned away to carry a glass of wine to Alex and she was able to watch the two men as they conversed. She remembered the icy dread she had felt when Alex had been wounded. It was nothing to the fear that now enveloped her when she thought of anything happening to Jack Clifton. She regarded his broad back. He was so strong, so assured, but even he was not proof against an assassin's knife or bullet. Deforge had promised to kill him, and she had no doubt that he would carry out that threat, if he thought Jack was involved. She squared her shoulders: she would talk to Alex tomorrow and make him promise not to divulge anything more to Jack Clifton. She finished her wine.

'I must go. I am promised to attend Parham House this evening.'

'But I thought you did not like Lady Parham above half.'

Eloise gave a little shrug. 'I do not, but I have hopes that I might be able to settle the question of Ainsley Wood this evening, so you see I must attend. I shall call upon you again tomorrow, Alex.'

Jack put down his glass.

'It is growing dark. I will escort you to your door, my lady.'

'Aye, please do, Jack,' said Alex, before Eloise could refuse. 'I'd rather not have her walking alone. It is only a step and you can be back in ten minutes.' He scowled. 'Do not argue with me, madam. Bad enough that you should risk your reputation by coming here!'

Jack grinned.

'I think we should humour him, my lady: opposition could render him feverish.' He held out his arm. 'Shall we go?'

Silently, Eloise allowed him to escort her out on to the street. The chill autumn night was already setting in and she was glad to push her hands deep into the large muff she was carrying.

'You said you were walking with Lord Berrow this afternoon,' said Jack, matching his step to hers. 'Was Lady Berrow with you, too?'

'No, she was not.'

'But she knows of your outing?'

Eloise shrugged. 'I presume so, Major. Why do you ask?'

'I think you should have a care, that is all.'

'Lord Berrow's estates border my own. We are neighbours. It is only natural that we should discuss matters together.'

'The gentleman may not see it in quite that way.'

She stiffened.

'Do not measure all men by your own standards, sir!'

'I do not,' he retorted. 'That is why I urge caution.'

She stopped and turned to face him.

'Major Clifton, allow me to know my own business,' she said angrily. 'I am perfectly capable of looking after myself.'

'I very much doubt that.'

She drew herself up.

'In case you have forgotten, sir, my husband was a military man and often absent. I am quite capable of running my own affairs and have been doing so for years!'

'No, I have not forgotten your husband, madam, which is why I am trying to protect you!'

She gave him an icy look and turned to walk on. He fell into step beside her, saying, 'While Mortimer is tied to his bed I would urge you to be more careful. You cannot deny that you are inexperienced in the ways of men.'

They had reached her house and she ran quickly up the steps. As the door opened to admit her she turned towards him and said in a low, shaking voice,

'During the past few weeks I have learned as much about men as I ever want to know!'

Chapter Thirteen

A quiet dinner alone did much to restore Eloise's good humour and by the time she set out for Parham House she was feeling quite optimistic. Alex was safe and recovering well, and although she was angry with Jack Clifton, she had to admit that it was very pleasant to have someone so concerned for her welfare that they were prepared to argue with her. Tony had been a kind and considerate husband, and Alex was a good friend, but neither had ever shown themselves quite so fiercely protective as Jack Clifton. She could almost believe he cared for her—but that was because he did not know the truth: he was far too honest to approve of the web of deceit she had woven with Tony and Alex. She leaned her head against the luxurious padding of her carriage and allowed herself to dream of what her future could be, if she could only destroy the journal and free herself from Deforge's clutches. Perhaps, once the secrets of her past were safely hidden she could start again; make a new life for herself that was not built on lies and deceit. And perhaps then Jack might be able to love her. It would not be easy, and escaping from Sir Ronald's clutches would be both difficult and dangerous, especially with Alex injured and unable to help, but she decided it was a future worth fighting for.

Parham House was hot, noisy and crowded. Eloise summoned up her society smile and wondered just how soon she would be able to get away. She took a glass of wine and scanned the room for Lord Berrow. During their walk that afternoon he had asked her most specific questions about her plans for the foundling hospital, and she had been encouraged to suggest he reconsider selling her the land at Ainsley Wood. When they parted he had hinted most strongly that if she attended the rout this evening he would give her his decision, so she had changed her walking dress for an evening gown of rose-coloured silk, secured the Allyngham diamonds about her neck and sallied forth to brave Lady Parham's barbed wit.

Despite her bold words to Jack Clifton, Eloise did not enjoy going about alone in town. She was used to turning off the gentlemen's flirtatious banter with a laugh and a witty rejoinder, but without Alex at her side she found their attentions a little more pressing, and it was necessary to give an occasional set down in order to keep the gentlemen at a distance. She could not be said to be enjoying herself at Parham House. The time dragged while she waited for Lord Berrow to arrive. She took a second glass of wine, then a glass of champagne, anything to occupy her. At last she was relieved to see the Earl approaching her, and she held out her hand to him, smiling.

'My lord, I am very pleased you are here! Such a squeeze. All the world and his wife must be present.'

Lord Berrow raised her fingers to his lips.

'My dear Lady Allyngham. You are radiant, as ever!'

'Thank you.' She looked past him. 'Is Lady Berrow with you?'

He chuckled.

'My wife is indisposed this evening, but even if she were not, we would not want her here upon this occasion, now would we?'

She realised he was still holding her fingers and gently but firmly pulled them away.

'No, I suppose not, if we are discussing business.'

'Business! Ha ha, well, if that is what you wish to call it.'

Her eyes slid away from him and as a distraction she beckoned to a passing waiter.

'Shall we take a glass of wine, sir?'

The room was very hot and the wine did little to cool her. Eloise wished she had sent the waiter to fetch her some lemonade instead. Lord Berrow seemed content to talk of trivial matters but she was impatient to get away.

'My lord, you said you would give me your decision on Ainsley Wood. Will you allow me to buy the land from you?'

'My dear ma'am, I shall be delighted to sell you anything your heart desires!'

'That is very gracious of you, sir, but it is only a small portion of land that is required.'

'Then it is yours.'

'I am so pleased. I shall instruct my lawyers to—'

Lord Berrow put up a hand.

'Yes, yes, of course, but there are a few little details I should like to talk over.' He held out his arm. 'Allow me to escort you out of this crush.'

She placed her fingers on his sleeve and was happy for him to precede her, his substantial bulk carving a path for her through the crowd. The double doors of the main reception rooms had been thrown open and Lord Berrow led her into the salon beyond. This room was just as crowded, but her partner carried on to a small corridor at one end.

'You appear to know the house very well, my lord.'

Eloise gave a nervous little laugh as he ushered her into a small, book-lined study and closed the door upon the noisy throng. A single branched candlestick and the glow from the fire provided the only lighting in the room, adding to her unease.

He tapped his nose, beaming at her.

'The advantage of spending years in town, one learns where one may be, ah, private in even the busiest houses.'

'But is this necessary, Lord Berrow? Would it not be better to discuss these things at your house, or even with my lawyer in the City?'

'Oh I don't see the need to involve the lawyers for this,' he said, drawing her down on to a sofa placed before a crackling fire. 'At least, not yet.'

He sat down beside her. She edged away a little, suddenly suspicious.

'My lord, I thought you had agreed to sell me Ainsley Wood.'

'I have indeed.' He moved closer 'But there are a few little details we must discuss.'

'Must we?'

'But of course. You know that I was not at all in favour of having a foundling hospital located so near to me.'

'So near? My dear sir, your house is quite five miles away from Ainsley Wood, and I have already said I would offer you a very good price to buy the land from you.'

'I am sure you would, my dear, and I am very happy to sell you the wood, but I think we need to discuss terms.'

'T-terms?'

'Oh, yes.' He was smiling at her, so close that she could see the tiny, broken veins in his cheeks. 'We are neighbours, after all, and it would be very pleasant to know that whenever I stayed in the area I should be welcome at Allyngham.'

'You and Lady Berrow may call at any time, my lord. Of course I did not receive visitors when I was in mourning, but—'

'You misunderstand me,' he murmured, his voice thickening. 'I shall call upon you *alone*, to enjoy those charms that you display so lavishly. Now let us seal our little bargain with a kiss, shall we…'

His arm slid around her waist and he pulled her to him. She turned her head and felt his hot breath on her ear. She pushed ineffectually at his chest.

'My lord, let me go! This is not what I intended!'

He chuckled, his mouth pressed against her skin. She felt his teeth nibbling at her neck. Her flesh began to crawl.

'How dare you. Leave me alone!'

'No need to be coy, my love, I have said you may have Ainsley Wood, and I will not object to you building your hospital, but you must give me something in return…'

He was forcing her back upon the sofa, his knee pushing between her legs and one hand firmly fixed upon her breast. She began to panic as she felt his weight pressing her down, pinning her beneath him.

His hot, rasping breath was warm on her face. She closed her eyes and tried to scream, but she could not get her breath and given the noise in the main salons she doubted if anyone would hear her.

Then, miraculously, she was free. The suffocating weight was lifted from her body and she opened her eyes in time to see Jack Clifton delivering a crashing blow to Lord Berrow's whiskery jaw. Gasping for breath, Eloise sat up and straightened her gown.

Lord Berrow spluttered and struggled to his feet.

'Damn you, sir, how dare you assault me!'

Jack stood over him, scowling blackly. 'From what I could see, *you* were assaulting the lady.'

'Not I,' blustered Lord Berrow, moving out of range of Jack's clenched fist. 'Lady Allyngham and I have an arrangement!'

'That is not how I perceived it.'

'Then ask her! She will tell you she came here willingly.'

Jack looked at Eloise. 'What do you say, madam?'

She crossed her arms over her breast, her whole body shaking.

'Please, make him go,' she croaked.

'Well, sir. You heard the lady.' Jack took a step forwards. 'You had best be off with you.'

Lord Berrow straightened his coat and cast an angry glance towards Eloise. She shuddered and looked away.

'Very well, madam,' he said coldly. 'It would appear I misunderstood you. I beg your pardon.'

With a stiff bow he turned and stalked to the door. There was a sudden burst of sound as he left the room, then the door closed again and relative silence settled over them. Eloise glanced up. Jack was still scowling, his black brows drawn together. She said in a small voice, 'I suppose you will say now that you told me so.'

The heavy frown vanished.

'I shall say nothing so ill mannered.' He walked to a side table and filled a glass from one of the decanters. 'Here,' he said, sitting down beside her. 'Drink this.'

She eyed the golden liquid doubtfully.

'What is it?'

'Brandy.'

He put the glass into her hand. Cautiously she took a sip.

She grimaced as the pungent aroma stung her senses. She held the glass away but Jack pushed it back.

'Drink it. It will put heart into you.'

Obediently she lifted the glass to her lips again. The brandy burned as she swallowed it but gradually its warmth seemed to spread through her body. The horror of the past few minutes faded and she no longer felt faint.

'It would seem I am in your debt again.' Her eyes

flickered over his face. 'Did…did you hear me cry out?'

'No, I came looking for you. Over dinner I questioned Alex about your interest in Lord Berrow. He told me that you had been trying to persuade Berrow to sell you some land.'

'Yes. I came here tonight because I thought…I thought he was going to agree to the sale.' She put her hands to her cheeks. 'But he wanted…'

'Hardly surprising.' Jack's hard tone heightened her remorse and she hung her head as he continued. 'When a beautiful woman seeks out a man to flatter and cajole him, is it any wonder if he thinks he can ask for certain favours? You have gone out of your way to give the impression that you are a woman of the world. No wonder Berrow thought you were his for the asking.'

'Well, I am not. I am not his or any man's!' She swallowed and said dejectedly, 'I do not suppose he will sell me that land now.'

'Was it so very important to you?'

Jack put his arm around her shoulders. She quickly damped the flicker of pleasure she felt at his touch. It was a gesture of comfort, nothing more.

'Yes. Did Alex tell you of my plans for a hospital?'

'A very little.'

'I want to build a foundling hospital, in memory of my husband.' His shoulder looked so inviting that she leaned against him. 'Tony knew there could be no children from our marriage. And I would have liked children, very much.'

'You are young, madam. There is still time.'

His words cut at her heart. She knew now that there was only one man she wanted to be the father of her children. He was sitting beside her now, his arm about her shoulders, having rescued her from another foolish scrape.

'Tony and I had talked about setting up a charitable foundation,' she said. 'When he died last year I thought it would be a suitable tribute to him. As an orphan myself I know what it is like to be alone. I was fortunate that Lord and Lady Allyngham took me in and raised me in comfort and luxury but I know that most do not have that advantage, and it is even worse for those poor babes born out of wedlock, or those whose mothers are too poor, or too ill to look after them. The children are left in church doorways, or worse, left to perish at the roadside. We have a good doctor in Allyngham who is very keen to help the poor. He sees the injustice of leaving these children to suffer. We have already financed a small school in the town but I want to do more. I have discussed with him my idea of a foundling hospital and there is some support from the church: we have set up a trust and agreed on a site to build the hospital, a piece of land from my estate, but it is a long circuitous route from the town, unless we can drive a road through Ainsley Wood.' She handed him the empty glass and gave a large sigh. 'Well, there is no help for it now. We will have to improve the existing lane.'

'No need to worry about that now.' He gently drew her head down on to his shoulder.

'No. I have been such a fool.'

'A regular little ninnyhammer,' he agreed, resting his cheek against her hair.

'I suppose I should go home, but I do not want to walk out, through all those people. I do not want everyone staring at me.'

'We do not need to leave just yet.' Jack leaned back against the sofa, pulling her with him.

'You will stay here?'

'As long as you need me.'

She sighed, murmuring, 'You are a very good friend to me, Major Clifton.'

Eloise closed her eyes. She was so very comfortable. The dim light, which had unsettled her when she had entered the study with Lord Berrow, now gave the room a cosy air. She felt safe, lying with Jack's arm about her and her cheek resting on his chest. The folds of his freshly laundered neckcloth tickled her nose. A strange inertia had invaded her mind and her body. Perhaps it had not been wise to take quite so much wine.

'I should not be here with you,' she murmured, snuggling even closer.

'You should not be here with anyone.'

She shook her head slightly.

'No, but definitely not with you. You are dangerous.'

'Not to you, my dear.'

She smiled as his fingers gently brushed a stray curl from her cheek.

'Oh, but you are.'

'I only want to protect you.'

The words rumbled against her cheek.

'How delightful that sounds.'

'It *is* delightful. Let me protect you from Deforge.'

'How could you do that?'

'I could force a quarrel on him. He is reluctant to meet me, but—'

She sat up, anxiety cutting through her drowsiness.

'No! No, if you do that his lawyer will publish the journal!' She clutched his coat. 'Promise me,' she said urgently. 'Promise me you will not challenge him.'

'How else would you have me deal with him?'

Her head was swimming, but it was imperative that she make him understand.

'I have no idea. I only know that if anything should befall him he has given instructions for the journal to be made public. If that happens—! No, please, Jack; tell me you will not call him out.'

'Very well, if that is your wish.'

She shook her head, wincing a little as something like a brick banged against the inside of her skull.

'No, you must swear it.'

'Very well,' he said solemnly, 'I swear I will not call him out.'

She looked into his eyes, frowning a little because it was so difficult to focus. At last, satisfied, she nodded and subsided against his shoulder once more. Everything seemed such an effort. She closed her eyes as Jack enfolded her in his arms again.

'But I still want to help you fight Deforge.' he murmured the words into her hair.

Secure within the comfort of Jack's arms, Sir Ronald seemed to pose no more threat to her than a troublesome fly. Her hand fluttered as if to swat him away.

'I can deal with him,' she said.

'He is a dangerous man, my dear.'

'To you, perhaps.' Deforge would not hurt her, at least not until he had made her his wife. That thought made her shiver, but she was resolved to wed him, if it was the only way to retrieve the journal. Once the damning evidence was destroyed then she would do what was necessary to escape a husband she hated. But Deforge had threatened to kill Jack. She could prevent that. She could protect him, just as she had always protected Alex and Tony—and now she knew that Jack was as dear to her as either of them. Her hand crept up to rest against his chest. 'Alex wants me to let you help us, but I cannot allow that.'

'Why not?'

She shifted impatiently. She was so tired. Why did he keep asking her questions?

'Because Deforge might kill you. Besides, you might discover the truth.'

'The truth? And what would that be?'

She shook her head.

'Oh, no, I won't be tricked into telling you.'

Even in her sleepy, comfortable state she knew she dare not tell him: he was far too good, too honourable. He would despise her for ever if he knew how deceitful she had been. And he would turn against Alex. She sighed.

'Poor Alex.'

'Why poor Alex?' asked Jack.

Had she spoken aloud? She pressed her lips together. She had drunk too much wine this evening and she must guard her tongue. She must not allow Jack to know any more of her secrets. And she must not allow him to fight Sir Ronald. She gave a little sob and Jack's arms tightened around her.

'Eloise? What is it?

She was drifting into oblivion, but even so she knew it was up to her to keep them all safe. As Sir Ronald's wife she could do that.

'Why poor Alex?' Jack asked again.

She said sleepily, 'I will marry him, and never see you again.'

'Curse it, no!' Jack exclaimed, sitting up.

Eloise remained slumped against him, fast asleep. Damnation, perhaps he should not have given her brandy, but she had been such a pitiful sight, pale and shaking so much he feared she might faint. Growling in frustration, he settled back against the sofa and gathered her against him. So she was going to wed Mortimer. Jack cursed under his breath. They weren't lovers; he knew that only too well. So why had they been at pains to make the world believe otherwise? And why marry now?

It had something to do with that damned journal. What secrets did it hold, if not a catalogue of the lady's scandalous affairs? His mind began to race with outlandish conjecture. Treason, spying, perhaps murder? He could not believe it, but even if it was true, did she think that by marrying Mortimer that would be the end of the matter? Deforge would publish anyway. If the contents were as scandalous as he had been led to believe then what life could she have? Marriage to Mortimer would not save her. They would have to go abroad, to live with the other exiles in Calais or Paris or Rome.

And he would never see her again.

His arms tightened around the slight figure sleeping

against his chest. He would not let it happen. Jack put his head back and stared at the ceiling.

'By heaven, what a coil.' He looked down at Eloise, her golden curls resting against his dark coat. She was an enigma. She had been at pains to hide her virginity from the world. She was happy for the world to think her fast and immoral, so what on earth was it that she dare not tell him? She had said it was not her secret, that others were involved. Suddenly he recalled Alex's words: *she was loyal to a fault… spent most of her time rescuing Tony and me from our more outlandish scrapes.* Perhaps she was innocent after all. Perhaps she was merely trying to protect others. It would certainly fit in with what he knew of the lady.

Jack sighed again. Conjecture was useless. There was only one certainty in his mind. She was his, however scandalous her past, and he did not want to see her married to Alex Mortimer.

Chapter Fourteen

Eloise was sitting at the breakfast table, her head on her hands when Noyes announced Major Clifton. Before she could tell him to deny her there was a heavy footstep in the passage and Jack entered the room. His knowing grin annoyed her.

'I did not know if you would be out of bed yet,' he said as the butler closed the door upon them. He eyed the untouched food upon the table and his smile grew.

'I have the most pounding headache,' she told him crossly.

'I am sorry for it.' He took a seat beside her. 'I find that a good meal helps.'

'I could not eat a thing!'

He buttered a piece of toast and handed it to her.

'Oh, I think you can. Try this.'

After a few pieces of toast and two glasses of water Eloise had to admit that she was feeling a little better. She knew she should not be entertaining a gentleman alone at breakfast, but several questions had been nagging at her since she had woken up that morning, and she needed Jack to answer them.

'How did I get home last night?'

Jack poured himself a cup of coffee.

'I brought you home in your carriage.'

'Thank you. I cannot remember leaving Parham House.'

'No, you were asleep at the time. I carried you out.' He grinned at her horrified stare. 'I waited until most of the guests had left, then put it about that you had been taken ill. However, I have no doubt that the Wanton Widow's latest escapade will be the talk of the town this morning.'

She dropped her head back into her hands.

'Until now my...*escapades* have been nothing more than conjecture.'

'And they are still. Your going off with Lord Berrow appears to have attracted little or no comment and by the time we left it was very late. No one can be sure how long we were alone together.'

'We should not have been alone at all!'

'I did not take advantage of your powerless state. Many men would have done so.'

'I know,' she muttered. 'I know and I am grateful to you.' She added in a low voice, 'I do not deserve your kindness.'

He put down his coffee cup.

'Elle—'

She recoiled at the use of her pet name: it was too intimate, too painful.

'No, please,' she beseeched him, 'do not say anything. I am in no fit state to talk to you this morning.'

He took her hand.

'Very well, but we must talk at some point. There must be no more misunderstanding between us.'

His clasp on her fingers was a bittersweet comfort. Once there were no misunderstandings he would not want to be near her.

'Yes, very well,' she said, fighting back tears. 'But not today.'

She looked up as the door opened and Noyes entered.

'This has arrived for you, my lady.'

The butler brought a letter to her on a small silver tray while a footman followed him into the room, carrying a large package. Her smile faded as she recognised the black scrawl upon the note.

'Thank you, Noyes. That will be all. Please, put the box down over there.'

'What is it?' asked Jack, when they were alone again.

Silently she handed him the note.

'Sir Ronald is back,' she said, her voice not quite steady. Steeling herself, she crossed over to the side table and began to open the parcel.

Jack scanned the letter. 'He will be at the Lanchester

Rooms tomorrow night and expects you to be there.'
She heard the note of disapproval in Jack's tone.
'They hold public balls there. Masquerades.'

'I know it.' She untied the string and lifted the lid
of the box. Inside she found an elegantly printed card
lying on top of a cloud of tissue. 'He has sent me a
ticket. And I presume this is the costume he wants
me to wear.'

Jack came over to her and while he perused the
card she lifted a heavy silk gown from the box and
held it up. The full skirts fell in folds of deep green
and orange to the floor.

'It is in the old style,' she said, observing the laced
bodice and straight, elbow-length sleeves.

'Even older,' muttered Jack. 'This goes back to the
time of the Stuarts. Look at the motif embroidered
here.' He lifted out a cream petticoat. 'Oranges. You
are to go as Nell Gwyn.'

She stared at him, then turned back to look again
at the gown with its wickedly low-cut neckline.

'He wants me to go out in public dressed as a…as
a…'

'An orange seller,' supplied Jack. His lips twitched.
'One cannot deny that Sir Ronald has a sense of
humour.'

'He is a villain!'

She dropped the gown back into its box as if it was
contaminated.

'Then do not go.'

She put out her hands.

'What choice do I have? You have read his letter: if I am not there he says the journal will be public by morning.'

He caught her hand.

'Elle, let him publish! I will take you out of town, tonight if you wish. I can protect you.'

She looked up at him. Her heart contracted at the concern she saw in his face. She reached up and touched his cheek.

'Then you, too, would be tainted by association,' she said softly. 'Besides, there is Alex. He is not fit enough for another long journey.'

He dropped her hand.

'And of course you cannot leave him.'

His cold tone cut at her. She said quietly, 'No. I will not leave him.'

'Yet you will not tell me what it is you have done that is so very terrible.'

She shook her head, not looking up. She heard him sigh.

'Very well, but you cannot go to the Lanchester Rooms unattended. I shall go with you.'

That brought her head up.

'No. It is too dangerous. I will not allow it.'

'Madam, you cannot stop me attending a public ball!'

Eloise looked up into his face, noting the stubborn set to his jaw. With a tired shrug she turned away and rested her hands on the table, bowing her head. Her brain felt so dull that she could not form an argument, especially when in her heart she knew she wanted him with her. She felt Jack's fingers on the back of her neck, rubbing gently, easing her tension.

'You need not be afraid. I will be in disguise. Deforge will not know I am present, but I will be close by if you need me.'

'Well, I must say, my lady, you looks a picture and no mistake.'

Alice stepped back to admire her handwork, a satisfied smile on her face. Standing before the long mirror, Eloise had to admit that the costume supplied by Sir Ronald appeared most authentic. From the brocade shoes with their leather-covered heels to the fontange headdress perched atop her golden curls she looked every inch a king's mistress. A whore. Eloise shivered. A green-and-gold mask had been supplied to hide her identity, but she allowed Alice to apply a coating of powder and rouge to her face to complete the disguise and the result was reassuring: Eloise did not expect to see any of her acquaintances at a public ball, but she would defy even as close a friend as Alex Mortimer to recognise her now.

'Your carriage is at the door, madam.' Alice interrupted her reverie by placing her cloak around her shoulders. 'I shall wait up for you, my lady, and won't rest easy until you are safely returned.'

With a nod and a brief, strained smile, Eloise hurried down the stairs and was soon on her way to Lanchester House.

She had never attended a public ball before and as she walked into the large echoing entrance hall her first instinct was to turn and run back to the safety of her carriage. Not that she could find fault with the bewigged and powdered footmen on duty at the door. Their livery was as fine as any she had seen, but the shrieks and unbridled laughter coming from the masked and disguised guests was very far from the genteel murmur of a *ton* party. Uncultured, nasal voices clashed with the over-refined accents of females whom she suspected to be the wives of wealthy tradesmen, dressed as fine as duchesses and gazing about them in surprise and disapproval at the free and easy manners of some of the revellers.

Eloise wanted to clutch her cloak about her but an insistent footman blocked her way and it was quite clear that she would have to give it up. As she moved to the stairs she put her hand up to her mask to check that the strings were secure, then, squaring her shoulders, she moved up the sweeping staircase towards the huge ballroom, where the strains of a boulanger could just be heard above the noise of the crowd.

In the ballroom she looked about her, dismay in her heart when she observed so many strangers, all attired in gaudy costume. She wondered if Jack was present. Perhaps he was one of the figures disguised head to foot beneath an enveloping domino. A waiter approached and offered her a glass of wine. She waved him away: she needed to keep a clear head tonight. She moved to the side of the room and turned to watch the dancing. It was not yet midnight but already the crowd was very wild. A Harlequin skipped passed and grabbed at her, trying to pull her on to the dance floor. Eloise dragged her hand free and stepped back even further, until she was standing at the edge of a small, shadowed alcove.

'Not inclined to dance tonight?'

Jack's low murmur drew a gasp from her and he added quickly, 'Do not turn. Keep your eyes on the dancers.'

She began to fan herself, holding the sticks high to cover her mouth as she replied,

'How long have you been here?'

'Not long. I saw you come in.'

'I am glad you are here. I did not expect it to be quite so…raucous.'

'Do not be afraid. I will let no one accost you.'

'Let me see you.' She wanted desperately to look at him. 'How shall I find you?'

She heard him chuckle.

'There are many black dominos here tonight. Best to let me find *you*.'

'Oh, but—' A laughing couple cannoned into her

and she was knocked back against the wall. They ran on, heedless, and by the time she had recovered and turned to peer into the alcove, it was empty.

Eloise wandered around the room. Her low-cut gown was attracting attention and she studiously ignored the many invitations from gentlemen to dance or to join them for supper. It was a comfort to know that Jack was nearby, although she could not see him. Her eyes sought out anyone wearing a black domino. There were several, but most were far too short to be Jack. She was so engrossed in her thoughts that she did not notice the gentleman in an old-fashioned coat and large black periwig until he spoke to her.

'So you came, Lady Allyngham.'

She stiffened immediately, but knew an irrational desire to laugh when she looked at the speaker.

'I had no choice.' Her lip curled. 'You see yourself as the merry monarch, Sir Ronald?'

He bowed.

'It seemed appropriate, since you are Nell Gwyn. Allow me to say how well you look in that costume, my dear.'

She waved her hand impatiently.

'Say what you have to say and let me leave this place.'

'I want your answer. Will you be my wife?'

'I have not yet decided.'

He placed a hand under her elbow and guided her, none too gently, to the far end of the room, where a series of pillars supported a minstrels' gallery. The area beneath the gallery was not lit, and the heavy columns cast deep shadows across the space. At first Eloise thought the area was deserted, but as her eyes grew accustomed to the gloom she could see that there were couples in each of the shadowy corners, their bodies writhing against the walls. She averted her eyes.

Sir Ronald turned to face her.

'My patience is running low, madam. I have given you time enough to make a decision. You know the consequences of refusing me. Are you prepared to suffer that? Your name disgraced, Mortimer branded a criminal.'

She snapped open her fan and began to wave it angrily.

'I am well aware of the risks, but what you ask...'

His lips parted in an evil grin. She took a step back and found a cold, unyielding pillar behind her.

'Would you rather I traded the journal page by page?' he said, leaning so close that she could feel his breath on her face. She averted her gaze and he continued softly, 'I could do that, you know.' He trailed one finger across the low scoop of her bodice. 'I would give you a sheet from the journal for each night you spend in my bed. As long as you pleased me, of course.' His lips brushed her neck and she froze, gritting her teeth to suppress the shudder of revulsion. He laughed softly. 'You do not like that plan, so I will be generous and honour my original offer: marry me and you shall have the journal immediately.' He grasped her jaw, forcing her to look at him. 'And do not think that you can ask Major Clifton to help you.' He took her arm and turned her towards the room again. 'Oh, yes, I know he is here, thinking he can protect you. Look—' his voice grated in her ear '—that is your precious major over there, is it not? In the black domino. But you see the two rustics on his right, and the piratical figure behind him? They are all my men. I realised at Renwick Hall that Clifton was likely to be a threat so I had him followed. I only have to give the word and they will cut him down like a dog.' Eloise gasped, her hand flying to her mouth. Deforge hissed, 'You have alarmed him. You had best signal to him not to approach. And quickly!'

The tall figure in the black domino had taken a few steps towards her. Behind him a huge bearded man in a pirate's costume was reaching for the gleaming, evil-looking blade in his belt. Frightened, she shook her head. Jack stopped and with a struggle she summoned up a reassuring smile.

Behind her, Sir Ronald murmured, 'Well done. You have averted a tragedy.'

'You would commit murder to achieve your ends?'

'Not I, my lady. It would have been a drunken brawl. No one could connect it to me.'

'You are an out-and-out villain!'

'No, I am merely protecting my interests. You have only to agree to marry me and Clifton will be safe.'

She shook her head and looked at him, bewildered.

'What happiness can there be with a wife that hates you?'

His thick lips parted into a leer and his grip tightened on her arm, the fingers digging into the flesh.

'Schooling you will be part of the enjoyment. And you must not forget that you bring with you the Allyngham fortune. So, madam. Your answer, now, if you please.' She swallowed nervously. A net was closing around her, cutting off every means of escape. At last she said in a low voice, 'You leave me no choice.'

'Then you will marry me. Say it.'

'Yes.' Eloise lifted her head. 'I will marry you.'

His triumphant look made her shudder. She watched him raise his hand, an innocuous gesture but immediately the shepherds and the pirate hovering behind the black domino melted away into the crowd.

'I shall send a notice to the newspapers in the morning, announcing that the wedding will take place on Friday next.' He held out his arm to her. 'My lady?'

She stepped away from him.

'If that is all you have to say to me I shall leave now.' She fixed her eyes upon his face. 'But be warned, sir. If anything happens to Major Clifton I promise you I shall cry off, do what you will with the journal!'

His hateful smile appeared.

'My dear, I think you care for the major even more than your good name. But have you told him what is in that journal? No, I thought not.' He leaned closer. 'Do you suppose the honourable Major Clifton will want any connection with the Allyngham family once he knows the truth?'

'That is none of your concern. I merely want your word that you will not harm him.'

'As long as you stick to our bargain the major is safe, but his continued well-being depends upon you.' He ran a finger down her arm. 'Be a good wife to me and there is no reason why Major Clifton should not enjoy a long and peaceful existence.' He gripped her arm and added, 'If you prove troublesome, however, I will make sure that your precious major meets a very slow and painful death. There are ways, you see; methods that would have even Jack Clifton begging for it to end. Do you understand me, my lady?'

Eloise shook off his hand. She said in a low voice, 'I understand you.'

'Then everyone is happy.' The smug note in his voice angered her but she said nothing and he

continued. 'I must hold a party, to celebrate our betrothal. It is short notice, but I believe the *ton* will
come, if only out of curiosity. What think you?'

She shrugged.

'Do as you please.'

'Oh, I will. It shall be next Tuesday, at my house
in Wardle Street, and I expect you to be at my side.
I shall be the envy of the *ton*, shall I not? The man
who won the Glorious Allyngham.'

Eloise turned away. She felt slightly sick. Sir Ronald
made no attempt to detain her and she hurried out
of the ballroom. She was aware of the black domino
shadowing her but she ignored him. She did not want
to talk to anyone, least of all Jack. She retrieved
her cloak and waited impatiently for her carriage to
arrive at the door. The black domino had disappeared
and her drooping spirits sank even lower. Did he
think that now she was leaving she no longer needed
his protection? Perhaps he considered his duty done,
and had returned to the ballroom to while away the
rest of the night with some pretty woman who made
no demands upon him.

'Your carriage, m'lady.'

The servant's sonorous tones recalled her wandering thoughts and she went out into the busy street.
Her own footman held open the carriage door and
she climbed in, closing her eyes with relief as she
fell back against the thickly padded seat.

'Thank heaven you are out of there.'

Eloise screamed and opened her eyes. Jack Clifton was sitting in the far corner of the carriage, his black domino merging with the shadows to make him all but invisible.

'I beg your pardon. I did not mean to startle you.'

'How did you get in here?' she demanded.

'I jumped in,' he said. 'From the street side. I want to know what Deforge said to you.'

'Sir Ronald knew you were present,' she replied cautiously. 'His people have been following you.'

'I thought as much.'

'You *knew*?'

She saw a brief flash of white as he grinned.

'That big oaf dressed as Blackbeard has been tailing me for days. His bulk makes him far too easy to spot.'

'But tonight there were others, I saw them.'

'The rustics? I saw them too—I had to throw them off my track before I climbed into your carriage.' He untied the strings of his domino and shrugged it off. 'They need not worry you, my dear.'

'But they might have killed you!'

'Not they! Trust me, they were never a threat to me. Only once have I been taken unawares, and that was by a beautiful woman on Hampstead Heath.'

There was a laugh in his voice but it awoke no response in her. He was far too reckless. If he would not protect himself then she must do so, even if it meant she would never see him again.

'But enough of that,' he said. 'Tell me about Deforge. I didn't like the way he kept leering at you.'

'He is growing impatient,' she responded quietly.

'And?'

Eloise hesitated. Sir Ronald's threats echoed uncomfortably in her head. At last she said, 'He wants my decision soon.'

'Hmm. Word is that he is rolled up and his creditors are pressing for payment. I thought he might have demanded you marry him at once.'

She forced herself to keep her eyes upon Jack. It was very dark in the carriage, but she would take no chances that he would catch her out in the lie.

'No. Not yet.'

'Not ever!' he growled. 'We will find some way out of this coil that does not involve you giving yourself to that fiend, or marrying Mortimer.'

She blinked.

'M-marrying Alex? How could you ever think I would do that?'

'You said so, at Parham House.'

Eloise was silent. She had only the haziest recollection of what had happened after Jack had rescued her from Lord Berrow. She was afraid she had given herself away and admitted her true feelings: now it appeared that Jack had misunderstood her.

He continued harshly, 'If you must marry anyone for expediency, then you will marry me!'

'M-marry you?' she gasped, surprised. 'What, what reason can you have for w-wanting to marry me?'

'Reason!' He gave a crack of laughter. 'If you want reasons—' He raised his hand and counted them off on his fingers. 'Well, for one thing it would foil Deforge, and for another Tony was a good comrade: I owe him my life.'

'That is very chivalrous, sir, but—'

He crossed the carriage to sit beside her. 'Not chivalrous at all, my dear. I have my own plans for you.'

She did not pretend to misunderstand. She swallowed, trying to clear the sudden constriction in her throat. His arm was around her and she allowed herself to lean against him.

'I thought you disapproved of me,' she murmured

He took her hand in his.

'I disapprove of the fact that you will not trust me with your secrets.'

'They are not my secrets to share.'

'Then I will not force them from you, but you must know that I am yours to command, now and always.' He put a hand under her chin and tilted her face up. 'I want you for my wife, Elle. My land isn't in such good heart as Mortimer's but with careful management and a little investment I know we can turn it around.'

We? The word made her heart give a little lurch. If only that were possible.

'I could want nothing better,' she whispered, sighing.

Jack kissed her and she clung to him, returning his kiss with such a passion that when he broke away they were both breathing heavily.

'I have only the one estate, now, plus a few acres at Brighton where I plan to build houses. Little enough to bring you, I know—'

'Do you think I care how wealthy you are?' Her fingers crept up to touch his cheek. 'Let us not talk of it now.'

He reached up and trapped her hand with his own.

'No,' he said thickly, 'Let's not talk.'

He slid his mouth over hers again and instantly she responded, her lips parting as his kiss deepened and she felt herself surrendering. She drove her hands through his thick hair, strong as silk between her gloved fingers. He unfastened her cloak and pushed it away, running his hands over her shoulders, his thumbs caressing her collar bones. Her skin was on fire beneath his touch. Her body remembered the delights of his lovemaking and she was overcome with an urgent need to repeat the experience. He planted a trail of feather-light kisses over her neck and she said, her voice not quite steady, 'When we reach Dover Street, will…will you come in and take a glass of Madeira with me, Major Clifton?'

He lifted his head to look at her. Even in the darkness she could see the gleam of desire in his eyes. He replied solemnly, 'I would be delighted, my lady.'

She stifled the voice in her head that urged caution. Tomorrow the announcement would be in all the newspapers, everyone would know that she was going to marry Deforge, but tonight—she closed her eyes. Tonight she would enjoy one last night with Jack before he was lost to her for ever.

Chapter Fifteen

Sitting in the darkened carriage with Eloise in his arms, a quiet, joyous elation swept over Jack. She was his, every instinct told him so. Whatever hold Deforge might have on her they would fight it together. When the carriage pulled up in Dover Street he jumped down and handed her out of the carriage. It was as much as he could do not to sweep her up as if she was a new bride and carry her into the house, but instead he must walk quietly beside her, exchanging idle chit-chat while they handed their cloaks to the butler and she requested refreshments to be fetched. Jack prowled around the drawing room while they waited for the butler to return, knowing that if he came within arms' reach of Eloise he would have to kiss her. He was almost painfully aroused, his body ached to hold her but he must go slowly, he must remember that she had little experience of love, despite her reputation. He watched her as she stood before the fire, pulling off her gloves.

There was a solemn, almost melancholy cast to her countenance.

'If you want me to leave—'

She glanced up and gave him a fleeting smile.

'No, truly, I want you here.' She turned away as Noyes came in and placed a heavy silver tray upon a table.

'Thank you, you may go now. And, Noyes…'

'Yes, m'lady?'

'You may go to bed. Major Clifton will see himself out.'

'But the bolts, my lady—'

She waved him away impatiently.

'I am quite capable of dealing with those. Now go to bed, if you please. And on your way tell Alice I shall not need her again tonight.'

There was no mistaking the butler's look of mingled shock and surprise. Eloise caught Jack's eye and blushed. She poured two glasses of wine and carried them across the room. Jack watched her, noting the way the wide skirts of her costume swayed with the movement of her hips as she walked. A smile tugged at his mouth.

'That gown suits you, but I do not like your hair to be so artificially contained.'

She stopped before him, a full wine glass in each hand but he made no move to take one from her. Instead he reached out and pulled off the headdress and tossed it aside.

'What are you doing?'

'Making you a little more like a king's mistress.'

Deftly he removed the pins and the gold curls cascaded over his hands. He spread his fingers and eased them into her hair, coaxing it to fall like a golden curtain around her shoulders. He nodded approvingly.

'Much better,' he said.

A shy smile lit her eyes.

'I do not believe Nell Gwyn ever appeared with her hair thus.'

'Not in public, perhaps, but in private. For her lover.'

She blushed profusely. Jack took the glasses from her and put them down on a side table. Time for wine later.

She kept her eyes on his face as he began to unlace the bodice of her gown. Her breasts rose and fell, temptingly close to his fingers but he resisted the urge to run his hands over their soft swell. She stood statue-like while he undressed her. The heavy skirts sank to the floor with a whisper and he continued, slowly discarding her clothes until she stood before him wearing only her chemise and a pair of creamy embroidered stockings.

'Now it is your turn,' he told her, smiling.

Shyly she reached out and began to unbutton his waistcoat. Despite the layers of material between them, her touch sent little darts of heat through his body. He experienced a jolt of excitement when she began to unfasten his breeches and, unable to restrain himself, he pulled her to him, his mouth seeking her lips. They finished undressing by the light of the guttering candles and then he drew her down on to the daybed.

Jack gently pushed her back against the padded silk. She did not resist. She was so trusting he tried to put aside his own urgent desires and concentrate on pleasing her. His kiss was long and languorous and he felt her relaxing, responding to him. When at last he raised his head, his heart sang out at the message he read in her eyes. They were dark and luminous and as he sat up she reached for him, pulling him back down against her. She gave him back kiss for kiss, tangling her tongue with his. Then he released her mouth and began to explore her body with his hands while he trailed kisses over her breasts and down across her stomach. Her body arched beneath him, pliant and yielding, inviting his touch.

Eloise closed her eyes, giving herself up to the sweet pleasure of his caresses. The past and the future were as nothing, she was aware only of the present: the crackling fire, the cool smooth daybed beneath her, Jack's hard body above and the faint, masculine scent of his skin. There was such an excitement building within her, such a cresting wave of joy waiting to burst that she could not keep still. Her body moved of its own accord and her skin was sensitive to the lightest touch. Jack's long fingers explored her, making her gasp with delight. At one point her body seized, and for one heady, heart-stopping moment she could not move, could not breath.

Jack stilled. He raised his head.

'Love?'

'No,' she whispered urgently, 'Go on, go on!'

She began to move against him, an instinctive, primal rhythm that she didn't understand. She wrapped her arms about him, pulling him on top of her, gasping as they were united, their bodies moving as one, faster, harder, the excitement building until they cried out together as the wave finally burst and Eloise clung to Jack as they collapsed back on to the daybed, gasping and exhausted.

Lying snug in the circle of Jack's arms, with his breath ruffling her hair, Eloise was aware of a sudden *tristesse*. The certainty she had felt earlier was gone, replaced by the thought that she should have sent him away. It would have been better not to know the wonder of being loved by Jack Clifton. She stirred. His hold tightened and he placed a soft, sleepy kiss on her cheek. She closed her eyes and pressed herself against him. No, she could not regret it. The memory of this night would be with her, a constant comfort in the bleak future that stretched ahead of her.

A cold, grey dawn was filling the London streets when Jack finally stepped out into Dover Street. His coat and waistcoat hung open and his neckcloth was missing but he didn't care. He felt alive and ready to take on the world. A sudden gust of wind reminded him that winter was on its way and he threw the black domino around his shoulders. Heaven knew what his friends would think if they saw him now. He grinned to himself. They would most likely think he had just left his mistress, and they would be right. Only she was more than his mistress. She was the woman he was going to marry.

When he reached King Street Jack ran up the stairs to his rooms, ignoring his man's remonstrations as he opened the door to him.

'Be done with your scolding, Robert,' he said, throwing himself on to his bed. 'I am going to sleep now, and I'd be obliged if you didn't wake me until at least noon!'

It was in fact some time past midday when Jack eventually awoke, and some hours more before he was bathed and dressed and Robert considered him fit to be seen. Having missed his breakfast, he was extremely hungry and decided to go off to White's to find something to eat.

As he turned into St James Street Jack spotted Sir Ronald Deforge descending the steps of the club. Jack frowned, the memory of the man's dealings with Eloise darkening his mood. He wanted to force a quarrel upon him and put a bullet through his black heart, but the villain had her journal and until Jack knew just what it contained he must go carefully. And he had given her his word he would not force a quarrel. He was thankful that Deforge did not see him, and had strolled away up the road towards Piccadilly before Jack reached the entrance to White's. There would be time enough to deal with Deforge later.

Jack found several acquaintances in the card room; they greeted him cheerfully and invited them to join him.

'Thank you, but no,' he said. 'I need to eat first.' He nodded towards a thin young man sitting by the window, his face as white as his neckcloth. 'What is wrong with Tiverton? He looks as if he is about to cast up his accounts.'

'Dished,' declared Edward Graham, shaking his head. 'He's just lost ten thousand to Deforge.'

'You have to admit the man's luck is in,' wheezed a portly gentleman in a grey bag-wig. 'Last night poor Glaister lost everything he had to him.'

'Well they say luck goes in threes, let's hope he's had his share.' Mr Graham slapped him on the back. 'But it's put paid to your hopes, eh, Clifton?'

Jack smiled.

'What's that, Ned? I don't understand you.'

'The Glorious Allyngham.' Mr Graham pointed to the newssheet lying upon the table. 'Seems Deforge has beaten you to it, old man.'

Bewildered, Jack picked up the newspaper, which was opened to display a large announcement. He stared at it, the letters dancing before his eyes.

'Aye,' said Mr Graham, resuming his seat at the card table. 'So Deforge is to marry Lady Allyngham next week. Damme if I'd have put money against his winning that trick! Waiter, bring me another pack of cards, will you?'

Slowly Jack folded the paper. Then, his appetite forgotten, he turned and walked out of the club.

'Major Clifton, my lady.'

Noyes barely had time to finish his announcement before Jack burst into the morning room. Eloise put down her embroidery and folded her hands in her lap. She had been expecting him, but she was not prepared for the violence she saw in his eyes. Her mouth went dry and she had to moisten her lips before she could speak.

'Won't you sit down, Major?'

He ignored her, and waited impatiently for the butler to close the door upon them before he spoke.

'What the hell is all this about?'

'All what?' She feigned surprise.

'This.' He threw the newspaper into her lap. 'The announcement of your marriage to Deforge. Will you tell me when that was agreed?'

She swallowed nervously and looked away from his furious glare.

'Yesterday. At Lanchester House.'

'And why did you not tell me?'

'Because I knew you would be angry.'

'Hell and confound it, woman, of course I am angry! Even more so because of what happened here last night.'

She rose from her chair.

'Pray lower your voice, sir. Would you have the whole world know our business?'

He laughed harshly.

'Your blatant actions last night can have left your people in no doubt of *our business.*'

She flushed and looked down at her hands. He came towards her and grasped her shoulders. She tensed herself for his tirade, but it did not come.

'Why did you do it, Elle?' His quiet tone flayed her even more than his anger. 'I thought that we understood each other. I thought you loved me.'

Too much to marry you!

The words pounded, unspoken, in her head. She shrugged off his hands and turned away.

'I...forgot myself.'

He pulled her round to face him.

'You must not do this! Send another notice, refute this and announce that you are going to marry *me.*'

Even as she raised her eyes to look at him in her mind she could see Deforge's men closing in, daggers drawn.

'I cannot. I gave him my word. Besides, there is the journal.'

'Ah, yes, that blasted book.' He let her go and took a hasty turn about the room. 'What is it, Elle, what have you done that is so bad you cannot tell me?'

She turned to stare out of the window. It was a bleak day, matching her mood. She said quietly, 'There are others involved: I cannot break faith with them, even for you.'

'So you would give yourself to this, this monster to protect other people. Hand over your fortune to a man who spends most of his day at the card table! Damnation, woman, he has already lost his own fortune and that of his first wife—he may even have driven her to her death! I will not allow it.'

She turned quickly.

'You cannot stop me.'

'I could put a bullet in him!'

'No!' she cried, alarmed. 'You gave me your word!'

'Hah! What do I care for that now?'

Even through her unhappiness she smiled at that.

'But you do,' she said. 'You are a man of honour.'
And I love you for it.

'But I will fight for what is mine.'

She said impatiently, 'Is that how you think of me, a chattel to be fought over and possessed?'

In two strides he was across the room and dragging her into his arms.

'You know it isn't. I think of you as my wife!'

She dug her nails into the palms of her hands to stop herself responding to him.

'No.' She forced out the words. 'I am tired of fighting the inevitable. I am going to marry Sir Ronald. It is agreed and I will not go back on it.'

'Not even for me?'

'Not even for you.'

His arms dropped away from her and the leaden band about her heart squeezed even tighter.

'I see.' He turned away and walked to the fireplace. For a few moments he stared moodily down into the flames. 'Does Mortimer know?'

'Yes. I told him this morning.'

'And he does not object?'

She hesitated, remembering the strong words that had passed between her and Alex. At last she said, 'Of course he objects, but he is still too unwell to do anything to stop me.' She raised her head and directed a look at him. Her heart was breaking but she met his eyes steadily, determined not to show him how much this was costing her. 'I have made my decision, Major Clifton. I…enjoyed our brief liaison, but it is over. Now we must say goodbye.'

She held out her hand. Jack stared at it, scowling blackly, then, without a word, he turned on his heel and left.

Chapter Sixteen

It was only to be expected that Sir Ronald Deforge's party would be the crush of the Season. He brought in his cousin, a colourless little widow of impeccable birth, to act as hostess, and even the creditors who had been baying at his door for the past few weeks had suddenly disappeared, reassured by the news that he was about to become master of the Allyngham fortune.

Any hopes Eloise had that her forthcoming marriage would pass off with little comment were dashed as the carriages turned off Oxford Street and queued up outside Sir Ronald's tall town house, waiting to disgorge their fashionable occupants. The interminable evening began with dinner. Eloise had tried to refuse but Sir Ronald insisted, pointing out that his cousin's presence would prevent any hint of impropriety.

'Although with your reputation I am surprised to find you worrying about *that*,' he said, with a grin that made Eloise long to slap his face.

'Until we are married,' she said frostily, 'we will observe every propriety.'

'Of course, my dear. I can contain my impatience a few more days.'

The dinner was long and cold, despite the dining room being on the ground floor and not far from the kitchen. Sir Ronald's cook was obviously unused to entertaining. The wine, however, was excellent, but she refused to take more than one glass. She was the only guest at dinner and her attempts to make conversation with her hostess could not be deemed a success. The widow was patently in awe of her blustering cousin and made no answer without first looking to Sir Ronald for approval.

'Once we are married I shall expect you to take over the running of my household,' said Sir Ronald, refilling his glass. 'I have no doubt that you are a very capable housekeeper.'

'I could certainly do better than this,' she retorted, pushing a piece of tough and stringy beef to the side of her plate.

'Well, we will not require two cooks when we are in town so I shall turn mine off,' he said. 'But what about the house—shall we live here, or would you rather I moved into Dover Street? You see, I am minded to be magnanimous about these things.'

The thought of Sir Ronald living in Dover Street appalled her. It had been her husband's home, not to mention the memories it held of the night spent in

Jack's arms. She could not bear to think of it being desecrated by the boorish animal now sitting at the head of the table.

The meal dragged on, the covers were removed and she was wondering how soon it would be before her hostess gave the signal to retire when Deforge said suddenly, 'Time is getting on. Our guests will be arriving soon and I have something for you. Come along to my study. Oh, don't mind Agnes,' he added, as Eloise's eyes flickered towards her hostess. 'She should be off now to make sure everything is in readiness for our guests. Should you not, Cousin?'

'Oh. Oh, yes, Ronald, immediately.' The thread-like voice could hardly be heard above the scraping back of her chair, and the little woman scuttled away. Sir Ronald picked up a branched candlestick and walked to a door at the far end of the dining room. Eloise hung back.

'How do I know this is not a trick?'

'What need have I of tricks? In three days' time you will be mine, you have given me your word. Now, if you please, madam.'

He led her up the stairs and past the main salon to a room at the back of the house. At the door he stopped.

'No one enters here without permission,' he said, fishing in his pocket for a key. 'Not even my valet.'

The room was very dark, and Sir Ronald held the

candles aloft as he entered. The light flickered over a large wing chair and across a number of tall bookcases. Eloise glanced about her nervously: a tall chest of drawers stood against one wall with a wooden-framed mirror and a number of small objects on the top. In the dim light she thought perhaps they might be snuff-boxes and scent bottles. She edged back towards the open door.

'This is your dressing room.'

'It is used for that purpose, yes, since it adjoins my bedchamber. Perhaps you would like to see where we will spend our wedding night?'

She fought down her panic.

'With the first of the guests about to arrive I think we should return to the salon with all speed,' she retorted.

Sir Ronald shrugged and moved towards the large mahogany desk by the window.

'I realised I have not given you a ring to seal our betrothal,' he said. He put down the candlestick and unlocked the centre drawer. Eloise watched as he pulled out a small leather box. 'I have no family heirlooms to give you, so I have bought you this.' He laughed. 'Let there be no secrets between us now, my dear. To tell you the truth I have it on credit, the jeweller knowing that I shall pay him just as soon as your fortune passes into my hands!'

He opened the box and held it out to her.

'There, I knew you would like it. Never met a woman who could resist a trinket.'

Eloise's gasp was genuine, but it was not the large diamond ring winking in the candlelight that had caused her exclamation. She had watched Sir Ronald pushing aside the contents of the drawer to get to the ring box, and nestling amongst the clutter she had seen a small, leather-bound book bearing the Allyngham crest.

Quickly she raised her eyes and gave Sir Ronald what she hoped was a warm smile.

'It is quite…breathtaking,' she said, moving around the desk. 'May I wear it now?'

'Of course.' Delighted, he pulled the ring from the box and slipped it on to her finger.

'There, now you have something to show the tabbies tonight.'

He shut and locked the drawer again, slipping the key into his pocket. She heard the thud of the knocker, and the sound of feet running down the stairs. Sir Ronald looked up.

'Now, shall we go and greet our guests?'

Eloise stood between Sir Ronald and his cousin as a steady stream of people made their way up the stairs towards her. Her smile was pinned in place and she greeted them all mechanically. If she had not been so busy with her own thoughts she might have felt a little self-conscious of their stares. Everyone was curious to know what lay behind the sudden betrothal, but her mind was elsewhere, thinking about what she had seen in the study. By walking around the desk she had managed to take a quick look through the unshuttered window. A pale moon illuminated the night, showing her that the room looked out on to a narrow yard bounded by a high brick wall. Half the space was taken by a small outbuilding that butted against the wall of the house, its roof only a few feet below the window ledge. And the journal was in the desk drawer. For the first time in days she began to feel a glimmer of hope.

'I am disappointed,' said Sir Ronald as he escorted Eloise through the crowded rooms. 'I know your friend Mortimer is indisposed, but I had hoped that Major Clifton would be here.'

'I do not see why he should be,' she replied shortly. 'He is no friend to you.'

'But I made sure to send him an invitation, because I know he is a special friend of *yours*,' he purred.

'You are mistaken.'

He turned to look down at her, an evil smile curling his lips.

'What is this, a lovers' quarrel, perhaps?' When she did not reply he laughed softly and patted her hand. 'What a pity. I had hoped he would be here tonight: I wanted him to know just what he had lost. But never mind, my love, I may even allow you to take him as a lover again, if he will have you once I have done with you.'

Disgusted, Eloise pulled her arm free and went her own way. The rooms were so crowded she thought it might be possible to spend the rest of the evening without talking to Sir Ronald. His comments about Jack Clifton had touched a raw nerve. She had heard nothing from him since he had walked out of Dover Street. A casual enquiry of Alex had elicited the information that Jack was preparing to leave town. Alex had questioned her closely, had asked if she and Jack had quarrelled and she had been at pains to laugh it off, but secretly she was forced to conclude that she had succeeded in driving Jack away.

Nothing of her melancholy thoughts showed in her face as she circled the room, talking and laughing with everyone. By the end of the evening her cheeks ached with the effort of smiling. She was so tired she could hardly stand and there was no attempt at deception when she told Sir Ronald that she was too exhausted to remain another moment, once the last of the guests had quit the house.

'If that is the case,' he said, 'then surely it would be easier to walk to my bedchamber than to take your carriage to Dover Street.'

She had no energy to prevaricate. He merely laughed at her look of revulsion.

'Very well, my sweet. Go home and rest.' He placed her cloak about her shoulders. 'I am engaged to dine at the Forbes' tomorrow night: Mrs Forbes did send me a little note to say that, having seen the announcement of our engagement, I might bring you with me, but it is a long drive to Edgeware and I want you to be looking your best for Keworth's party on Thursday.'

'Thursday! But we are to be married on Friday. I need to prepare.'

'No. You will accompany me to Keworth House. His lordship's parties are always well attended. I want everyone to see you at my side.'

She grimaced.

'A card party! I have no interest in gambling.'

'But I have, and I want you beside me. You need not play.' He ran a finger down her arm. 'You may stand by my chair and bring me good fortune!' He laughed as she shrugged him off. 'I want everyone to see that I am lucky in cards *and* in love!'

With barely a nod she left him, and made her way downstairs to the tiled hall, where a vacuous-looking footman was waiting by the door.

'Your carriage is sent for, m'lady, but it ain't here yet,' he mumbled as she approached.

Eloise gave him a tired smile and moved towards a large button-backed arm chair. 'Then I shall sit here and wait. Unless, of course, this is your seat?'

The lackey jumped and looked a little flustered. She suspected he was unused to being addressed in anything but the curtest of terms.

'No, m'm, that seat's only used by Stevens, the master's valet, when he waits up for Master to come in o' nights.'

'Well, it is very comfortable. I have no doubt Mr Stevens has a little sleep while he is waiting for his master, what do you think?' She twinkled up at him and the lackey flushed, shifting uncomfortably from one foot to the other. Then he nodded.

'Aye, m'm, I think he does. Ah, and here's your carriage now, m'lady.'

Eloise hurried out, relieved to be leaving the gloomy and oppressive house at last. But the depression that had enveloped her for much of the evening had lifted. She had a plan.

Alex Mortimer was stretched out on the daybed in his morning room, struggling to eat his breakfast one-handed when Eloise was shown in.

'Thunder and turf, Elle, you cannot come in here!'

'Fustian,' she replied calmly, pulling off her gloves. 'Farrell told me you were going to get up today.'

'Yes, but I am not yet dressed. It is most improper for you to walk in here as if we were related. I won't have it!' He gave her a quick, searching look from under his brows. 'Unless you have come to tell me you're not going to marry Deforge after all.'

'No, I am not going to tell you that, although I hope now it might not be necessary.' She could not quite keep the excitement out of her voice. 'The journal is at his house, Alex! I saw it in his desk when I was there last night. I suppose he had his lawyer deliver it, ready for the wedding on Friday.'

'Very likely.'

'Or perhaps it has been there all the time,' she mused, 'and he only told me otherwise to make sure no harm came to him. It is in his study, which is at the back of the house, on the first floor.'

'And what has that to say to anything?'

'Well, it should not be too difficult to break into that room and take the journal.'

Alex's knife clattered on to his plate.

'Are you out of your mind? You know the penalty for stealing!'

'The journal is not Sir Ronald's property, and once it is destroyed—'

'Eloise, you know if I was fit I would do this for you, but it is as much as I can do to climb the stairs at the moment.'

She looked at him, her bottom lip caught between her teeth.

'I thought, perhaps, you might speak to Major Clifton for me…'

'Well, you thought wrong,' he retorted brutally. 'Jack has left town.'

'L-left?' A chill rippled through her, starting in her core and spreading rapidly throughout her body. 'He's gone?'

'Yes. When he came to see me yesterday he said he was off to Staffordshire.' Alex scowled at her. 'I take it you quarrelled with him.'

'Not, not quarrelled, exactly.' She looked down at the gloves held tightly between her fingers. 'He was very angry about my marrying Sir Ronald and I told him it was none of his business.'

'What? After all he's done for us?'

'No, what he has done for *you*,' she flung at him, angry colour burning her cheeks. She was filled with a disappointment as bitter as gall. 'As far as I am concerned, Jack Clifton has been nothing but a nuisance!'

'Oh, nuisance, is it? Well you had best look at what he's left you, over there.' He waved towards the side table. 'I was going to bring it to you later today but since you are here you may as well read it now.'

Eloise picked up the letter and broke open the seal. The thought flashed through her mind that Jack had written to her, but the hand was unfamiliar, and as that first flare of hope died away she had to concentrate to make sense of the words. Alex pushed aside his breakfast tray and waited for her to finish reading. At last she looked up.

'I don't understand,' she said slowly. 'This is from Lord Berrow, agreeing to the sale of Ainsley Wood.'

Alex nodded.

'Aye. Jack brought it round to me last night.'

'But…but why did he not bring it to me?'

'He said he didn't want to see you again, and from what you have just told me I can't say I blame him! He persuaded Berrow to sell you the land so you can build the road to your foundling hospital. Jack suggested you should get the papers signed today. Once you marry Deforge you will lose control of Allyngham and your fortune.'

Hot tears pricked at her eyelids.

'Oh. That was so very good of him.' She hunted for her handkerchief.

'You were a damned fool to turn Clifton away, Elle.'

'What else could I do? Deforge threatened to kill him if he interfered.'

'I would back Jack Clifton against a dozen men like Deforge.'

She shook her head.

'I could not take that risk. Until last night I thought that any attempt to thwart Sir Ronald would result in the journal being published, and if M-Major Clifton was involved then he would be implicated in our disgrace.'

'So you sent him away.'

'Yes.' Eloise wiped her eyes. 'It is done, and that's an end to it.' She looked again at the paper. 'But I do not understand: after my last…meeting with Lord Berrow I was sure he would not sell. What made him change his mind?'

Alex grinned.

'Jack saw him coming out of the house at the end of the street. Kitty Williams's house.'

She stared at him.

'But Mrs Williams is a...'

'Exactly. Jack made a few enquiries, found that for a price the fair Kitty was more than willing to divulge all the sordid details of Lord Berrow's visits to her establishment. Then he went to see the old hypocrite and told him that if he didn't want the whole world to know about his dealings with that Cyprian and her sisters, he should sell you Ainsley Wood.'

'And Lord Berrow agreed?'

'Aye, immediately,' Jack said. 'It seems he was eager to protect his reputation. He was especially anxious that his friend Wilberforce should not find out about it, nor his wife.'

'Then, then we can go ahead with the foundling hospital.' She folded the paper and put it in her reticule. 'That is wonderful news. I must write to the major and thank him—'

'No.' Alex interrupted her. 'Jack said to tell you he wants no thanks from you. He is doing this for Tony, because he wants a lasting memorial for a fallen comrade. I think you have hurt him very badly, my dear.'

'I know.' She put her hands to her cheeks. 'I

know, and I am sorry for it. But it is not as if he l-loved me.'

'No?'

She heard the disbelief in Alex's tone and she shook her head.

'No. He told me himself that he was in love with Sir Ronald's first wife. That is why he is so keen to challenge Deforge.'

'That may of course be an added reason—'

'It is the *main* reason,' she interrupted him. 'My reputation is sadly tarnished, Alex.'

'But Clifton knows now it was all a lie—!'

'But the world believes it, Alex! How could a man as good, as honourable as Jack Clifton live with that, when he has carried the memory of a sweet, innocent woman in his heart for so many years?'

Alex did not answer and a long silence fell over the room. She struggled to smother her unhappiness. She had succeeded only too well: Jack Clifton had left town and he wanted nothing more to do with her. He was safe from Deforge and his henchmen. That was what she had planned, so she had no reason to feel aggrieved, and certainly no reason to be surprised. He was gone. Even now she could feel the loneliness settling over her like a heavy cloak. Eloise squared her shoulders: there would be time for tears later. Now she had to decide just how to proceed.

She looked at Alex. He still had one arm in a sling and by his own admission he was unable to walk more than a few steps. He could not help her. There was only one solution. Having made up her mind, she looked up, saying brightly, 'I had best take this paper to my lawyer and have him deal with it immediately.'

'And what of the other business—the journal?'

'You must not worry about that, Alex.'

'I always worry when I see that look on your face.'

She gazed at him, her eyes very wide.

'What look?'

'That innocent, butter-would-not-melt look. I insist that you tell me what you are planning, madam. No, don't walk out on me—Elle—*Eloise*!'

But she was already at the door and as she closed it behind her she heard his angry exclamation and the clatter as his breakfast tray slid to the floor.

Chapter Seventeen

Jack was putting the finishing touches to his neck-cloth when he heard voices on the stairs outside his rooms. He nodded to Robert.

'Go out and send them away. Tell them I've already left town!'

He shrugged himself into his waistcoat, scowling as he heard the low rumble of voices growing louder. Damn Robert, could he not even obey a simple order?

'Sir, 'tis Mister Mortimer, and he says he knows you are here and he must speak with you.'

Jack's frown turned to a look of exasperation as he watched Alex limping into the room.

'What the devil are you doing here?' he demanded. 'You are as pale as your shirt!'

He quickly lifted the half-filled portmanteau from the chair. 'You had best sit down.'

Alex was leaning heavily on his stick and with a grimace he lowered himself on to the chair.

'Yes, well, I wasn't planning on coming this far today!'

'You walked here? Damned fool.'

'No, of course I didn't walk! I took a cab, but just those stairs to get up here have taken their toll.'

Jack waved his hand impatiently.

'And what has brought you here? I don't suppose you came to see me off.'

'It's Elle,' said Alex without preamble. '*I* can't help her, so I need you to do so.'

Jack looked towards Robert, dismissing him with the slightest movement of his head. 'Does Lady Allyngham know you are here?'

Alex shook his head.

'She came to see me this morning, and I did as you asked. I told her you had already gone.'

'Thank you. Now I suggest you go home and let me get on with my packing.'

'But this is important, Jack!'

'Not to me! I am done with her. She does not want my help; she has made that very plain on more than one occasion.'

'This is not about what Elle *wants*. I am afraid she is going to do something foolhardy.'

Jack gave a bitter laugh.

'There would be nothing new in that! No, she has chosen her path. God knows I tried to befriend her. I even thought—but she is done with me. She is going to marry Deforge. I won't try to stop her.'

'But the fellow's a rogue!'

Jack shrugged. 'I have told her what I think of the man,' he said coldly. 'If she chooses to ignore it then I can do nothing to help her. I only hope she fares better than his first wife.'

Alex waved his good hand.

'I am not talking about her marriage,' he said impatiently. 'I think she has conceived some madcap scheme to recover the journal!'

Jack looked at the pale face staring up at him and bit back a stinging retort.

'Alex, tell me why I should put myself out any more for this woman? She is not at all grateful for anything I have done so far and at our last meeting she made it very clear that she wanted nothing more to do with me.'

'I thought you loved her.'

Jack looked away. He picked up his brushes from the dressing table and threw them into the portmanteau.

He said coldly, 'It is impossible for me to love someone who is not honest with me.' He turned, subjecting Alex to a fierce glare. 'From the very beginning she has refused to share her secrets with me. I wanted to help her—hell and damnation, I wanted to *marry* her, regardless of the crimes she may have committed in the past, but I am convinced now that there is no future for us. She is determined not to confide in me. She does not trust me.' He snapped shut the portmanteau. 'All she will say is that the secrets are not hers to share.'

'She is correct,' said Alex slowly. 'But they *are* mine. And I will share them with you.'

There is an hour when the fashionable London streets to the west of the City are silent and deserted, between the night-soil cart rumbling through to collect the pails and the moment when the cook's boy emerges, yawning, and waits to follow his master to the market.

Eloise stood in the shadows, looking across the street at Sir Ronald's imposing town house. The windows were dark and the only light from the house was the dim glow of a lamp shining through the fanlight. With her heart thudding heavily against her ribs, she slipped across the road and into the deep shadows of a side alley. She ran freely and realised with some little shock that it was more than ten years since she had last worn breeches. She had bought them that afternoon at one of the less fashionable bazaars off Bond Street. Her maid had been surprised at her purchases but she had explained that she was buying a set of clothes as a present for a young relative. Even as she counted along the windows to find the right house, part of her mind was thinking of what she might do with the clothes when this night's work was over. *If* she was successful.

The third set of windows from the alley belonged

to Sir Ronald's house. Everything was in darkness. She had been watching the house for some time, and thought that by now everyone would be asleep, even Sir Ronald's valet, who would be dozing in his chair by the front door. She only hoped that his master would not come back early: it was well known that Josiah Forbes preferred dancing and theatricals to cards, but he and his wife were exceedingly rich and influential, so those receiving an invitation to one of their select little parties deemed it expedient to make the long drive out to Edgeware. For once she was thankful that her reputation as the Wanton Widow had so far spared her that treat.

She crept along the dark, narrow alley, trying not to think of the dirt and debris beneath her shoes. The brick wall was a good six feet high, but she had climbed higher. Not for a long time, of course: not since she was a girl, making up wild adventures at Allyngham with Tony and Alex. How long ago that seemed now!

'Can I help you over the wall, my lady?'

Eloise smothered a scream as she spun around to peer at the black shape towering over her. It was far too dark to see, but there was no mistaking the deep, mellow voice, and even as her heart settled back into a steady beat she felt her fear subsiding.

'Jack! What are you doing here?' she hissed.

'I have come to help you.'

Her spirits lifted. She said gruffly, 'I thought you had left town.'

'No. Alex was worried about you and since he is not fit enough to help you, it seems I must.'

The elation she had felt a moment ago was somewhat dimmed. Could it be that Jack was doing this for Alex's sake? From his angry tone it seemed likely. She reached out in the darkness and gripped at his coat with her fingers.

'You must go away, Jack, now,' she urged him. 'It is far too dangerous for you. If *I* am caught, then Sir Ronald may be angry, but he will still want to marry me to gain control of my fortune. I may even be able to placate him, if I am alone…'

He silenced her by pressing his fingers to her lips.

'Let us be quite clear about one thing, madam, you are *not* marrying Deforge, whether we succeed tonight or we fail. Now no more talking or the sun will be rising before we get out of here!'

His tone brooked no argument. Eloise allowed herself to be lifted up on to the wall and she nimbly swung her legs over and dropped to the ground on the other side. Jack followed a moment later. Fitful moonlight illuminated the yard in shades of blue and black, and she concentrated on finding the best route up to the study window. She scrambled on to a water barrel and from there climbed on to the roof of the outhouse. Her soft shoes made no noise on the tiles: she gave a fleeting smile, remembering Alice's comments that a pair of solid leather boots would be more fitting for a schoolboy than dancing slippers. That, of course, was before she had shocked her maid into silence by explaining the real reason for her purchases.

The moon slipped behind a thick cloud, plunging her into momentary darkness and she stopped, unable to see her way. She felt Jack's hand on her shoulder, steadying her. As the darkness eased she moved forwards until she was standing directly beneath the study window. When she had been inside the room with Sir Ronald she had noted that the window had a new sash frame, secured only by a brass fastener. She took out her penknife and reached up, planning to slide it between the two frames and push back the fastener. Behind her she heard a faint snort and Jack leaned close to breathe his words into her ear.

'You need to grow another six inches to reach the catch, my dear. Allow me.'

In an instant the deed was done and Jack was carefully pushing open the window. Another moment and they were both standing in Sir Ronald's study. The moon shone directly in through the window, bathing the room in a silvery light and making it unnecessary for Eloise to use the tinderbox and candle she had thoughtfully tucked into her pocket. She moved swiftly to the desk, penknife in hand, but once again Jack forestalled her.

'Did your education include picking locks?' he whispered.

'Of course not.'

'Then let me do this. If we are careful no one will know we have been here.'

From his pocket he drew a thin length of wire. It was bent at one end and he carefully inserted it into the drawer lock. He gently moved the wire until she heard a faint but distinct click and Jack pulled open the drawer.

'Where did you learn that?' she breathed, wide-eyed.

He turned his head to grin at her.

'Some of the men in my regiment came from the stews and rookeries of London. They would have been very much at home here.' He reached into the drawer and lifted out a small, leather-bound volume. 'Is this what you have been looking for?'

With shaking hands Eloise took the book and ran her thumbs over the embossed cover. An ornate letter *A* was enclosed in a circle of acanthus leaves: the Allyngham family crest. Quickly she pushed the journal inside her jacket.

'Thank you,' she whispered, fastening the buttons of her coat. 'Let us go now.'

She watched Jack slide the drawer back into place and lock it again. He straightened, looking around him as he put the metal rod back into his pocket. Eloise touched him arm.

'We must go,' she hissed.

Jack raised his hand. He was looking towards the wing chair, where a shaft of moonlight fell upon a bundle of straps lying over one arm. He walked over and picked them up. Eloise thought at first it might be a belt, or a dog's leash, but when Jack held it up she saw the straps were connected into an intricate webbing.

'What is it? It looks very much like a pony's head-collar, only it is far too small.'

'This is no head-collar,' murmured Jack, carefully draping the harness back over the arm of the chair. 'It is something much more interesting than that.'

There was a thud from somewhere below and she froze, her heart beating so hard she thought it might break through her ribs.

'The front door,' hissed Jack. 'It must be Deforge returned. Quickly!'

He pushed Eloise towards the window. She slithered out on to the roof and descended hastily to the yard with Jack close behind her. He threw her up over the wall and she huddled in the shadows until he joined her. As soon as he reached the ground he took her hand and they set off at a run out of the alley.

Jack did not stop until they had crossed Oxford Street and were out of sight and sound of the highway, where carts and wagons were beginning to make their way into the town. At last he slowed his pace and Eloise was able to catch her breath. She pulled her hand from his grip and leaned for a moment against the wall. She felt very light-headed. When she had set out that night she had been nervous, but determined upon her course of action: as soon as Jack had appeared her fear had diminished—in a strange sort of way she was even enjoying their adventure.

Jack was watching her, his hands on his hips and his feet slightly apart. She was pleased to note that he, too, was breathing heavily. In the dim light she realised that he had come dressed for the night's work: he had replaced his modish jacket and light pantaloons with a tight-fitting black coat, black breeches and stockings, and instead of his snowy white neckcloth he wore a dark woollen muffler wrapped around his neck. She glanced down at her own apparel and a quiet laugh shook her.

'We look like a couple of housebreakers!'

'We *are* a couple of housebreakers.'

'Are we safe now, do you think?' she asked him.

He took her arm again.

'As safe as one can be on the streets of London at this time of night,' he retorted, making her walk on. 'Of all the ill-judged starts! Don't you know how dangerous it is to come out alone at night?'

She put up her chin.

'How do you know I didn't take a cab to Wardle Street?'

'Because I followed you.'

She pulled her hand free and stared up at him. The flaring street lamp cast deep shadows across his face. Eloise could not see his eyes but she could almost feel the anger burning there.

'Alex told me you had left town.'

He let out a long breath, as if controlling his temper.

'That was my intention. I was finishing my packing when Mortimer came to tell me he was anxious about you.'

'But he knew nothing of my plans!'

'He knows *you*. Once he learned you were not accompanying Deforge to Edgeware this evening he guessed you were up to something. I merely had to watch your house until you made your move. I was not fooled when a slip of a lad emerged from the servants' door in the middle of the night.'

He began to walk on again, and she fell into step beside him.

'Then I am very grateful to you.' She tucked her hand into the crook of his arm. 'I am *very* glad you came, Major.'

He put his hand up and briefly clutched the fingers resting on his sleeve and her spirits rose a little. Perhaps he was not quite so angry with her. She glanced around, suddenly anxious.

'Sir Ronald's men, the ones who were following you—'

'No need to worry about them any longer. They are even now on their way to the coast where they will be pressed into service on one of his Majesty's frigates.' His wicked grin flashed. 'Deforge is not the only one who has fellows willing to carry out his more—er—dubious orders.'

'Oh.' She digested this in silence for a few moments.

'I shall write to Sir Ronald immediately,' she said, 'to terminate our engagement.'

'No, do not write to him just yet. I was careful to close the window when we left so I hope our visit to Sir Ronald's house will not be noticed, and if that is the case I do not believe he will discover the loss of the journal immediately. I understand he is attending the Keworths' party tomorrow, that is, tonight. Do you go with him?'

'Yes, I am engaged to join him there, but now—'

'I want you to go, Eloise. Act as if nothing has changed. I have a plan to rid the town of Sir Ronald Deforge for good, but it will work best if he does not suspect anything.'

When they turned into Dover Street, Eloise noticed that the lights were still burning in Kitty Williams's house.

'I have not thanked you for securing Ainsley Wood for me,' she said. 'For making Lord Berrow agree to sell it.'

'I want no thanks for that.'

'You have been very good to me. It is more than I deserve, after I was so impolite in sending you away.'

'Hush, now. We will talk later.' They were opposite her house and Jack stopped. 'When you get inside, make sure you burn that damned book.'

'I will.'

He led her across the road and followed her down the area steps to the basement door. The scrape of the bolt told Eloise that her maid had been looking out for her. She looked back at Jack.

'Will you not come in?'

'No, dawn is breaking and I must get back. I would have no one guess just what we have been doing this night.'

She was disappointed, and her hand fluttered as if to detain him. He caught it and held it for a moment.

'You have the journal now. Destroy it before it can cause any more harm.' He raised her fingers to his lips. 'And no sooner have we secured the good name of Allyngham than I shall be asking you to change it!'

Eloise sat before the kitchen fire, tearing sheets from the leather-bound book on her lap and feeding them into the flames.

'Never seen anything like it, in all my born days,' muttered Alice, bustling around behind her. 'Running about the town dressed as a boy and breaking into houses! Why, miss, I've never heard of such a thing. Even Master Tony's most outlandish tricks never included thievery!'

'Enough, Alice,' said Eloise, frowning. 'I told you I was merely recovering my property, it was not stealing.'

'And heaven knows what would have become of you if Major Clifton hadn't been there to protect you. Still, all's well that ends well, as they say, and now that you have burned that book you have no need to marry nasty Sir Ronald Deforge. I must say I was never in favour of that, even when you explained to me why it must be so. And unless my ears was deceiving me, it's Mrs Clifton you'll be before the year's out. You couldn't wish for more, could you, my lady?'

Eloise did not reply. She pushed the last of the pages into the fire and sat back. The euphoria of the last few hours had melted away, replaced by a heavy depression.

There was no mistaking Jack's last words; he meant to marry her, but even if his plan worked and Deforge was no longer a threat, she must still tell him the truth about her marriage. He had not asked to read the journal: he was willing to forget her past but she could not. He had said he wanted no secrets. Well, there would be none.

An inner demon whispered that it was not

necessary: Jack need never know. She clasped her hands together so tightly the knuckles showed white in the firelight. No. He had to know. If he loved her then perhaps it would not matter, but she was not sure how deeply he cared for her. He desired her, she knew that, but love—she dared not believe it. She was an obligation, the widow of a comrade, left to his care. And perhaps part of her attraction was the fact that in marrying her, Jack could thwart Sir Ronald. But could Jack really love her for herself? She found it hard to accept. She was so different from his first love, the incomparable Clara. She trusted him not to expose her, but once he had taken his revenge upon Sir Ronald, once he no longer needed her help, she must tell him the truth about herself, and give him the chance to walk away.

So you would throw away your chance of happiness. The demon in her head would not be silenced. *Do you think he can love you, once you have shattered his opinion of Tony and destroyed his friendship with Alex? You have only to keep quiet and you can all be happy.*

'No. I will not lie to him.'

'I beg your pardon, my lady?'

Eloise started, blushing as she realised she had spoken aloud.

'Nothing, Alice.' She pushed herself out of the chair. Suddenly she felt desperately tired. 'It is time for bed, I think.'

Chapter Eighteen

A sleepless night did nothing to relieve Eloise's depression, but neither did it shake her resolve to tell Jack everything. And once the truth was out, she doubted very much if he would want her for his wife.

She dressed quickly and dashed off a note to Alex, telling him that the diary had been destroyed and asking him to call. She sent her groom to deliver the message and remained at the window, watching, until his return.

'Well,' she demanded, 'did he send me an answer?'

Perkins tugged his forelock.

'Mr Alex says to give you his regards, m'lady, but I'm to tell you that he is gone out with Major Clifton and he will see you at Keworth House tonight.' The groom nodded, smiling. 'I must say it is good to see Master Alex looking so well, ma'am. Left off his sling, he has, but he is still using a cane.' He winked at her. 'He'll do his best to put that aside before he has to walk you to the altar and give you away, I'll be bound!'

'That is enough of your insolence, Perkins, you may go now!'

Eloise hunched her shoulder and turned away from the groom's knowing grin. That was the problem with having retainers one had known since childhood, they were more like family than servants. Her irritation died away: at least she would still have Perkins and Alice to keep her company in her lonely future. She put a hand up to her cheek, her dilemma growing greater the more she considered it. By confessing everything to Jack she could lose Alex's friendship, too, once he realised she had divulged the truth.

These depressing thoughts combined with her fears that Deforge might discover the theft and call upon her. She tried to stay calm, telling herself that there was no longer any danger, but she knew that Deforge was capable of revenging himself upon those who moved against him. Jack might have removed some of Sir Ronald's henchmen, but there would be others. Her anxiety made the day one of the longest Eloise had ever spent and it was with some relief when the time came to change her dress and order her carriage to take her to the Keworths' card party.

'Shall I be coming with you, m'lady?' asked Perkins, when she descended the stairs, the candles glinting from the diamond cluster at her neck and the tiny diamond drops hanging from her ears.

Eloise looked at the groom as he stood before her, twisting his cap in his hands. She had received no word from Jack or Alex all day, and at that moment Perkins seemed to be her only friend in the world.

'Yes, if you please,' she nodded. 'Jump up on the back and stay with the carriage.'

Keworth House was ablaze with light when the Allyngham town coach rumbled up to the door. Reluctantly she prepared to alight. She had no idea what Jack was planning. He had asked her to trust him and she would do so, but once this was over she knew he would ask her to marry him, and she would have to tell him the truth. In her imagination she saw the blaze of desire die from his eyes, to be replaced by a look of revulsion. It could not be avoided. Better now than in the future.

A light drizzle was falling. She put up her hood and grasped her cloak about her, glad that the chill night air gave her some excuse for her trembling. However, once she was inside the house there was no escape: she was obliged to straighten her shoulders and make her way to the main salon, no sign of her inner anxiety showing in her face.

The news of her betrothal was still the talk of the town and there were more congratulations to be endured as she made her way up the grand staircase. She was relieved to move into the candle-lit salon where dozens of little tables had been set up and nothing more than a gentle murmur disturbed the players who were intently studying their cards. Lord and Lady Keworth were renowned for their card parties. In the past Eloise had always declined their invitations because she found nothing to amuse her in games of chance, but looking around the room she realised how few of her acquaintance shared her view, for the cream of society was seated around the room.

'We are delighted to have you join us tonight, Lady Allyngham,' her hostess beamed. 'We are very fortunate to have so many friends here tonight.' Lady Keworth bent an arch smile towards Lord Berrow, who was passing at that moment. 'You, too, are a veritable stranger to our little parties, my lord.'

Unable to ignore his hostess, the Earl stopped and gave a little bow.

'It is unfortunate that I am so often otherwise engaged…'

Lady Keworth laughed and tapped his arm.

'Well, I am very glad that you are not engaged elsewhere this evening, sir, especially when we have such delightful company.' She glanced towards Eloise, gave her an encouraging smile then turned away to greet another guest.

Lord Berrow looked around him, clearly uncomfortable to be left in Lady Allyngham's company. She held out her hand to him.

'My lord, I am glad we have met: I wanted to thank

you personally for allowing me to buy Ainsley Wood. It was very generous of you.'

His lordship flushed.

'Oh, yes, well,' he muttered, 'it is in a good cause, after all.'

'Indeed it is, sir,' she replied warmly. 'When the trustees are drawing up their records I shall make sure your generosity is recognised.'

With an inward smile she watched him puff out his chest.

'Oh, no need for that, dear lady,' he said, looking considerably more cheerful. 'We must all do a little something for those less fortunate, eh?'

He gave a fat chuckle and looked as if he would say more but Sir Ronald's voice cut across the room.

'Ah, and here is my lovely bride. Come along over here, my dear, and join us.'

Play was suspended as everyone's eyes were fixed upon Eloise. Not by a flicker did she betray her nerves. She nodded to Lord Berrow and moved across to Sir Ronald. He was sitting at a table with several other gentlemen, including his host and Mr Edward Graham. Lord Keworth rose and began to offer Eloise his chair but Sir Ronald waved at him.

'Sit ye down, sir. Lady Allyngham ain't one for cards, are you, my dear?' He reached out and caught her wrist, pulling her closer. 'She will stand beside me, my lucky charm.'

'Damme, sir, I think you may need it,' laughed Mr

Graham, giving Eloise a good-natured bow. 'There are a number of gamesters here tonight, ma'am, some of 'em quite reckless. The game is bassett, you know: I fear the play will be very deep.'

She glanced around at them all and managed a smile.

'Then pray be seated, gentlemen and go on with your game. Sir Ronald is quite correct, I am more than happy to observe the play, if you will let me.'

'Bless you, my lady, of course you may watch,' declared Lord Keworth, picking up his cards. 'Though tedious work you may find it. Once Deforge has his mind on the cards, nothing will sway him!'

Lord Keworth was right; Eloise found it very dull standing at Sir Ronald's shoulder while he played. Cards were taken and discarded, wagers were made and she found herself surprised at the high stakes. Glancing around the room, she realised that although the players at every table were doing their best to win, none had the intensity of those pitting their skill against Sir Ronald.

A light-hearted game of quadrille was just breaking up and she used the diversion to move away. As she did so Lady Parham beckoned to her.

'My dear Lady Allyngham, I was so sorry to miss Sir Ronald's little soirée.' She glanced at the diamond winking on Eloise's finger. 'It was such a surprise to hear that you are to be married, and to Sir Ronald, too.' She hesitated before giving another of her thin smiles. 'I had not thought him one of your *particular* favourites.'

Silently Eloise inclined her head and moved to pass on but Lady Parham stepped in front of her.

'I had thought Mr Mortimer had the advantage, especially since you have known him for so long. He is your neighbour at Allyngham, is he not? It must have been *such* a comfort to have him so close while your husband was away.'

The implication was plain. Eloise realised she had played her part as the wanton widow far too well. She replied evenly, 'Mr Mortimer has always been a very good friend, Lady Parham.'

'And what does he think of your betrothal to Sir Ronald?' The sly look that accompanied these words angered Eloise, but at that moment there was a distraction at the door. She looked up.

'You had best ask him that yourself, ma'am,' she said, smiling in relief and surprise as she watched Alex limp into the room with Jack close behind him. Until that moment it seemed to Eloise that she had hardly been breathing. Now her heart swelled with pride and pleasure as the two gentlemen greeted their hostess. Alex was looking a little pale and leaning heavily upon a cane. Jack, standing tall and dark beside him, looked at the peak of fitness. Surely there was nothing to fear while she had two such champions.

'Lady Allyngham, I fear you have forgotten your role this evening.'

Sir Ronald's voice boomed out once again. Her eyes narrowed angrily. She wanted to tear the ring off her finger and throw it in his grinning face. She looked across the room at Jack, who gave the tiniest shake of his head. Putting up her chin, Eloise fixed her smile and walked back to Sir Ronald.

'Stand close, my dear, you are here to bring me luck.'

He reached out and put one arm possessively about her hips. She forced herself to stand passively until Sir Ronald released her and returned his full attention to the cards. Jack was watching them, but his countenance was inscrutable. She must play her part until he gave her a sign. She watched the game progress, alarmed at the large amounts the gentlemen were prepared to wager on a single card. As banker, Sir Ronald had the advantage, controlling the cards and dealing them with practised ease. Across the room Jack and Alex were talking to Mr Renwick. They were moving closer, but so slowly that the tension made her want to scream. No one at the table had eyes for anything other than the play. Mr Graham had thrown in his hand and now sat with his head bowed, rubbing his eyes. Another gentleman pulled off a ruby ring and placed it on his card, only to see it join the growing pile of notes and coins in front of Sir Ronald.

'Hell's teeth, Deforge, you win again!' With a laugh Lord Keworth stared at the cards Sir Ronald turned up on the table. 'What luck!'

'And skill, Keworth,' murmured Sir Ronald, smiling. 'Although having my future bride at my side is undoubtedly an advantage.' He glanced up at that moment and saw Jack standing nearby. His smile grew more unpleasant. 'It is a case of winner takes all, I think. What say you, Major Clifton?'

'Oh, undoubtedly,' replied Jack, 'Only tonight I do not think the winner will be you.'

His words were quiet but uttered with such cool conviction that a sudden hush fell over the table. The players were very still, while other guests drew closer, drawn by the sudden tension in the air. Sir Ronald raised his quizzing glass and stared at Jack, his smile turning into a sneer.

'Oh, I think you are wrong there, Clifton. You only have to look at the fortune on the table to see how successful I have been. And tomorrow, you may come to the church to watch me claim this beautiful woman as my bride.'

Jack's slow smile was even more menacing than Sir Ronald's.

'I think not.'

Eloise eased away. All eyes were upon Jack and Sir Ronald: there was violence in the air, she could almost taste it. She wondered what had become of Alex. She could not see him, but there were so many people standing around the table now that her view of the room was quite limited. Lord Keworth gave an uncertain laugh.

'Gentlemen,' he said, 'There are tables and cards enough for everyone. Perhaps, Major Clifton, you and Deforge would like to settle your differences with a game of picquet.'

'My dear Keworth, we have no differences to settle,' said Sir Ronald, rising to his feet, his cold eyes fixed upon Jack. 'The major does not like to lose.' His lip curled in an ugly smile. 'Losing to me seems to be your lot in life, does it not, Major? First your childhood sweetheart and now Lady Allyngham. But you must resign yourself to it. You have no choice because, you see, I hold the winning hand.'

'Aye,' said Jack steadily, 'you hold all the aces.'

Deforge gave a soft laugh.

'I am glad you realise that, Clifton. Now if you do not mind—'

'Not only aces,' stated Jack, raising his voice a little, 'but kings and queens, too.'

There was a movement in the crowd. Alex stepped up behind Sir Ronald and pulled his coat off his shoulders.

'What the—!' Deforge gave a snarl of rage, but the coat was already halfway down his arms and he could only struggle against Alex's hold.

Lord Keworth sprang to his feet. 'Good God, Mortimer, what do you mean by this?'

'I think it is quite clear,' said Jack.

Alex yanked the coat even further, revealing a web of leather straps around Deforge's left forearm. Sir Ronald stood before them, his fists clenched as he glared at the horrified faces around him. Jack stepped around the table and pulled a card from beneath one of the straps.

'I was right, you see. A king.' He withdrew a second. 'And a queen. You have already played the knave, have you not, Deforge?'

With a roar Sir Ronald turned on Jack but immediately Alex grabbed him and held him fast. A low murmur broke out and rippled around the room.

'By God,' muttered Mr Graham, 'the man's nothing but a cheat!'

Lord Keworth stared across the table, shaking his head in disgust.

'And to think I called you friend,' he muttered. 'I think you can release him now, Mortimer. I will have the servants escort Sir Ronald from my house.'

Alex stepped away and Deforge angrily shrugged himself back into his coat, his heavy pock-marked face almost purple with rage and humiliation. He looked at Eloise.

'Come, madam. We are leaving.'

'I will not.'

His eyes narrowed and he said menacingly, 'You are promised to marry me, my lady. You know the consequences of denying me.'

Slowly she withdrew the diamond ring from her hand and placed it on the table.

'You coerced me, but that is all at an end now.'

Jack stepped up beside her.

'There will be a notice in tomorrow's newspapers, announcing that the engagement has been terminated,' he said. 'In the circumstances I do not think anyone will be surprised. Lady Allyngham will not dishonour her late husband's memory by marrying a cheat.' He fixed Sir Ronald with a steady look. 'You have no hold over the lady now, Deforge.'

Sir Ronald stared at him.

'What have you done?' he ground out, his chin jutting pugnaciously.

Jack merely smiled. Two burly footmen appeared behind Sir Ronald and Lord Keworth said coldly, 'I would be obliged if you would leave my house immediately, Deforge. You will not touch the money lying on the table,' he added, as Sir Ronald glanced towards it. 'I do not need to tell you that you are no longer welcome here.'

An expectant silence hung over the room. Eloise found herself stiff with tension as Sir Ronald cast a venomous glare in her direction. She returned his look with a haughty stare until at last he looked away. One of the footmen put a hand upon his shoulder and with a snarl Sir Ronald shook him off. He straightened his coat and headed for the door. As he passed Eloise he stopped and turned towards her, his eyes menacing. Immediately Jack stepped in, as if to shield her.

'Just go, Deforge. If you have not left town by the morning it will give me very great pleasure to call you out!'

Eloise caught her breath. The two men glared at one another for a long, angry moment before Sir Ronald turned and flung himself out of the room. Jack turned back to her, the angry light in his eyes replaced by something much softer. He said quietly, 'It is over, my lady. Now you may be easy…'

She struggled to concentrate. His voice seemed to be coming from a great distance. Blackness was closing around her. The last thing she saw was Jack's face smiling at her before the darkness overwhelmed her and she fainted.

Jack did not hesitate. As Eloise began to fall he swept her up into his arms.

'Ah, poor thing,' exclaimed Lady Keworth. 'Bring her this way, Major, into my sitting room.' She led Jack out of the salon and across the landing to a small, cosily furnished parlour. 'I will have the fire banked up…'

'No, thank you,' said Jack, gently laying his precious burden on a chintz-covered daybed and sitting down on the edge. 'I think it was the heat in the salon that caused Lady Allyngham to faint. It is quite warm enough in here.'

Alex appeared in the doorway.

'Is she all right?'

Lady Keworth hovered over the daybed.

'Lady Allyngham will be very well, I am sure. Perhaps you would like to leave her with me…'

'No!' Jack softened his first, instinctive response by directing a charming smile at his hostess. 'I feel responsible for Lady Allyngham, I shall look after her.' He pulled off her gloves and began to chafe her hands. 'But perhaps a glass of water?'

'Yes, yes, of course.'

Alex stood aside to allow Lady Keworth to hurry away.

'I did not see,' he said, stepping into the room. 'Did Deforge attack her?'

'No, she has fainted, nothing more,' said Jack, not looking up. 'Is he gone now?'

'Aye. Keworth's men showed him to the door. He was looking as black as thunder, as well he might. No one will receive him after this night's work.' He glanced down. 'She's stirring.'

Jack felt the little hands tremble and his own grip tightened.

'Be easy,' he murmured. 'You are safe now.'

She looked up at him, her eyes as dark as sapphires. Her fingers clung to his and only the knowledge that Alex was in the room prevented him from pulling her into his arms.

'Aye,' said Alex, coming to stand beside him. 'It is over, Elle. Deforge is finished.'

Lady Keworth bustled back into the room with a glass of water.

'Well, my dear, I am so glad to see you have come round,' she said. 'Such a fright you gave us, but I am sure you will be better now.'

Eloise struggled to sit up. Jack went to rise but her slender fingers clung to his hand so he remained perched on the edge of the daybed.

Lady Keworth held out the glass. 'There, my dear. Are you sure there is nothing else I can do for you; shall I summon a doctor?'

Eloise's fingers were shaking when she took the glass and Jack immediately reached out to help her, putting his hand over hers to steady it. She cast a swift, grateful look in his direction before turning to address Lady Keworth.

'Thank you, ma'am. I am sure I shall be very well, if I may only rest here quietly for a little while.'

The lady hovered uncertainly.

'I shall look after Lady Allyngham, ma'am,' said Jack again. 'I am sure you want to return to your guests, they will be growing anxious.'

'Well…' Lady Keworth hesitated and Alex stepped up.

'Indeed, ma'am, we should go: so much excitement—we would not wish it to spoil your card party. You may be easy, madam; before he died at

Waterloo, the late Lord Allyngham consigned his wife to Major Clifton's care.' He held out his arm to her. 'Let us leave them now, I am sure they have much to discuss!' He looked back over his shoulder as he escorted the lady from the room, giving Jack a grin and the suggestion of a wink.

Chapter Nineteen

'I thank Providence for Alex Mortimer,' said Jack, unable to suppress a smile. 'I thought our hostess would never go away. He has closed the door upon us, too. I fear your reputation will be ruined after this, madam, unless you agree to marry me.' He turned to Eloise, but his smile quickly disappeared when he saw her pale cheeks and the stricken look in her eyes. He said quickly, 'Dearest heart, what is it?'

She shook her head.

'Please, do not call me that!'

He took the glass from her shaking hands and placed it on a small side table.

'Now, Elle,' he said, taking her in his arms. 'What is all this?'

She put her hands against his chest to hold him off.

'I c-cannot marry you!'

'No?' He let her go and she turned away, hunt-

ing for her handkerchief. Silently he handed her
his own.

'No. At least,' she muttered, dabbing at her eyes,
'not until you know the truth about me.'

He smiled.

'I know everything I need to know about you.'

She choked back a sob. How was she ever to explain it to him? He put his hands on her shoulders
and she jumped, moving to the far end of the sofa.

'Please,' she said quickly, 'do not touch me, not
until I have t-told you.'

'There is no need—'

'But there is!' she cried. 'I w-would have no secrets
from you, Jack, not any more. But once you know
everything I am very much afraid you will want
nothing more to do with me.' She turned back towards him, her hands clasped so tightly the knuckles
gleamed white. 'I must tell you. I could not bear for
you to find out in the future and…and hate me.'

'I could never hate you.' He reached out and
took her hands. He said quietly, 'Elle, if this is
about Allyngham and Alex, I know. Alex told me
everything.'

'He did? But…when?'

'The night we broke into Deforge's house. I was
determined to leave town. I told Alex that if you
would not trust me then I wanted nothing further to
do with you. So he told me what you would not—
what you felt you could nott—out of loyalty to your

husband and your friend. After all it was their secret, was it not?'

She gazed at him wide-eyed.

'You are not…outraged?'

He smiled at her.

'Despite your reputation, my lady, you really have led quite a sheltered life. No. I was not scandalised to learn that Alex and your husband were lovers.'

'But…in the eyes of the law it is a criminal offence—men can be hanged for it.' She squeezed his fingers, not sure that he understood her. 'Lives have been ruined, reputations lost—Tony and Alex were so careful to protect their secret. Tony knew his name would be disgraced for ever if the truth came out—no respectable person could ever acknowledge him.'

'Then perhaps I am not quite so respectable as you think me,' replied Jack, smiling slightly. 'Alex's disclosure did not shock me. I was more shocked to learn that you had married Allyngham to protect them both. Mortimer said that you are very loyal and he is right, is he not? A little too loyal, perhaps. You were prepared, nay, willing, to be thought fast—a wanton widow indeed!—rather than have anyone suspect the truth.'

She bowed her head.

'I am glad Alex told you,' she said quietly. 'I did not want to betray him, or Tony. But neither could I let you marry me without you knowing the truth.'

'Thank you,' he said, giving her a smile that tugged

at her heart. 'Once I knew you were a maid I suspected the affairs in the journal might be Allyngham's rather than yours, but I was at a loss to know why you would not trust me with the secret, until Mortimer explained it all.'

'I am so very sorry.'

'Elle, you have done nothing wrong,' he said quietly. 'You were merely protecting those you loved.' Jack squeezed her hands. 'What a burden for you to carry! I admire your loyalty towards Tony and Alex, my dear.'

She bit her lip.

'I seem to have spent my life looking after them,' she murmured.

'And now I am going to look after *you*,' he told her, smiling. 'Tony said that you deserved better, I didn't understand him at the time, but now, I hope I can be a worthy husband for you. I shall obtain a special licence: we can be married and away from London within a se'ennight, what do you say to that?'

'It—it sounds delightful, if you are sure you still want to marry me.'

'It would be an honour to marry Tony Allyngham's widow,' he told her solemnly.

She closed her eyes, suddenly exhausted by the events of the evening. Jack leaned forwards and kissed her cheek.

'Poor love, you look very tired. I should take you home.'

She nodded.

'Yes, if you please.'

'Wait here, then. I must find Alex and tell him we are leaving. And I must speak with our hosts.' He gave her a rueful smile. 'It may take some time: you will not mind being left alone here?'

'No, I shall be well enough, but please, be as quick as you can!'

Alone in Lady Keworth's elegant sitting room, Eloise reclined upon the daybed, her arms folded over her stomach. She was aware of a little seed of happiness inside her, but she was afraid to allow it to grow too much. She was very weary, but she did not want to sleep, only to lie still and go over in her mind all that Jack had said to her. He knew the truth and he still wanted to marry her. She went back over his words again. He cared for her, he desired her, she knew that, but at no time had he told her loved her. She hugged herself a little tighter. Perhaps, given time, he might grow to love her for her own sake, and not just as his comrade's widow.

A light scratching on the door made her sit up.

'Come in.'

A liveried footmen stepped into the room. He carried her blue silk cloak over his arm.

'If it please your ladyship, Major Clifton is waiting for you with the carriage.'

She rose and followed him out of the door, throwing her wrap over her shoulders.

'This way, madam.' He pointed to the backstairs. 'The major thought you might like to leave by the side door, rather than go out through the main salon.'

'Of course.' She followed the servant down the stairs, smiling to herself. How thoughtful of Jack to know she would not wish to speak to anyone.

The side door stood open and she could see her carriage drawn up on the street, the flickering streetlamps illuminating the Allyngham crest on the door. A fine drizzle was falling and Eloise threw her hood up over her hair. The footman went out before her, opened the door and handed her into the waiting carriage. Almost before she had climbed in the door was closed behind her and the carriage pulled away with a jerk, toppling her on to the seat.

'Goodness, Herries is eager to get home tonight!' she laughed, addressing the figure lounging in the far corner of the carriage.

Her laughter died and a cold, sick dread came over her as Sir Ronald Deforge leaned forwards.

'I, too, am very eager, my lady, but we are not going to Dover Street.'

Eloise shrank back into the corner of the carriage.

'How did you get here? Where are my people?'

'Trussed up in an alleyway, along with one of Keworth's lackeys. We needed his livery.'

'So the footman was one of your hirelings.' Her lip curled. 'I did not think you would stoop so low.'

'I have not resorted to housebreaking,' he retorted. 'Do not look so innocent, my lady: I gather from Clifton's words that you have somehow managed to retrieve Allyngham's journal.'

'Yes,' she said defiantly. 'It is destroyed. You have no further hold over me.'

He laughed gently and a shiver of fear ran down her spine.

'Since you are here now, I think I have quite a substantial hold over you, madam.'

Eloise bit her lip, her eyes sliding towards the carriage door. Sir Ronald said coldly, 'If you are thinking of leaping out, my dear, let me assure you that it will not help you: you might easily break a limb in the process and in any event my men would catch you and bring you back immediately.'

'Where are you taking me?'

'To Redlands, a little property of mine near Thatcham. It belonged to my late wife—all that remains of her not inconsiderable fortune. Being a gambler is an expensive business, my dear: I need the Allyngham fortune to replenish my own.'

'So you have abducted me,' she said, her voice heavy with anger. 'When it is discovered that my servants have been attacked and I am missing, everyone will guess you are the culprit.'

'But that may not be for some time, madam, and

how are they to know where we have gone? We shall be at Redlands in a few hours: the rector there owes his living to me: I have the special licence in my pocket.' She saw his evil grin appear. 'We shall have our wedding today, as planned.'

'I will never marry you!'

'Oh I think you will, madam,' he said softly. 'And you will learn to please me, if you do not want me to hand you over to my stable hands for their plaything.'

'You will not get away with this,' she retorted. 'When they come after me—'

'They!' He gave a cold, cruel laugh. 'Who do you think will put themselves out to chase after you, madam? Mortimer is not fit to ride, and as for the rest, do you think they care what happens to a woman with a reputation such as yours? That leaves only Major Clifton, and what can one man do against myself and the three fellows travelling on the top? You have overplayed your hand, my lady: the *ton* will say that the Wanton Widow has received no more than she deserves!'

Eloise glared across the carriage at Sir Ronald, who lounged carelessly in his corner. Perhaps he was right and the *ton* would leave her to her fate. She had no doubt that Jack would try to find her, but even if he had Alex to help him how long might that take?

Sir Ronald rubbed his chin thoughtfully. 'And yet Major Clifton is such a resourceful fellow, he will go to great lengths to do me a disservice,' he purred. 'I think I shall hire a room at Maidenhead and take you there, just to make sure of you.'

She curled her lip.

'Do you think that will save you from him? It will only make him more determined to kill you!'

'I am well aware that Clifton wants to put paid to my existence. He wants revenge upon me for marrying his childhood friend, the love of his life. You are little more than a pawn in this game, my dear. Did you think you could ever replace Clara in his heart? She was a veritable angel, my dear, as pure as you are wanton. Taking you from me might redress the balance a little, but where would be the satisfaction for him if I had already bedded you? He will not want you then, madam, knowing that I have already sampled your delights. How could he ever lie with you after that, knowing that I had enjoyed you?' He laughed. 'But this is mere conjecture. No one knows our direction and it is most unlikely that they will find us before I have wed you. And once we are married I shall make sure you have no opportunity to escape me.'

'And will you kill me, like you killed your first wife?'

'Is that what Clifton has told you?' Sir Ronald gave a bitter laugh. 'Aye, he would like to believe that. Much more comfortable for him to think I was villain enough to beguile Clara into marrying me and then find a way to dispose of her once I had run through her fortune!'

'Is that not the truth?' she challenged him.

'Far from it. Clara was a sweet, innocent beauty. We were madly, hopelessly in love within weeks of being introduced. Such passion could not last, of course, and I confess that her devotion outlasted mine. She liked to live at Redlands, I preferred town. Once she knew she was with child she settled down, although she seemed to think I should come and live with her. I kept putting it off, making excuses why I could not join her, until it was too late.' He paused and turned his head to gaze out of the window. 'I was in London when she drowned herself, driven mad with grief at the loss of her baby. Our son.'

'I am so very sorry,' murmured Eloise.

He turned back to her, saying harshly, 'You need not be. Clara has been dead for three years and unlike your precious major I gave up mourning her long ago. Truth to tell, I cannot say that her death was anything but a relief. I had grown very weary of her maudlin airs and clinging ways. You, my dear, have so much more spirit.' He stretched out his foot and rubbed it against her leg. She quickly drew back, pulling her skirts about her. Sir Ronald merely laughed again. 'By Gad, madam, it will be amusing to bend you to my will.'

Eloise returned no answer but huddled in the corner, staring resolutely out of the window, watching the dark landscape flying by. Jack would come after her, she was sure of it, but she was less sure of his reasons for doing so. Sir Ronald's words had lodged themselves in her brain. Her reputation, even her actions in giving herself to Jack, proved her to be far beneath the paragon that was his first love. She knew he wanted to marry her because she was Allyngham's widow, but what if he also he wanted to thwart Sir Ronald? Would he still want her once Deforge had taken her to his bed? Even if by some chance Jack decided upon the right road, there was little chance he would catch them before they reached Maidenhead.

Chapter Twenty

They rattled on and Eloise kept her gaze firmly fixed upon the window. She forced herself to consider her position. It did not look promising. Sir Ronald might dress as a fop but he was too strong for her to overpower him, and she did not even have a hatpin with which to defend herself. Once he had her alone in a room she feared all would be lost. The idea of his hands on her body made her shudder with revulsion. She shifted closer to the window and peered down. She had never considered the distance from a carriage to the ground before, but now she was determined that if they slowed at all she would attempt to run away. Sir Ronald took out his watch and held it, turning it towards what little light there was coming into the carriage.

'We shall soon be at Maidenhead, my dear. You had best prepare yourself.' He leaned across to run his finger along her cheek. 'What, still not speaking to me?' She flinched away and he sat back, chuckling. 'You will soon learn to enjoy my caresses, Eloise.'

Her stretched nerves noticed immediately when the pace slackened. They were entering a village: the dark outlines of buildings could be seen on either side of the road, although not a light was visible from any window. She tensed, surreptitiously noting the position of the door handle. The carriage slowed still further and began to turn off the road towards the lighted yard of a large inn. Sir Ronald was peering out of the window beside him.

'What the devil, this isn't the Bear—'

Eloise seized her chance. She sprang up, released the door catch and leaped from the carriage as it turned off the road. She landed heavily and rolled over, hoping she was clear of the wheels. Her voluminous cloak billowed out and settled around her even as she scrambled to her feet. She could hear Sir Ronald's outraged roar and knew she had only seconds to escape. As she raised her head she saw there was a line of horses stretched across the road, blocking the way. That was why the carriage had turned off the highway.

It took her a moment to recognise Lord Keworth and Mr Renwick amongst the horsemen. A glance back showed her that more men were surrounding the carriage, their pistols directed at the coachman and the two accomplices who were clinging to the back straps of the coach-body. Sir Ronald had jumped down and was coming towards her. Eloise quickly moved towards the horsemen.

'Thank God we have found you, Lady Allyngham!' Lord Keworth dismounted and held out one hand to her, the other levelling a pistol at Sir Ronald. 'That is far enough, Deforge. Stand, or I shall shoot!'

'Elle!' Jack was running towards her. 'Elle, dearest! Are you all right?'

His voice was shaking, and suddenly she felt close to tears. With a sob she threw herself on his chest.

'Yes, yes,' she said, 'I am well enough now.'

'Why did you jump from the carriage?' He held her away from him, staring into her face. 'If he touched you—!'

Eloise shook her head.

'No, but he p-planned to hire a room and—' She broke off, shuddering, and Jack pulled her back into his arms.

'Then thank God we were in time.'

She leaned against him, secure within his embrace while all around them was confusion.

The riders were dismounting and moving forwards to stand around them, effectively cutting off Sir Ronald's escape. She could hear a familiar voice barking orders to the men on the coach.

'Climb down now, me boys, and steady does it: there's more than one finger here itching to pull the trigger!'

She raised her head.

'Perkins?'

'Yes,' said Jack. 'It is thanks to your groom that we were able to find you so soon. He was returning from a local gin shop when he saw your carriage pulling away from the side door at Keworth House. If the speed of its departure hadn't made him suspicious then the fact that a Keworth footman scrambled up on the back told him something was wrong. He immediately raised the alarm and had the presence of mind to follow the carriage until he ascertained that it was leaving London by the Great West Road. We followed, and thankfully, even at this hour of the night there were enough people abroad to notice your flight.'

'And you all came to find me,' she said, looking around at the familiar faces. 'I am very grateful.'

'Not at all, dear lady.' Lord Berrow pushed forwards and gave a little bow. 'When Major Clifton set up the hue and cry we were all most happy to oblige!'

'Very touching,' sneered Deforge, glaring at them all. 'Especially when you know you would all like to have the wench for yourself!'

'Enough!' barked Lord Keworth. 'You will keep a civil tongue in your head when addressing the lady.'

'Lady? I know better,' cried Sir Ronald. 'She has taken you all in with her smiles and fine airs, but she is nothing but an imposter! She was never a virtuous wife to Allyngham—their marriage was a sham, a cover to mask her husband's unnatural practices with Alex Mortimer! No *lady* would have agreed to such a pretence. Who knows what went on in their bedchamber between the three of them? And she knew, she *knew* when she married him that Allyngham was a—'

He got no further. Jack stepped forwards and smashed his fist against Sir Ronald's jaw. Deforge's head snapped back and he crashed to the ground.

'Well done, Clifton, just what was needed,' declared Lord Berrow, coming forwards. 'I have no doubt Mortimer would have done the same, had he been well enough to ride with us.'

'Aye,' declared Lord Keworth. 'A dastardly act, to accuse Mortimer, a man who you know is already wounded and in no condition to demand satisfaction.'

'Not only Mortimer, but Allyngham, my friend and neighbour,' roared Lord Berrow, turning to glare at Sir Ronald who was slowly picking himself up. 'Why, you filthy scoundrel, how dare you attempt to blacken the name of a hero of Waterloo? One, moreover, who is no longer alive to defend himself! Tie him up, gentlemen.'

'It is true!' cried Deforge, struggling as Renwick and Graham secured his hands with a length of whipcord. 'And I had the proof, before they stole it from me! Ask them,' he spat. 'Ask Clifton to deny that he broke into my house!'

Putting her hand up to prevent Jack from uttering an angry retort, Eloise took a step away from him and looked at the men gathered around her. She said clearly, 'But of course, knowing that he had the means to blacken my husband's good name, I went to Wardle Street to retrieve it. I climbed in through his window at dead of night, stole the proof and burned it!'

An instant's shocked silence was followed by hearty laughter. Jack took her hand.

'As if any woman would have the nerve to do such a thing,' he murmured, grinning at her.

'Curse you,' snarled Sir Ronald, 'I shall swear to it, on oath!'

'Do you think, sir, after your behaviour tonight, anyone will take your allegations seriously?' retorted Mr Renwick.

'Aye,' nodded Lord Berrow. 'You had best beware, Deforge: false accusations of this kind are punished very severely. Come, gentlemen, let us take this villain and his cronies back to town. We shall haul them before the magistrate in the morning.'

'You may use my horse,' offered Jack. 'I shall drive Lady Allyngham home in her carriage.'

'I'm coming with you, m'lady,' put in Perkins, walking up at that moment with the major's man, who added,

'And if you'll allow me, madam, I can handle a coach and four: it'd be an honour to drive you.'

'Thank you,' she murmured.

'Aye, thank you, Bob,' said Jack, putting his arm about Eloise. 'Now, if that is settled, tell that rascally landlord to bring us some fresh horses and we'll be away.'

The first grey streaks of dawn were edging into the sky as they rumbled back towards London. Eloise sat beside Jack in the dark carriage, her head on his shoulder and her hand snugly held in his comforting grasp.

'I was so frightened,' she murmured. 'I never doubted you would come for me, but I did not know how soon, or if you would be alone.'

Jack put his arm about her.

'After he had ruined the card party so spectacularly this evening, the gentlemen were only too pleased to have an excuse to come after Deforge,' he said, resting his cheek against her hair. 'And your groom's quick thinking put us on the right track immediately. I have quite forgiven him for hitting me over the head on Hampstead Heath.'

'And me?' she asked shyly. 'Have you forgiven me for being so foolish?'

'Of course. The person I do find it difficult to forgive is Allyngham for marrying you. And for committing a record of his indiscretions to paper. Damnably irresponsible for such a clever man.'

Eloise was silent, leaning against Jack and listening to the thud of his heart.

'I think he began his journal because he was away from home and missing Alex,' she said at last. 'He continued to write it when he was at Allyngham for those few short months before Waterloo. I did not know what was in it and when it went missing I was not unduly concerned: I thought perhaps Tony had destroyed it himself. From what Sir Ronald told me I believe now it was stolen by a servant I had turned off for dishonesty. I knew the man had taken a few pieces of clothing when he left—a few shirts and a pair of boots.' She gave a little sigh. 'Things of such little value I did not pursue it. I thought the poor man would have a hard enough time of it, being turned off without a reference. He was illiterate, so he had no idea what was in the journal.'

'And you think he passed it on to Deforge?'

'Yes.' She shuddered. 'It was not until Deforge left me one of the pages in the gardens at Clevedon House that I realised just how, how *explicit* Tony's journal was, and how dangerous that could be. Not to me.' She sat up and looked at him, her eyes begging him to understand. 'Not to me, but to Tony's name, and of course to Alex, if it became public knowledge that they were...*lovers.*'

He put up a hand to stroke her cheek.

'So you had to protect them, just as you had always done.'

'Yes.' She nodded. 'We grew up together, you see. Tony and Alex were two years older and I thought they were wonderful, everything older brothers should be. They were never cruel, or spiteful, as boys often can be to a younger child, and we were always friends. We were allowed to run wild at Allyngham. Tony was the leader; he liked excitement and danger. Somehow I seemed to be the one who found ways to extricate us when Tony's madcap schemes went awry. Even when the boys went off to school I was still the one they called upon in a fix. I remember I sold my pearls once, when Tony became embroiled with a moneylender and was too afraid to tell anyone in the college, and he certainly would not tell his father. But he paid me back as soon as he was able,' she added quickly. 'Tony was always very generous. And very kind.'

'Kind!' Jack muttered an oath under his breath. 'I do not call it *kind* of him to wed you, to rob you of the opportunity to marry the man of your choice, to have children—'

She sat up and put a finger to his lips.

'He *was* my choice. I loved him as a brother. And Alex, too. I wanted them to be happy. It was always plain to me that theirs was a very deep and abiding love. Alex still feels the loss, more keenly than I.'

'Allyngham should not have married you!'

She shrugged.

'I had to marry someone. I was the poor relation, brought up with the family but expected at some time to repay their kindness by making a good marriage of my own. Lord and Lady Allyngham did not attempt to force me into a marriage, but it was apparent—never said but always implied—that I *must* marry.' She paused, looking back into the past. 'Tony was army mad, so Lord Allyngham bought him a commission. Then his elder brother died and Tony was the heir. Suddenly his family were pushing him to marry—whenever he was home on leave they would invite a series of young ladies to meet him. Of course he did not want to wed any of them. He was far too kind to allow any woman to marry him unless she knew the situation and he could not risk *telling* anyone, so when he suggested that we should wed, it seemed the perfect solution, for all of us. Lord and Lady Allyngham never liked the match, but when they saw that Tony was adamant they relented.'

'And how old were you then?'

'I was seventeen.'

'And he explained everything to you? You knew you were entering a sham marriage?'

'I knew Tony could never love a woman as he loved Alex.' She raised her chin and looked directly into his eyes. 'That was all I needed to know. Sir Ronald thought Tony had…had corrupted me, but that is not so. Tony and Alex were always very discreet when I was present. I think I had a much happier marriage than many women. Tony always looked after me, always treated me with the utmost kindness. To the outside world he was the perfect husband.'

'Except in one regard.'

A slight flush tinged her cheeks.

'I never noticed the lack,' she said softly, 'until I met you.'

A low growl escaped Jack and he swept her into a crushing embrace. She clung to him, pressing her body against his as she gave him back kiss for kiss. Tiredness forgotten, Eloise found her body responding to his caresses. When at last he raised his head she lay in his arms, her head thrown back against his shoulder as she gazed up into his face. Suddenly she could not bear the thought of being apart from him for even a moment. She reached up and touched his cheek.

'How, how soon can we be married by special licence?' she whispered.

'Ah. I have been thinking about that.'

'Oh. I—um—I thought you wanted to be married with all speed.'

'Yes, I know that is what I said, but after all that has happened I am afraid I have changed my mind.'

Eloise struggled to sit up. It was impossible to read his expression in the darkness, but his words sent her heart plummeting. Swallowing, she began nervously to smooth her gown over her knees.

'I, I quite understand,' she said, trying not to cry. 'I am aware that you consider yourself under an, an *obligation* to Tony, but after all you have done for me, I think you have more than fulfilled that duty.'

'Why, I think so, too.'

Her heart sank. Eloise gazed out of the window where the dawn was washing the landscape in shades of dirty grey. So he had reconsidered, he had realised how damaging it would be to marry her. He would have to love her very much indeed to risk everything for her. And he did not love her, he loved Clara Deforge. With great resolution she turned to face him.

'Jack, there is something else I must tell you.'

He was leaning back in the corner of the carriage, half-asleep, but now he opened his eyes and regarded her.

'More secrets?'

'Not exactly.' She did not smile. 'When I was in the carriage with Sir Ronald, he—he mentioned his first wife.' Jack did not move but she knew she had his attention. She continued, 'He, um, he told me that he and Clara had fallen hopelessly in love when they first met and, and although their passion had cooled a little by the time she drowned herself, I do not think he wished her any harm.'

She waited, holding her breath, for his reply.

'And you believe him?'

'Yes.' She nodded. 'He had no reason to lie to me.'

She took his hand. 'I wanted you to know that, Jack. I know it will hurt to think that she was not faithful to you, but she and Sir Ronald really did love one another.'

'Thank you for telling me.'

He closed his eyes again. Anxiously she studied his face. There was no guessing his thoughts. After a few moments Jack opened his eyes and looked at her.

'I beg your pardon,' she whispered. 'I thought it might help...'

He smiled.

'It does. I am glad, truly, that she was not unhappy.'

She blinked rapidly. 'I am sorry that she did not always love you...'

'I am not. Not now. I did love her, but that is in the past, and knowing that she made her choice for love, not greed, or ambition—I will let her rest now.' He reached out to stroke her cheek. 'Did you think I still loved her? I don't, you know. She will not come between us.'

She nodded, the knot of misery still tight in her chest. She had been foolish to think a respectable man would want her for a wife, but even as her hopes crumbled she realised that she did not want Jack to suggest she become his mistress: she had thought him different from those other men. She had thought him truly honourable. A lump filled her throat. It was her own fault; she had always been too fanciful. She knew very well that even honourable men had mistresses. Eloise had never considered herself in the role of a mistress, and she would not, even for Jack. Especially for Jack. She blinked, hard. Alex wanted to go home to mourn his lost love. She would return to Allyngham and do the same. As Jack went to pull her into his arms she held him off.

'Please,' she said, her voice not quite steady. 'I know you think me fast, I know I have given you every reason to do so, but please, no more! I quite understand why you no longer wish to marry me, but—'

She heard Jack chuckle.

'No, you don't understand, Elle. Come here.' He pulled her back into his arms. 'I never said I didn't want to marry you, but I will not wed you by special licence, my foolish love, because I intend to marry you with as much pomp and ceremony as we can muster, and that will take a little time to arrange. The only decisions you have to make, my sweet, are what you will wear, and whether you wish to be married from Allyngham, or from Henchard.'

She stared at him.

'Truly?' She put one hand up to his face, her fingers rubbing against the faint dark stubble on his cheek. 'You would really do that for me?' she said wonderingly. 'But, but *why*?'

He gazed down at her. Even in the grey dawn light she could see the warm glow in his eyes.

'Do you really have to ask?'

'Y-yes,' she whispered, hardly daring to hope. 'Yes, I do.'

'Because, my sweet innocent, I want the whole world to know how much I love you.'

'Oh,' she said, tears welling in her eyes, 'you r-really love me?'

'To distraction,' he muttered, hugging her even tighter. 'I cannot imagine life without you!' He kissed her savagely. 'I want you for a wife, Elle. A lover, a friend—a partner to stand beside me against the world!' He kissed her again. 'And we will be married in a positive *fog* of respectability.'

With a little sob she threw her arms about his neck.

'Oh, Jack, it is what I hoped, what I dreamed of, but never dared believe…'

'Well, you may believe it now,' he murmured, gently nibbling her ear. 'And as long as you love me, there is nothing to stand in our way.'

'I do,' she told him, hugging him tightly. 'I love you more than I ever thought it possible!'

He gathered her to him and kissed her, gently at first, but as the kiss deepened his arms tightened protectively around her. She leaned into him, revelling in the way his body hardened against hers. He swung her round and pulled her across his lap, covering her face and neck with kisses while she clung to him, exulting in the hot, passionate embrace. When at last he released her they were both panting. She lay in his arms, her head resting on his chest and the steady thud of his heart beating against her cheek.

'Happy now?' he murmured, dropping a kiss on her hair.

'Mmm. Jack?'

'Yes?' He began to nibble her ear.

'Your plans for a respectable marriage,' she murmured, closing her eyes as his lips trailed gently across her neck, painting a line of warm kisses on her skin. 'The banns, a new gown—this will take at least a month. Does that mean I must hire a chaperon, and only see you in company until our wedding day?'

His mouth was moving across the soft swell of her breast, but at her words he raised his head and looked at her. There was sufficient light in the carriage for her to see the gleam in his dark eyes and what she read there sent a delicious tingle running down to her very toes.

'Well,' he said, giving her a wicked smile, 'I don't think we need to be *quite* that respectable!'

* * * * *

HISTORICAL

Large Print

INNOCENT COURTESAN TO ADVENTURER'S BRIDE
Louise Allen

Wrongly accused of theft, innocent Celina Shelley is cast out of the brothel she calls home and flees to Quinn Ashley, Lord Dreycott. Lina dresses like a nun, looks like an angel, but flirts like a professional – the last thing Quinn expects is to discover she's a virgin! With this revelation, will he wed her before he beds her?

DISGRACE AND DESIRE
Sarah Mallory

With all of London falling at her feet, wagers abound over who will capture the flirtatious Lady Eloise and her fortune. Dashing Major Jack Clifton has vowed to watch over his late comrade's wife, but her beauty and behaviour intrigue him. The lady is not what she seems, and Jack must discover her secret if he is to protect her…

THE VIKING'S CAPTIVE PRINCESS
Michelle Styles

Dangerous warrior Ivar Gunnarson is a man of deeds, not words. With little time for the ideals of love, Ivar seizes what he wants – and Princess Thyre is no exception! But to become king of Thyre's heart, mysterious and enchanting as she is, will entail a battle Ivar has never engaged in before…

MILLS & BOON

HISTORICAL

Large Print

COURTING MISS VALLOIS
Gail Whitiker

Miss Sophie Vallois has enthralled London Society, yet the French beauty is a mere farmer's daughter! Only Robert Silverton knows her secret, and he has other reasons to stay away. However, Sophie is so enticing that Robert soon finds that, instead of keeping her at arm's length, he wants the delectable Miss Vallois well and truly *in* his arms!

REPROBATE LORD, RUNAWAY LADY
Isabelle Goddard

Amelie Silverdale is fleeing her betrothal to a vicious, degenerate man, while Gareth Denville knows that the scandal that drove him from London is about to erupt again. In Amelie, Gareth recognises a kindred spirit also in need of escape. On the run together the attraction builds, but what will happen when their old lives catch up with them?

THE BRIDE WORE SCANDAL
Helen Dickson

From the moment Christina Atherton saw notorious Lord Rockley she couldn't control her blushes. In return, dark and seductive Lord Rockley found Christina oh, so beguiling… When Christina discovered that she was expecting, Lord Rockley knew he must make Christina his bride…before scandal ruined them both!

MILLS & BOON

HISTORICAL

Large Print

LADY ARABELLA'S SCANDALOUS MARRIAGE

Carole Mortimer

Sinister whispers may surround Darius Wynter, but one thing's for sure—marriage to the infamous Duke means that Arabella will soon discover the exquisite pleasures of the marriage bed…

DANGEROUS LORD, SEDUCTIVE MISS

Mary Brendan

Heiress Deborah Cleveland jilted an earl for her true love—then he disappeared! Now Lord Buckland has returned, as sinfully attractive as ever. Can Deborah resist the dark magnetism of the lawless lord?

BOUND TO THE BARBARIAN

Carol Townend

To settle a debt, Katerina must convince commanding warrior Ashfirth Saxon that *she* is her royal mistress. But the days—*and nights*—of deceit take their toll. How long before she is willingly bedded by this proud barbarian?

BOUGHT: THE PENNILESS LADY

Deborah Hale

Her new husband may be handsome—but his heart is black. Desperate to safeguard the future of her precious nephew, penniless Lady Artemis Dearing will do anything—even marry the man whose brother ruined her darling sister!

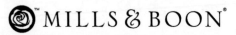

HISTORICAL

Large Print

LADY FOLBROKE'S DELICIOUS DECEPTION

Christine Merrill

Confronting her errant husband after being snubbed, Lady Emily Longesley finds that he has been robbed of his sight and doesn't know her! Emily longs for a lover's touch. If she plays his mistress, can he finally begin to love his wife?

BREAKING THE GOVERNESS'S RULES

Michelle Styles

Governess Louisa Sibson was dismissed for allowing Jonathon, Lord Chesterholm to seduce her. Now she lives by a strict set of morals. But Jonathon *will* get to the bottom of her disappearance—and will enjoy breaking a few of her rules along the way…!

HER DARK AND DANGEROUS LORD

Anne Herries

Exiled Lord Stefan de Montfort rescued Englishwoman Anne Melford from the sea, taking her to his French château. The spirited beauty fires within him a forbidden desire. Now he's determined to break one last rule and claim her as his bride!

HOW TO MARRY A RAKE

Deb Marlowe

Mae Halford mended her heart after rejection by Lord Stephen Manning. Now she's ready to find a husband—only the first man she bumps into is Lord Stephen himself! Romance may blossom once more—but will their adventure lead to the altar?

 **MILLS & BOON**

HIST0811 LP

HISTORICAL

Large Print

MISS IN A MAN'S WORLD
Anne Ashley

Georgiana Grey disguised herself as a boy, and became handsome Viscount Fincham's page. Having come home love-struck, she must return to London for the Season. When she comes face-to-face with him again, her deception is unmasked…

CAPTAIN CORCORAN'S HOYDEN BRIDE
Annie Burrows

Aimée Peters possesses an innocence which charms even the piratical Captain Corcoran. Then he discovers the coins stitched into her bodice—what secrets does Aimée hide behind her naive façade?

HIS COUNTERFEIT CONDESA
Joanna Fulford

Major Falconbridge can see that Sabrina Huntley is no ordinary miss! With their posing as the Conde and Condesa de Ordoñez, he doesn't know which is worse—the menace of their perilous mission, or the desires awakened by this tantalising beauty…

REBELLIOUS RAKE, INNOCENT GOVERNESS
Elizabeth Beacon

Despite hiding behind shapeless dresses, governess Charlotte Wells has caught the eye of notorious Benedict Shaw. Charlotte declines his invitation to dance—but this scandalous libertine isn't used to taking no for an answer!

 MILLS & BOON